The Soul

A Spirit Trilogy Novel

d. Nichole King

The Soul

First Print Edition: October 2016

Limitless Publishing, LLC
Kailua, HI 96734
www.limitlesspublishing.com

Formatting: Limitless Publishing

ISBN-13: 978-1-68058-831-6
ISBN-10: 1-68058-831-1

Dedication

For my readers.
Thank you.
For everything.

Chapter 1

"I look like Godzilla's wife," I said to myself, peering into the full-length mirror behind my bedroom door. I picked at the royal blue graduation gown that was big enough for me and my Siamese twin. I pulled the material out at my sides as far as it would allow to prove my point to the mirror. My reflection agreed with me. Unfortunately, the Villisca school board did not.

Fashion fail of the century.

Seriously, these robes needed to be redesigned a hundred years ago. I mean, I understood the whole school spirit thing, but why couldn't I wear one of the fifteen Villisca Blue Jays t-shirts I'd inherited over the course of my single year here? That would demonstrate more school pride than this atrocity.

Besides, graduating today was not my idea. I had no intention of walking across a stage to receive my diploma. Rumor had it, if you didn't show up they'd mail it to you, so I didn't see why the fanfare was necessary. Last month's hell was still fresh in my mind, and this whole celebration didn't seem fitting to me.

Especially when I'd be leaving tomorrow.

I slipped my feet into white flip-flops, giving a passing glance at the new two-inch footwear Mom had requested. At least I'd be comfortable.

I took a final look at my tent-reflection, grimaced, and swung the door open. Lucas, with his fist raised to knock, stood on the other side. His green stare ran the length of my body and back up before he lowered his hand.

"Now *that* is sexy." He nodded his approval, a small smirk the tell-tale sign of his teasing.

I glared at him. "Oh shut up."

"No, I'm serious. Smokin'."

I went to slug him, but he disappeared and I hit the air instead. From behind me, strong, cool arms circled my waist and pulled me against a solid body. He dipped to my neck, and his lips brushed over my skin.

"I love you, Carrie," he said. Then in my head he added, *"You don't have to come with me tomorrow, you know. You can go home with your mom."*

Since we'd returned from Jessica's funeral, Lucas had often tried to convince me to go back to Texas. He wanted to protect me, which was sweet, but I'd proved time and time again that I could take care of myself…with a little help.

Plus, Lucas's soul-search wouldn't only affect him. Half of his soul now resided in me. He needed me.

"Not a chance. I'm going with you," I said, like I did every time. "I meant it when I said we'd do this together."

I spun around in his arms, facing him. I lifted up on my tip-toes and kissed him. "I love you, and I'm not giving up on this. We'll find your soul *and* we'll find a way to be together."

"Carrie…" he murmured against my mouth.

At the sound, something inside me lurched. Like I'd just been tackled by Mike and all of his teammates at the same time.

A needle jabbed into my heart, and if Lucas hadn't been holding me up, I'd have slumped on the floor. In pain, I clutched my chest.

Miles away, a voice called out to me, but I couldn't tell whom it belonged to. It sounded muffled, as if I had cotton jabbed into my ears.

Not again.

Incenamus, the supernatural bond we shared, had only grown since I died and Lucas brought me back to life. He used a spell to rip his own soul apart and replaced my dead one with half of his. The pull to the rest of his soul now tugged at me too, like I could feel its instability growing the longer his spirit remained separated from it. Being corporeal most of the time, Lucas had lost most of that connection. Judging by the wailing in my head and the emptiness behind my ribs the last few weeks, I, on the other hand, seemed to have gained it.

Slowly, the pressure lessened and I lifted my head. Lucas stared down at me, concern lining his brow. "You all right?" We didn't know why this was happening, and I'd witnessed this expression too many times.

Luckily, whatever my spasms were, they didn't last long. A couple of times since they started I'd passed out, but I didn't today. I inhaled and blew the air out through puckered lips as the last of the pain exited my body. "Yeah. I'm fine."

I locked my knees to hold my weight again, and my arms fell from around Lucas's neck. He examined me, his stare doing a thorough assessment of my body before settling on my chest.

"Hey, I have eyes, you know. They're up here." I snickered at the tiny smile he offered at my joke. He placed a palm over my heart before his gaze floated up to mine.

"The seizures are getting stronger, aren't they?" he asked.

"I'm fine," I repeated.

Gingerly he cupped my face, a wash of cold caressing my skin. "No, Carrie, you're not. My soul, the piece that resides in you, is calling out for the rest. If we don't find it soon, these episodes might happen more often."

I groaned. "You make it sound like a supernatural form of epilepsy."

His jaw clenched. "Maybe it is."

"And if we don't unite..."

Wintery lips pressed hard on mine as he cut off his own thought. I didn't want to think about it either. We'd been through too much together to consider any other outcomes than the one we sought. The power of Incenamus bonded us, and tomorrow we'd begin our journey to make sure it stayed that way. Anything less was unacceptable.

"Carrie!" Grandma Renae's voice echoed up the stairwell. "It's time to go!"

"Be down in a minute!" I hollered back.

I groaned again. A reel of every possible disaster ran though my head. My parents—Mom *and* Griffin—would be in attendance. In fact, the only reason they weren't at the farmhouse pre-G-day was by my request. They'd been civil at Jessica's funeral, sure, but that was different. Today was all about me, or so I'd been told. Graduation was supposed to be fun. Exciting. A once-in-a-lifetime experience.

Whatever. Those things were reserved for kids whose parents were still together, who were graduating with their best friends at their sides, and who had some idea what they were going to do come September.

I had none of these things. Jessica, my BFF, was dead. Stacy, my ex-BFF, wouldn't return my calls. And did I mention that Griffin brought his twenty-six-year-old secretary fiancée with him to Villisca? Obviously she'd be at the ceremony too.

Absently, I glided the heart-infinity charm along the silver strand at my neck. Lucas had bought me a new chain after Carver broke the original one. I never took the necklace off now.

My attention wandered to a photo on my vanity. The picture had been Jess's idea, and Stacy had cringed at the burnt orange t-shirt Jess tossed her. Of course she put it on to match Jess and me, but her expression had resembled mine with the graduation gown minutes ago. Then we did the Hook 'em Horns signal as Jess's mom snapped the picture. It had only been two years ago, but it felt like another lifetime. Someone else's lifetime.

The uncertainty of the future coupled with the

horrors of the past was too much. Slowly, Lucas turned my face to him. He'd heard and seen everything in my head, and the tenderness in his gaze almost undid me. "Nothing beautiful ever really dies," he whispered.

Warmth flooded through me from the inside out. He cocooned me in his arms and kissed the top of my head.

"I always thought Jess was the prettiest of the three of us," I confessed.

Lucas's chest vibrated with his chuckle. "I was talking about friendship."

"That too."

"Come on, Mrs. Godzilla," he said, unhooking my grip on his waist. "You have a diploma with your name on it."

I felt the corner of my lip lift, my mood lightening, and I nudged him with my shoulder. "Call me that again and I'll get my reptilian husband to eat you."

"You're just saying that because I'm already dead and you know I'd come back for you."

"You want to test that theory?"

His eyebrows shot up in a challenge. "Do *you*?" His stare held mine for a long second before he captured my mouth in another kiss.

"Carrie! You're going to be late!" Grandma yelled again, but I ignored her. Lucas had me trapped in his embrace, and I imagined our perfect life. No graduation. No divorced parents or too-young fiancée. No broken friendships. No death.

And as he leaned in, I answered his question in a whisper.

"I already have."

Chapter 2

Forty-four seniors didn't take up much room in the gym where our graduation was to be held. Back in Sherman, my old class would be spread over the football field or crammed into the auditorium, depending on the weather. But this was the tiny village of Villisca. We didn't have an auditorium, and the football field seemed like overkill for this few a number. Two rows of metal chairs in front of a make-shift stage were sufficient. Spectators had plenty of room in the bleachers.

As luck would have it, the R last names sat directly behind the Cs. My best friend in this town and I had barely spoken since I told him Lucas's and my relationship wasn't any of his business. After that, he started to look at me differently, like he was disappointed in me. Lucas told me to give him space and he'd come around. I wish he'd hurry the hell up.

From the seat in front of me, Mike twisted, and for a second, I thought he would speak to me. I'd settle for a one-syllable word at this point. Instead he chin-upped fellow teammate Logan Rinner, who sat beside me. Mike's gaze drifted over me though before he turned back around.

Hello to you too.

The small gymnasium filled. A few stragglers shoved their way past those blocking the doors from the cafeteria. I caught sight of Mandy, Mike's little sister, among them, squeezing through the crowd. In Sherman, eight-year-olds stayed glued to their parents at events like this, but here in Villisca no one batted an eye at lone kids. Determination crunched up her face as she huffed by Mr. Graundelin, her last roadblock to the bleachers. Her overdramatic expressions made her even cuter. Once through, she blew out her cheeks and climbed up to sit with her parents. Beside them strung the line of my family.

Griffin. Secretary. Grandpa. Grandma. Lucas. Mom. The seating order seemed to have been decided beforehand. At least they resembled civility. I hoped it would stay that way.

The dimple on Lucas's cheek sank deep as he grinned at me. He nodded knowingly, probably reading my thoughts regarding the family seating chart. He was still better at slipping into my thoughts than vice versa.

"Welcome VHS class of 2016!" our too-peppy principal announced, her arms open wide as if anticipating a group hug.

NGH, lady.

"Is this over yet?" I mumbled to myself.

In front of me, Mike's shoulders vibrated. He must have heard me, because he tilted his head back slightly and whispered, "In a hurry? *Hot* date or something?"

"Don't be a jerk, Mike," I said.

"I'll take that as a no."

I leaned back against my chair, fighting the urge to cross my arms. Megan said he talked to her a few times after the fire at the Axe Murder House. He asked a lot of questions about witches and ghosts and necromancers, and he borrowed a few of Vanessa's books on various supernatural subjects. I'd hoped all the research would have made him more understanding toward Lucas and me, but apparently not.

I spaced off during the remainder of the ceremony. A couple students and a teacher presented speeches about—I don't know—following your dreams, probably.

"So I'd like to leave you with this: you get one shot at life; follow your dreams," Gabby, the valedictorian, finished. Then she flashed a camera-friendly smile.

Applause erupted as if she just announced the cure for cancer, mostly from the adults in the bleachers. The student section was less enthusiastic. I clapped three times.

The one positive about today was that the distribution of diplomas at Villisca High took a grand total of fifteen minutes. When the principal presented Mike his, he raised the leather folder above his head with the world's largest grin on his face. He hollered out his success, to which the rest of the football team blasted out whoops along with him. Regardless of Mike's earlier comment, I chuckled at that. His parents stood up and cheered, and Mandy did one of her famous pinkies-in-her-mouth whistles she usually reserved for games.

I didn't make a show after receiving mine; it *was* only high school. I simply shook hands with Mrs. Costa, offered a tight-lipped glance toward my cheering section, and made my way back to my cold, metal chair.

"Congrats, Reese," Mike murmured after I sat down, not making eye contact, which was Mike's version of remorse.

"Thanks. You too."

Following the closing statement, we did the throw-our-caps-in-the-air-for-the-parental-photo-op, then played rummage-on-the-floor-for-it as camera flashes went off like fireworks. Seriously, it was the most clichéd graduation ever.

Afterward, Grandma and Grandpa and the Carsons ushered Mike and me together for a picture. For all they knew, we were as tight as ever. Mike put his arm around my shoulder and hugged me against him.

"Play it up," he told me. Then he put on the cheese, sticking his tongue out and holding up his new diploma.

"Cocky," Lucas mouthed to me, referring to Mike. I gave a small shrug in reply, because irritated at him or not, Mike was Mike and cockiness usually worked for him. Sometimes it was even an endearing trait.

"Okay, you two," Mrs. Carson said. "Now a serious one, please."

I let off a smile as Mike repositioned himself

beside me. This time, he threaded his fingers with mine as if Lucas wasn't two feet away. A twinge of pain that didn't belong to me twisted in my heart, and I looked up at Mike. Hazel irises gazed at me, intense and apologetic, and I didn't understand why until his mouth crashed onto mine. His arms tightened around me, keeping me close. Sorrow draped over my soul—Lucas's soul—like a veil. The depth of it overtook my shock, and I sucked in air through the kiss.

Slow and gentle, Mike released me. He studied me for a reaction. I knew our audience waited too. Lucas's expression was a mix of anger and despair, but he didn't move toward us.

Heat warmed my skin, anger overpowered the flood of emotions swirling inside me, and I did the one thing I never thought I'd do. I pulled my arm back and smacked my best friend across the face. Without a word, I walked away.

***

I sat in my car, torn between feeling ashamed and proud of my actions. Mike had no right to do what he did. Still, had he deserved the handprint I left on his cheek?

"The boyfriend part of me votes yes," Lucas said, materializing in the passenger seat.

"Do you have another part besides the boyfriend part?"

"The small part that understands why he did it."

"Is that why you didn't intervene?" My tone sounded more hurt than I felt.

"And cause a scene?" He smirked. "Besides, I think you handled it."

I huffed. "Speaking of causing a scene, someone could have seen you, you know," I said, changing topics to how he showed up in my car out of thin air. "It's daylight, and this place is swarming with people."

"They're preoccupied with post-ceremony photo shoots and after parties. Which we need to talk about."

I shook my head adamantly. "I'm not going to Mike's party. Not after what he did."

"That's not what I meant."

"Then what did you mean?"

"Your parents. I think you should go to the dinners alone."

Tension flowed out of my shoulders and I felt them slump. "No. Why?"

"Because they came all this way to see you, not me. You've been away for months now, and they miss you." His voice softened, and I realized he was thinking of his own family, the one he didn't remember.

I pressed my hand into his, feeling his coolness collide with the warmth of my own skin. "I want you with me, Lucas. I don't…" I pursed my lips, the image of my mother crying as she told me *Griffin* was leaving flashing through my mind. "I don't think I can do it alone." In a whisper, I added, "I don't want to."

Lucas was quiet for a moment, the scene in my head playing out for him too. "Carrie, they're your parents. They're not cambions or demons. They love you and want what's best for you," he said, reaching over the center console and pulling me toward him. "And if you decide not to come tomorrow—"

"Stop trying to convince me not to go with you. It's a done deal."

"I'm not trying to convince you, but I need you to be sure. I don't know what'll happen once we get there."

"I do," I said. "We'll accomplish what we came for and then live happily ever after."

***

I'd been played. Somehow Lucas had distracted me, then persuaded me to go out to lunch without him. I guessed that meant it was officially "girl time," which would have been great under other circumstances. Today, though…not so much.

Maylee, I assumed by the nametag, placed our plates in front of us. She laid the ticket face-down at the edge of the table. "Can I get you anything else?"

"I think we're good, thank you," Mom answered for the both of us. After our waitress left, my mother pulled out the big guns. Up until now, we'd done mostly small talk—weather, her job, Grandma's antique store. Neither of us mentioned the post-graduation Mike incident. "So, are you all packed to come back with me to Texas tomorrow? You only have a few months before classes begin at UT."

"I only graduated today. Do I really have to make this decision right now?" College and my plans for tomorrow were topics I wanted to evade forever.

"You make it sound like I sprang this on you last minute when we've been talking about it for weeks."

Clarification: *she'd* been talking about it for *months*.

"Then a few more days won't hurt, right?" I showed off a toothy smile she flagged as fake in less than a second.

She sighed and grabbed her coffee mug. "You've avoided the question since I arrived two days ago." Mom never did miss much, and after nine months apart, her mom-dar seemed to work perfectly fine. Damn it.

This conversation had to happen, I knew that, but that didn't make it suck any less. She was right though. My time for stalling was officially up.

Here goes nothing.

I took a deep breath and let it out thin and slow to buy an extra moment or two. My eyes never left my plate. "Okay. Well, I'm, uh…taking the semester off. Lucas and I are leaving for his hometown in North Carolina tomorrow."

Her mug hit the edge of the table, a small wave of dark brown spilling over the rim. With wide eyes too shocked to blink, she didn't even notice that her hand was covered in coffee.

Silence dropped like a weight, and I wondered if she was breathing. She opened her mouth as if she was going to respond, but only half a nonsensical noise came out.

Finally, she regained her composure and cocked

her head to the side. "Is this about sex?"

Say what?

"What? Mom, no. I…" had no response for this. Nothing.

She stared at me, apparently expecting me to complete the sentence. If she kept her neck at that angle too much longer, she'd be sore in the morning.

She must've realized I wasn't going to talk, because she straightened her head and softened her brow. Great. It was lecture time.

I wasn't interested.

"Carrie," she began, "You and Lucas are close; I see that. But, honey, you just finished high school, just started life. The first boy you think you love might not be the one you'll always love. What about that Mike boy? He's obviously smitten with you."

She was speaking from experience with Griffin. Parents never wanted their kids to make the same mistakes as them. The difference was that I wasn't her. And Lucas wasn't Griffin.

I wasn't in the mood to comment on my prick of a best friend.

"I'm an adult now—eighteen. I'm capable of making my own decisions. And if I fail, I fail. At least it will be on my own terms, and I'll have no one but myself to blame." I leaned forward to take her hand when I saw the tear slide down her cheek. Knowing how hard this would be for her and seeing it were two different things, and a part of me wanted to take back what I said. But this was my life, and I needed to be the one controlling it.

"Mom, I've only thought as far out as one

semester. I'm not putting off college forever. There are some things I have to figure out first."

She wiped away the tear, but the husk in her voice remained. "You've had a hard year, baby, and I'm so sorry about that. If I could do it all over again, make difference choices, I would."

"I know, Mom."

Mom let out a sniffled snicker. "When did my little girl grow up?"

I laughed. "When we weren't looking."

She sat thoughtful, gliding her thumbs over the backs of my hands. "I'm not going to lie; I'm disappointed that you're running off to another state with a boy and forsaking school."

"I know."

Her gaze narrowed, and I worried what came next. "But."

There's always a but. Maybe this will be a good *but?*

She paused, examining me over her glasses. "I understand. You gave me the time I needed, and I want to step back and give you the time you need."

My worry vanished as quickly as Lucas from my bedroom at the sound of Grandma climbing the stairs. "Thanks, Mom."

"You didn't think you were the only one who grew this year, did you?" She winked at me, and I realized how her face held its natural colors again. She wore a little makeup, the bags under her eyes had all but disappeared, and the blue-green of her irises sparkled more than I'd seen in years.

"Have you told your dad yet?" she asked, her tone turning serious again.

I fought the groan in my throat. She'd complimented my growth a second ago, so I couldn't let the groan out and ruin it for myself. "We're doing dinner tonight. I'll tell him then."

"And the wedding? Still not going?"

"Why should I? He didn't need me for a divorce; he doesn't need me to get re-married." Yep, there went my attempt at adulting. I swiped up my grilled chicken and took a bite, hoping this conversation was over.

It wasn't.

Mom straightened. "Because he's your father. And you need to forgive him."

I lifted my eyes to her. "Have you?"

"I'm getting there. The hardest part of forgiving someone is convincing yourself that you should. The rest will come."

My thoughts trailed to Stacy. Griffin.

To Lucas and the reason he didn't cross over when he died.

If only it were that easy.

***

After lunch with Mom, I called and asked Lucas to reconsider. His answer hadn't changed and true to his word, he didn't show up at the restaurant in Council Bluffs that evening. So I sat in my car, watching the clock pass the seven p.m. mark before I got out and walked through the door at Murphy's a few minutes late on purpose. My logic? Them waiting for me was more comfortable than me waiting on them.

While Mom picked somewhere homey and local, this place was a few towns over and had clean floors and shiny silverware. The hostess had already seated my party.

Griffin and Ami faced an empty chair, presumably mine. Ami wore a pleasant expression and too much makeup, including fake eyelashes. Beside her, Griffin tugged at his collar and bobbed his head at whatever she was saying to him. When he noticed me walking toward them, he scooted his chair back and stood up.

"Hey, princess," he said, and I wondered if he expected a hug.

The only move I made was to pull out my own chair and sit down. "Hey."

Ami beamed at me. This was technically our first meeting. "What a great graduation ceremony, Carrie. You should be very proud of yourself and your accomplishments."

Is she for real?

In the name of politeness, I answered, "Thank you." Ami probably remembered her high school graduations very clearly, and the last thing I needed was for her to go into "I remember when" stories of eight years ago in an effort to "make a connection" with me. God, was this evening over yet?

Thankfully our server asked for my beverage choice, which knocked off a whole twenty seconds of uncomfortableness. In hindsight, I should have pondered my selection longer.

Griffin nodded at me, his idea of a conversation starter. "Your mom said you got accepted to UT. Good choice. I think you're going to like it there."

How quickly my parents had gone to referring to the other as the parent who belonged to me. I was the one thing, the only thing, they shared. Not like glue, though, because I didn't stick them together. I was more like a traveling trophy—important yet homeless.

"Yeah, except I won't be taking classes until spring semester," I offered. Ami's reaction to my announcement meant jack shit to me, and really, Griffin's didn't mean much more.

"Have you chosen a major yet?" Ami asked, as if I hadn't said what I said. My choices didn't matter to her, nor should they. She was here to play nice.

"No."

"Wait a second. Why aren't you going this fall?" Griffin's voice rumbled with part confusion and part irritation.

"I'm taking the semester off," I answered, more coolly than I intended.

"Doing what?" His tone deepened, and any nervousness he'd had when I arrived disappeared like the wedding ring Mom gave him twenty years ago when he'd promised till death do they part. Suddenly, the man in front of me morphed into my two-years-ago father, the one who used to have some say over my life.

I didn't want to fight in public, so I went into survival mode. Answer questions with as little snark as I could muster, giving away as little as I could.

"Traveling."

"To where?"

"South."

"Carrie Anne Reese," he warned. Like he had the

right.

Blood boiled in my veins, and I fought to keep it from rising to the surface. "North Carolina."

"What's in North Carolina?"

I had enough of this Q&A. Plus, the vein in Griffin's neck pulsed more erratically with each of my answers. It wasn't my intention to piss him off. To calm the waters, I would have to offer a little more information.

"Lucas's family," I said. A part of me wanted him to understand the way my mother had. Understanding, not approval, was my end goal. "After his sister died, he left and hasn't been back. I want to go with him for moral support."

Griffin placed his elbows on the table and rested his chin on the tops of his folded hands. "This will take the whole summer along with a semester of school?"

"Maybe. I don't know, but I don't want to put a time limit on it."

His mouth formed a straight line, something he did to intimidate me. It worked wonders when I was six. "Lucas is okay with you abandoning school, family, to run around with him for months?" he asked, eyebrows perked.

"Griffin," Ami said softly. She must know this expression too.

"No, no. I want to know what kind of a boy thinks this is acceptable, Ami," he said.

If my arms were long enough and I wanted to cause a scene, I would have reached across the table and smacked him across the face like I had Mike. But since my arms were short, I used words for the same effect. “The grieving kind. You know, like your daughter over her best friend? Have you considered that maybe I *can’t* go back to Texas right now? With Jessica not there?” I felt my nostrils flare as heat rose to my cheeks. Somehow I managed to stay calm despite the rising anger. “And for your information, it was my idea, not his. He wanted me to go to school. I refused. You lost a say in my life when you walked out of it.”

The urge to scoot my chair back, stand up, and leave the restaurant ached in my legs. From the corner of my eye, I saw Ami stare at Griffin, chewing nervously on her lip. Griffin’s gaze burned into me, and I returned the heat.

I don’t know how long we sat like that, exchanging fire. It seemed like forever, but I stood my ground. Didn’t move. Didn’t speak.

Finally, Griffin’s shoulders rose and fell in a deep sigh, and he folded his arms in front of him. “You always were stubborn. Inherited it from me, I suppose.” He glanced at the blonde beside him, and unspoken words passed between them. Then he returned to me. “Go to Carolina, but if you need *anything*, you call me. We clear?”

“Yes,” I answered, already deciding I wouldn’t need a damn thing.

Griffin nodded, and we dropped back into uncomfortable silence until the server came for our orders.

After the waitress left, Ami cleared her throat. “So, did the dress fit okay?”

Dress? What dress? I was about to ask when I suddenly remembered the unopened box I’d shoved in the back of my closet after Christmas.

The wedding. My bridesmaid dress.

“Yeah. Fits great,” I lied.

“I thought you’d like the color. Griffin showed me a picture of you and your friends at prom, and I commented on how lovely the color of your dress went with your eyes.”

My eyes were brown. No color went with brown. Whatever. I hadn’t even agreed to be *at* their shindig, let alone be a part of it. But I didn’t say anything.

The rest of dinner dragged on with Ami asking questions and keeping up the pleasantries. I didn’t offer much, but she acted like she didn’t expect me to. I appreciated that. If it weren’t for her marrying my dad, I might have liked her.

Outside the restaurant, Griffin hugged me and kissed my hair. “I love you, princess. Be careful out there.”

“I will,” I assured him.

Ami didn’t hug me. “It was wonderful to finally meet you, Carrie. I’ll be in touch as the wedding gets closer.”

“Great,” I said without enthusiasm.

I got in my car and didn’t look back to see if they’d left the sidewalk yet. All I wanted was to get out of there. As I pulled onto the highway, a tingle fluttered up my stomach and settled in my chest. A cool breeze swept over my cheek, caressing me. My heart stuttered, and Lucas appeared in the passenger seat beside me.

“I don’t want to talk,” I said out loud.

“I wasn’t going to ask.”

I drove on, trying to clear my mind. What a crappy last day in Villisca, and it all began with a graduation I didn't want to attend in the first place. At least this day would end with Lucas by my side.

Lucas let out a small snicker. I felt him in my head, but I was used to it by now.

"What's so funny?" I asked.

He scratched his forehead, relieving an itch he didn't have. I concentrated on opening my soul to break into *his* thoughts. I pushed, pounded, then grunted in frustration. The tiny grin on his face unnerved me.

"You're on edge. Maybe you should let me drive," he suggested.

"Maybe you should tell me what's so funny," I retorted.

Lucas laughed, his lone dimple appearing and reminding me that I couldn't stay irritated at him for long.

"I have a surprise…of sorts," he said.

"Of sorts? What kind of sorts?"

"Pull over. Relax. Enjoy the rest of the ride, okay? After today, you could use some time to cut loose and have fun."

I couldn't argue with that. Plus, I usually enjoyed Lucas's version of fun. And judging by the sexy glint he shot me as I pulled his Jeep onto the gravel shoulder, tonight would be no exception.

Yep, I could totally deal with that. Bring on the stars, the moonlight, and Lucas's skin on mine.

Chapter 3

Not. Fun.

Are you freaking kidding me?

I heard the country-pop beat of Luke Bryan booming from the hay field before Lucas parked the Jeep. I couldn't believe this was his idea of "cutting loose and having some fun" all of a sudden.

His explanation? I wasn't allowed to leave the state until I made amends with Mike. Lame. So, so lame.

"He kissed *me*, remember?" I said.

"I was there." He reached for my hand, cooling it with his touch. "Lead the way."

So I did. I re-opened the Jeep door and hoisted myself up to get back in. Unfortunately, Lucas stopped me.

"Nice try, Carrie, but I'm pretty sure the party is in the opposite direction."

"I disagree," I muttered, but I shut the door at his insistence and walked toward the sound of "That's My Kind of Night." Congrats to Luke Bryan and all, but this was totally *not* my kind of night. Three bonfires erupted from the ground, all surrounded by square hay bales used as benches. Pick-up trucks with their tailgates open served as dance floors, and the senior members of the football team hovered around the kegs.

"'Sup, Carrie!" Logan hollered over the music.

I did a small wave in his direction, hoping it would satisfy him. It didn't.

"Get that girl a beer!"

Drunk Logan was incredibly loud. Drunk Logan apparently also followed his own orders. Holding two red Solo cups, he obstacle-coursed his way over to us. I watched carefully; Drunk Logan was surprisingly light on his feet.

He thrust a cup at me and one at Lucas. "I was wondering when you were going to show up. Mike doubted you'd come, but I knew better! You wouldn't miss an opportunity to *part-ay* one last time with me!" He rolled his hips and bit his lower lip seductively before hooting into the night sky.

Drunk Logan clearly didn't know me.

"Where's Mike?" I asked, ready to do what I came for and get the hell out.

"Wanting another kiss, huh?" Logan winked at Lucas and managed to undress me with his eyes at the same time. Drunk Logan was also a douchebag.

"No. Where is he?"

"I don't know. Somewhere. Around…" he slurred, lassoing a finger in front of his face. "Here." He pointed in the direction of the field where no one was. Real helpful.

"Great. Thanks, Logan."

"You are welcome, baby. And when you're

ready to dance, you come and find me, okay? I gots better moves than Mikey and this guy." He thumbed at Lucas.

"I bet you do."

"Yes, I do." He nodded at me, like I'd actually consider his offer.

I peered around him, taking a quick scan of the area. Dancers crowded the truck beds, but Mike wasn't one of them. The outlines of a few couples moved inside the cabs, making out. I wasn't going to check that out. He wasn't with the rest of the team at the make-shift bar either.

I swung toward the bonfires, and there he was. At least, I was pretty sure it was him. I couldn't tell with the blonde straddling his lap.

I chugged my beer, because what the hell? It was an after graduation party and Lucas used the word "fun." Besides, I needed a bit of alcohol in my system to face my cocky best friend. I was on a mission now. I tossed the empty cup to Logan and strode over. Behind me, I heard Logan whistle, presumably at my ass. Yeah, I'd had enough of Drunk Logan.

"Ow, dude!" he grunted, and I figured Lucas hit him.

The couple sitting on the bale beside Mike and his company stood up to leave. Perfect timing. I didn't have to look to know that Lucas hadn't followed me. For the first time today, I was thankful for his absence. I lifted a red cup from some girl on my way over, so unlike me, but it felt good right now.

"Hey!" she cried, but didn't move to get it back.

It was half-drank anyway.

"Hello, *friend*," I said as I plopped down on the now-empty square bale. "Great party. Logan's having fun."

"You made it," he replied, voice monotone.

"Yep." I stuck my hand out to his squatter, whom I didn't recognize from school. "Hi, I'm Carrie. I'm the one responsible for that handprint on your boyfriend's face."

She puckered bright red lips. "Uh…maybe I should leave you to it." She swung a leg over and straightened her too-short skirt in front of me, one of her ass-cheeks giving me a little show. I suppressed a snort.

"Another beer, Mike?" she asked.

"Sure. Thanks."

She walked away, and Mike's gaze bored into me. "What the hell, Carrie?"

"I could ask you the same thing."

I sucked down my drink as Mike studied me. I hated the taste of beer, but as a light-weight, I already enjoyed the slight buzz I had. He massaged the stubble on his chin before he shook his head and laughed. "Damn it, Carrie. You're a pain in the ass, you know that?"

"You're a crappy friend, you know that?"

"I've told you a thousand times: I don't want to be your friend."

"Yeah, well, that's all I'm offering, and even that's close to being off the table."

"I'm not sure we have much to discuss, then." Hard hazel eyes, darker in the light of the fire, stared back at me.

"So that's it? All or nothing?" I fought to mask the hurt in my voice. I guess I hadn't expected that response.

"What do you want from me? Slumber parties in pink pajamas? Pillow fights after baking cookies? Painting our nails with little flowers on them?" He wiggled his fingers at me. "Shit, Carrie. You're running off with ghost-boy tomorrow for God knows how long, and I'm leaving for college at the end of July. We had a year. Year's over. Time to move on."

I swallowed, convincing myself that the burn in my eyes was because of the bonfire smoke. "You don't mean that."

His eyebrows flicked upward. "You sure?"

"After everything we've been through? Yeah, I'm sure."

I wasn't sure—I hoped.

"Keep telling yourself that."

The blonde sauntered back over and handed Mike his new beer. He knocked it back and threw the empty cup into the fire. Then, to her delighted squeals, he grabbed the girl's hips, yanked her down on him, and kissed her the way he had me earlier.

"I think you're jealous," I murmured, only half-meaning it.

"You know what I think?" he said, unlocking his lips from hers. "I think you don't know what the fuck you want."

My jaw trembled. "You're drunk."

"Doesn't mean I'm wrong."

I didn't understand. From my first days in Villisca, he'd been there for me. We'd had movie nights, rode horses on Sundays, and when I started school, he had included me with his friends. Months ago, he'd even risked his life for me. But now? Now he acted as if none of that mattered. Like our friendship meant nothing to him.

A tear snaked down my cheek, and I didn't bother wiping it away in front of him. Maybe he wouldn't notice it was there if I left it alone. I chucked the rest of my beer into the fire. When I turned to leave, the last thing I heard was the blonde's breathy giggles.

***

Lucas wasn't at his Jeep. My body felt like it was being squeezed in from all sides, and I wanted to puke. In two months, I'd lost my three best friends. How much more did I have to lose?

I staggered back to the party and went to the "bar." Alcohol masked pain, right? I grabbed a cup off the table and emptied it down my throat. Then I grabbed another.

Logan came up behind me and grinded against me. "Ready for that dance?"

I shoved him away before gulping down my second drink. God, it was disgusting, but unlike Stacy, Mike didn't serve strawberry daiquiris and piña coladas, and I had to deal with it.

As I reached for a third, someone grabbed my wrist. "I think you've had enough."

"I don't care what you think," I said, facing Mike.

"You care what Rob and Renae think, and so do

I. I'm not sending you home too drunk to walk through the front door."

"I'm not your responsibility," I seethed, pissed and hurt and pissed some more.

"You're on *my* property."

"So? Everyone else here is too, and I don't see you policing them."

I must have gotten through to him, because he loosened his grip. He looked me over, conflict glazing over his once laughing stare. Then he let go completely, giving up.

He held his hands up in surrender. "Fine. By all means, drink yourself unconscious."

I glared at him for a second before pushing my way past and stumbling between two of the pick-up trucks with dancing senior girls.

Where's Lucas?

As soon as I thought it, I spotted him talking with someone in the middle of the field, away from the party.

I marched over. Luminous irises like fire locked onto me as I trampled over the grass. Stupid hay field. Stupid party. Stupid everything.

"Let's go," I said when I reached him.

I'd interrupted something, but so what? He was the one who'd brought me here against my will. Now he could take me home.

"Carrie, are you okay?"

The girl was the first to speak. I glanced up, squinting through the dark to make out her features.

"Megan. I didn't realize you'd be here." I swallowed the bile rising in my throat. My head was fuzzy and heat coursed through my veins.

"Mike invited me," she said, giving me a onceover. "Are you drunk?"

"That might explain why I couldn't feel her," Lucas murmured. "Come here."

He tucked me in against him. No longer holding all my own weight, I felt a little less dizzy, Lucas feeling a little more solid.

"Alcohol severs our connection, huh?" I asked, massaging my temples in hopes of some clarity.

"Not severs. Impairs," Megan explained.

"So if I want him out of my head, I just need to get sloshed. I'll remember that," I said, sounding more whiny than I meant.

They ignored me.

"All right," Lucas said, maybe resuming their private conversation. "But we need to be more careful this time. With part of my soul inside Carrie, we're not taking any risks."

"It's a gamble, Lucas, regardless," Megan said. "Nothing like this has succeeded before. Hell, I don't even know if it has ever been attempted. At least"—her eyes flicked to me then back to Lucas—"you know what I mean. It's only a myth."

"I'm buzzed, not dead. I can still see and hear, you know," I informed them.

Again, they ignored me.

"Any sign of Reid?" Lucas continued.

"No, nothing. I've tried every tracking spell I could find. It's like he's vanished."

I felt Lucas's chest expand under my ear. "He's out there somewhere. Keep trying."

"I will."

"How's Vanessa?"

Megan blew out a long sigh. "Mom's not doing well. If a necro doesn't show up soon…" She trailed off and bowed her head. "I don't know what will happen. I'm not leaving Villisca, though. Not as long as I can be of help."

"What's going on? What's wrong with your mom?" I asked. No one had said anything to me, and I'd just seen Vanessa a few weeks ago. She seemed fine. Tired, sure, but fine.

This time, my inquiry was not ignored.

"She's sick. Exhausted from the influx of spirits coming day and night," Megan answered.

"Doing the necromancer's job is hurting her?"

Megan nodded. "Everyone has their place and time on this earth. Everyone has a purpose, Carrie. Being a necromancer isn't hers."

"Villisca should have had one by now," I said, repeating what Megan told me months ago. Necromancers had to answer some kind of call in order to be instated into their position. Megan didn't know what that entailed. "Where are they?"

"I wish I knew."

***

I fell asleep on the way back to my grandparents' house. To their knowledge, I was going to Mike's party, so they didn't wait up. I awoke when I felt the familiar tug in my stomach, like my skin and bones were being stretched and forced through a keyhole.

Teleporting, my brain supplied.

Lucas and I appeared in my bedroom, me in his

arms, and I breathed out a long exhale of relief.

"That was most fun I've had all night," I murmured, half-awake.

"I owed you."

"Yeah, and you still do."

"I'll hold your hair back when you throw up later," he teased, the smirk on his face making me hum out what was supposed to be a giggle.

"Okay, deal."

My head pounded, and the sliver of moonlight peeking through the curtains was enough to kill my eyesight.

Darkness, oh how I love you.

I let Lucas lead me to my bed, because my balance sucked. He draped warm blankets over me. Beside me, the mattress sank as Lucas laid down. He spooned my body perfectly, except for the stupid duvet that separated us. It kept me from freezing, as if I cared about that.

I didn't have the energy to argue, though. Actually, I didn't have the energy for anything but deep, deep sleep.

My last night in Villisca. In the morning, Lucas and I would begin our forever.

Together.

Chapter 4

A few weeks shy of a full year here, yet nothing had changed. Not on the outside anyway. My grandparents' farmhouse with peeling white paint on the picket fence stood silent behind me. Goldie, my horse, stomped a back hoof by the fence as if irritated that I was leaving her.

"You'll always have a room here, Care," Grandma Renae said. "And a job."

"You have Megan again this summer," I reminded her. "One of her knows more than two of me anyway."

Grandma pulled me into her again. "You sure you want to go?"

"I'm sure, Grandma." I hugged her. "You take care of Grandpa, okay?"

"I'll do my best, but you know him—stubborn old man."

I let go of her and turned to Grandpa Rob. My understanding, wonderful grandfather always seemed to get me. "You work too hard" was the first thing out of my mouth as I wrapped my arms around his sweaty neck. Already by ten a.m. he'd been in the fields for hours. Mike was out there now, somewhere, continuing the chores. Our conversation from last night played out in my head again, and I had to force it away.

"Gotta eat." Grandpa always smelled like Old Spice. "You planning on being at your dad's wedding?"

"I'm not sure I'll be able to make it," I told him honestly. That was how much I respected my grandfather.

"Well…think about it while you're gone. You being there might be good for the both of you."

I released him and looked up into the glossy brown eyes I'd inherited from him. His were always so gentle, the kind that made you like him immediately. In fact Grandma once told me it was Grandpa's eyes that made her say *yes* to their first date and *yes* to his marriage proposal. They were eyes that knew things—tough things—yet remained thoughtful.

"I don't see how me going would be good for me," I said, peering over my shoulder at Lucas.

Grandpa put a hand on my shoulder, bringing my attention back to him. "You will, Care Bear. You will."

I studied him for a second. His solicitous smile held a hint of mystery that his eyes lacked. It was the only sign that he kept anything hidden.

I smiled back, letting him know I was on to him. "Okay, then. Keep your secrets."

He just nodded at me with that knowing gaze of his.

"Sir," Lucas said, extending his hand to my grandfather. "I'll take good care of her. I promise."

Again, Grandpa nodded as he shook Lucas's hand. "All right." He glanced at his watch. "You kids had better get going if you're going to make it through Nashville by sunset."

I'd made motel reservations outside of Nashville. Lucas insisted he could drive straight through, but I'd done my research and I disagreed. With Congress Inn and Tennessee State Prison located in Nashville, there were at least two decent sized rifts to Hell within that city—and a couple outside—which meant greater chances of wandering demons. I wasn't going to risk it, even with Megan's protection spells shrouding Lucas's Jeep.

Obviously that wasn't Grandpa's reasoning for us to get through the city before dark. He knew nothing about the supernatural world around us. No, he just hated when I drove at night.

"Yeah, we'd better," I said, giving my grandparents one last look. "Thank you. For everything."

Watching them through the glass, I closed the Jeep door. Lucas slowly backed out of the gravel drive. When we reached the end, Grandma and Grandpa waved, and they didn't stop until I could no longer see them out of the rearview mirror.

Lucas reached for my hand. *"It's not too late to turn around,"* he said inside my head.

"Yes, it is. The moment you tore your soul in half and gave it to me, it became too late," I answered out loud. "And we're not coming back until you have a spirit, body, *and* soul."

"You're confident," Lucas noted in a way that suggested he might not be.

"Yeah. I am." I studied him, waiting to see if he'd give more away. He didn't.

I took one last look out my window, and my heart jumped into my throat. Mike stood in one of Grandpa's fields, close enough to the road for me to see him following us with his stare, but not close enough for me to see his expression.

Then again, it didn't matter. He'd already said his goodbye, and I didn't need a second one.

In fact, I never wanted to hear that word again.

***

A few miles outside Villisca, I kicked off my shoes and settled in. We had a long drive, and I might as well be comfortable. I twisted to either side of me, my back cracking with each movement. I rolled my neck too and tucked my legs under me. Yep, all comfy.

Lucas laughed. "You're like a cat."

"Meow!" I rubbed my cheek on his arm and made purring noises.

He petted the top of my head. "Megan gave us some travel reading. You interested?"

I checked the backseat. Two stacks of ancient books rose up from the middle. I hissed at the sight.

"What else are we going to do?" he asked, his eyebrows in a flirtatious peak.

"It was your idea to take the stupid Jeep. You could have just teleported us there, and we could be doing *else* right now." I tried and failed to contain my grin.

"Want me to pull over?"

"Would you?"

"No."

"Why did you ask then?" My voice rose playfully.

"To see that crazy gleam in your eye. It's cute when you get all worked up over little things." Lucas snickered.

"Crazy, huh? You ain't seen nothing yet."

"I'm looking forward to it. For now, though…" He nodded toward the backseat.

"Light reading." I grabbed whatever book was on top and grimaced at the title. I flipped it around to show Lucas. "Not English. How much you wanna bet what's inside isn't English, either?"

"My life."

"Ha. Ha."

I opened the book anyway and groaned. Yep, not English.

"It's Latin," Lucas said.

"That's nice. But knowing what it is doesn't mean I can read it." I closed the book and reached for another one. "*Latin to English Dictionary*. Helpful. So are all these in Latin?"

Lucas shrugged. "Only one way to find out."

"Why did she send us a bunch of books in a dead language?"

"I read Latin."

I frowned. "Have you ever wondered how you remember stuff like that and not more important things?"

"It wasn't until I came across it that I realized I

could read and understand it."

"Maybe Susan Taylor was right. Maybe your memory is returning in bits and pieces."

"I don't recall any of the stuff Reid told me though. I've tried. Nothing's there." He tapped his thumb on the steering wheel. "I think I need some sort of outside stimulus to trigger the memory. Something physical I can touch or see. Like the Latin. Like the stars."

"I guess it's good, then, that we're heading to where it all happened. Should have a ton of triggers."

"Yeah, hopefully." The corner of his lips curved up, but his gaze stayed on the road.

I examined the covers of a few more books. A couple I recognized, because I'd seen Megan reading them before. Most, though, I didn't. I had no interest in digging into a book I didn't understand. What was the point?

Halfway through the pile, one caught my eye. By the golden chemistry beaker imprinted on the cover, I assumed the book was about potions. Again, a language I didn't know graced the top, but I opened it anyway. The first page contained pictures of plants and—

Please tell me those aren't intestines.

"Pig intestines," Lucas said, rubbernecking.

"Disgusting."

I kept scanning the pages. Megan wrote notes in the margins, half of them in English. I read those but couldn't make much sense out of them:

For stronger antidote, add extra 5

ml.

Slower titration yields better accuracy and more potency.

DO NOT exceed 411.6° F.

I continued through the book, occasionally recognizing some words that resembled their English counterparts—at least *my assumptions* of their English counterparts. Toward the end of the book Megan's handwriting littered an entire page. Notes were written, circled in red, then scribbled out, and even her *notes* had notes. She'd done the same thing with the actual text. Another few page turns and I realized the rest of book was much the same. In fact, there were no other potion titles.

This is one long, complicated potion.

I went back to the beginning of the section, curiosity fueling me. The bottom of the second page was missing. I shot a quick peek over at Lucas.

"Anything interesting?" he asked, smiling, presumably because I'd found something worthwhile.

"Actually yes. What does *res-tit-ue ani-man ad in-fer-os ded-u-cent-ur* mean?" I asked, fumbling out the pronunciation.

His smile fell. "Let me see."

I lowered the book and pointed at the title. "Right there. The whole spell or whatever is in—"

"Latin. Yeah."

"Except for Megan's notes."

When he didn't answer, I asked again. "So what's it for?"

"It's a potion for—Carrie?"

Dizziness washed in without warning, and I barely heard Lucas say my name. Suddenly, the world around me began to spin. Faster and faster until the colors were a whirl that all blended into a haze of sickly brown. I hunched forward, cradling my head between my knees.

I held my breath. Counted—

One. Two. Three. Four...

My head exploded in pain. My heart pounded, thudding harder and harder, like it too was close to exploding. I tried to inhale, but air caught in my throat.

I can't breathe.

Images flashed through my mind: trees. A winding road. Reid. 314.

A graveyard. People stood around a coffin, wearing black. The picture blurred, and the faces became unrecognizable.

Then they were gone. Replaced by a tombstone.

And etched in marble was a name:

Lucas Reynolds.

Chapter 5

Something hard jabbed me in the back, but it wasn't enough to rouse me completely. Stuck somewhere between asleep and awake, I wasn't sure what was real and what was a dream. Pictures moved in and out of my mind. Voices funneled through my ears. Some I recognized. Some were too fuzzy.

Two voices seemed close, though. Wherever I was, they were there too. Only snippets of their conversation came through. The rest faded out, and I figured I was slipping back into unconsciousness.

"…the potions book. She wants to know about it."

Lucas—the voice belongs to Lucas.

"I guess you can either tell her or lie to her."

And Megan.

"I'm not going to lie to her," Lucas murmured. "But I can't tell her the truth until I know it's going to work."

"We've been toying and testing the formula for months now, Lucas. It may never work."

"I can't get her hopes up just to have them shattered."

"There's only one way this can end. She'll be shattered either way."

"No. I won't let that happen."

"You may not have a choice…"

Blackness enveloped me again as spasms rocked my body. My heart tore down the middle, and I knew it was Lucas's pain I felt.

"This will kill her, won't it?" Lucas asked.

"The seizures? I don't know, Lucas. I'm trying to freaking walk on water here. None of this has been recorded in any book I know of. We're on our own, but you knew that when you decided to split your soul."

Lucas's tone hardened. "Then take. A guess."

"I have a theory, based on what little information we have."

"Lay it on me."

"A soul must be reunited with its spirit or both will cease to exist. This we know. We also know your soul has been calling for you. But by choosing to stay corporeal, you've lost your ability to feel it beckoning to you. When you used the power of Incenamus to bring Carrie back to life, you did two things. One, you cut whatever time you had to find your soul in half. And two—and this is my theory—you created a supernatural magnet. Broken souls cannot survive apart, even less so than souls without their spirits."

"So this will keep happening until what? I reunite with the other half?"

"Maybe. Or until her half breaks free."

A tense silence draped over them.

When Lucas answered, the husk in his voice made him barely audible. "Incenamus gave her life back to her. Are you saying it can take it away?"

"It's a possibility. I'll keep researching, see what I can find."

"And until then?"

"I can give her a potion. It won't stop the halves from trying to reunite, but it might stop the seizures."

"No. No more potions for her."

"Then what the hell do you want me to do, Lucas?"

"Save her."

A long pause.

Then Megan's voice lowered. "*I* can't."

***

Sunlight splashed over my eyelids, and I rolled away from it with a moan. The soft scent of leather hit my nostrils, forcing me awake.

Car leather, I realized.

It took me a second to remember why a leather backseat touched the tip of my nose. Hadn't I called shotgun? I was pretty sure I had. In fact…I lifted my leg and confirmed my suspicions. Bare feet. I only did that if I was riding in the front.

But now I was in the back. And the engine wasn't running.

I sat up and looked out the window into the blinding sunlight. I squinted, focusing on the convenience store entrance. The shadow behind the glass extended an arm and pushed the door open. He carried a bottle of water.

I opened the Jeep door to climb out, but as my feet hit filthy cement, I pulled them back in. Gas station ground was the worst kind for bare feet.

"Good morning, my beautiful snoring girl."

"I don't snore. Is it seriously morning already?"

Lucas gave me the water. "No, but you've been out for almost eight hours."

"No way? So where are we?"

"A couple hours outside of Nashville."

I snapped my attention to the opposite window. Sure enough, dusk was approaching. "We're not going to make it to our hotel before sunset, are we?"

"It'll be close."

Thirsty, I sucked down half the water. Amazing. Then I finished it off and gave the empty bottle back to Lucas. "Okay, where are my shoes? My turn to drive."

Lucas twirled the keys around his index finger, eyebrows raised. "After you just slept like the dead?"

I tried to swipe the keys from him but missed when he yanked his arm up. "No, after I put on my shoes and pee."

He caught the keys in his palm. "To Nashville? At twilight?"

"I thought you said it wouldn't be a big deal?" I reminded him. I batted my eyelashes too, to rub in his own words.

"Because *I* would be driving."

I got out, small rocks, spit, and whatever other nastiness I didn't want to think about sticking to the bottoms of my feet...all to challenge my overprotective boyfriend. "You afraid, Lucas Reynolds?"

"Terrified."

I pulled up to my tip-toes, eyeing his fisted hand above his head. "We've outmaneuvered demons before when I was driving. I'm sure we can do it again." I used *we* to make him feel better, but we both knew it was me.

He smirked. "It's not the demons I'm concerned about. Those I can handle."

"Oh, really? Then what are you worried about?" I let my tone turn flirtatious to match his.

"Female drivers. They account for eighty percent of car accidents."

I puckered my lips to hold back a giggle. "I call bullshit."

"Okay, one hundred percent, then."

"Now I know you're lying."

"One hundred percent of females I let drive my car have wrecked it."

I wrapped my arms around his neck and led his mouth down to mine. "Give me the keys."

"And if I say no?"

I ran the tip of my tongue over his lips. "You'll find out what crazy really means."

"That sounds more like a promise than a threat."

"What if it's both? You can't get one without the other."

Lucas laughed, and from the corner of my eye, I noticed him lowering his hand. "You've gotten better at this game. Okay, but on one condition."

"Depends on the condition."

"Any sign of dizziness, you tell me immediately."

I'd never had more than one spell in a day, so this deal was as safe as it could get. "Condition granted," I said.

He placed the keys in my palm, and I flashed him a smug smile before I danced around him to the driver's seat.

"Um, Carrie?"

I twisted to face him. "Yeah?"

"Shoes? Bathroom?"

"Oh, right." I dove in and retrieved my sandals. I used Lucas's body to help me keep balance as I brushed off the soles of my feet and put my shoes on.

"I'm gonna regret this, aren't I?"

***

Car accident. Fantastic.

We'd been stopped on the interstate for forty minutes. Not crawling along either. Stopped.

"Semi tipped over," Lucas said, reappearing at my side. "There's grain all over the road. We'll be here a while."

"There's no way we'll make our reservations by dark then. Maybe we should check into the first hotel we see," I suggested. Not that we were seeing much of anything at the moment.

"Now who's scared?" Lucas teased.

I raised my hand as if in school. "Me. I am."

"We're protected in here." He lowered my hand and kissed my fingers. I didn't miss the way he scanned the darkening horizon behind me as his lips moved from one finger to the next. Or the small flutter of nerves beating their wings against my soul. Those had to belong to Lucas, because my nerves usually told me to vomit.

Lucas's mouth lingered on my ring finger, his gaze frozen on the driver's side window.

"Lucas?" I murmured. "What's out there?"

He blinked, his focus only half returning to me. "Nothing yet."

A chill raced up my spine. "You've said this before and then Reid turned up."

"It won't be Reid this time."

"So something *is* coming." The stir in my stomach almost had me reaching for the door handle. I swallowed the rising fear and tightened my grip on the steering wheel. If I had to, I could haul ass down the shoulder.

"There's a golden glow moving up from the treeline over there." He pointed out the location to me since I couldn't see the auras of supernatural beings.

I twisted to where he indicated. "Gold is angels, right? They won't hurt us."

"No, they won't."

"They ignore the dead," I said, a little surprised at the ice in my tone.

"The dead are dead, Carrie. They don't need protecting."

"From demons? Yes, you do. You said once that because your soul doesn't belong to Heaven or Hell, it's up for grabs. The only *things* I've seen try to make a grab for you have red pupils and horns.

How is that fair?"

Lucas gave a half-grin accompanied by a nod. "Life isn't the only thing that's not fair."

I held my breath and counted to five before blowing it out slowly. Only part of my frustration exited with the air. "Okay, so what are they doing here?"

"The angels? I don't know. It looks like they're creating a barrier, but who they're guarding and from what is anyone's guess."

I swallowed. "Demons?"

"Maybe. Could be cambions, other humans, a natural disaster. Sometimes they protect humans from themselves."

"So what are we going to do?"

Lucas glanced out the windshield to the double row of vehicles lining the interstate. His jaw clenched. "We wait and hope this jam starts to move."

Then his eyes widened at the horizon.

Cautious, I followed his gaze. Only half a day from home, and already I thought of how slim our chances of returning were. I expected to see the same line of trees as before, with the angels, but Lucas's attention darted in the opposite direction.

"Stay here. You'll be fine."

"Lucas, what the hell? Where are you—"

And he was gone.

Damn you, Lucas!

I screamed the words in my head as loud as I could, hoping to pierce our connection so he'd hear me as loudly as I wanted him to. I probably screamed it out loud too, because the kid in the vehicle beside us gawked at me. Or maybe he'd witnessed Lucas's disappearing act. At the moment, I didn't care.

I threw my head back and growled out my frustration. What else could I do? I was human, and I was stuck.

The line of cars didn't move, so out of curiosity, I scanned over the tops of the trees Lucas had said were shining gold.

Angels were here. So what? Lucas had told me once that they were everywhere. Why had that thrown him?

I reached back to massage the ache in my neck. The kid in the car was still looking at me, and it was beginning to freak me out. As a child, I remember my mom telling me not to stare. I wondered why this boy's mom wasn't doing the same. Instead, she kept her head down as she typed on her phone.

I peered off in the other direction, the way Lucas had gone. I didn't know what I expected to see. It wasn't like he'd stay in corporeal form to chase whatever he'd seen. I didn't see Lucas, but I didn't see *nothing* either.

Glowing.

Silver.

How can I see that?

I rubbed my eyes to wipe away the obvious hallucination. I couldn't see ghosts when they're invisible. I was human.

I opened my eyes again and the silver mist disappeared. Now there was nothing but a forest.

***

The sun went down exactly two minutes ago. I knew because I had nothing better to do than count the seconds that dragged on excruciatingly slow. At one point I even considered asking the little boy beside me if he had a deck of cards. Maybe then he'd stop staring at me. Because so far, he hadn't.

Geez, kid. Read a book.

I turned the radio on, searched every station, then turned it off. If something happened to Lucas, I assumed I'd feel it inside me, right? Incenamus was like that sometimes. Usually more for Lucas than for me.

I tapped my nails on the steering wheel. Chewed on my thumbnail. Glanced out my window.

Hey, kid.

When I twisted back around, Lucas sat in the seat beside me. My breath caught at the sight of him. His hair was disheveled. His skin paler than normal. White-lipped, he bowed his head into his hands for a second before combing them through his hair.

"What happened?" I asked, reaching out to touch him but stopping short. I knew I couldn't physically hurt him, but he looked so fragile.

Sluggishly, he pointed out the windshield. "Cars should be moving soon. The accident is cleaned up."

"Good."

He clearly didn't want to talk, and strangely, neither did I. My heart weighed a thousand pounds, my skin crawled with regret, and an emptiness I didn't recognize filled my stomach.

These sensations didn't belong to me, but I felt

them as if they did. Because they were Lucas's.

"I'm glad you're back. That you're okay," I murmured anyway.

"Yeah." He kept his head down.

I forced a smile to lighten the mood and nodded toward the Buick parked next to us. "Besides, the kid over there is creepy."

The corner of Lucas's mouth twitched. Then he tilted his head to where I'd indicated and frowned. "What kid?"

"The one in that blue car, right there."

Lucas's eyes searched mine, his brow furrowing. "Carrie. There's no kid in that car."

"Yes, there is. He's…" I turned to see if he had finally found something else to do than stare at me. But the only person in the vehicle was the woman in the driver's seat.

The kid was gone.

Chapter 6

We finally arrived at our motel. Stars glittered above us, and I kept studying every corner until Lucas unlocked our room door. I didn't think I'd ever been happier to be in a motel room. I grabbed my phone and plopped down on the edge of the bed.

Lucas decided to take a shower, even though his bodiless form didn't really need one.

"I need to clear my head," he said. Typically he disappeared to do this, but I figured he wanted to be alone and stay close to me at the same time.

So that left me with nothing but my own thoughts. And my thoughts were telling me I was crazy.

I needed a good dose of reality after seeing not only the silver mist of a ghost in the forest, but a kid who turned out to be a figment of my imagination. He'd seemed so real. I really needed Jessica right now, my down-to-earth best friend, the one who knocked sense into me time and time again. Unfortunately, I couldn't call her anymore. Because the dead didn't have phones. I sighed out my grief at the thought of her.

Instead, I decided to try my other bestie. Or used-to-be-bestie.

I'd dialed this number so many times in the last month, I was sure my cell phone would start calling Stacy on its own soon. I hit *send* and waited.

"If you have reached this number on purpose, then leave me a message and I'll get back to you ASAP. If you reached me by mistake, no problem. Mistakes happen. And if you are Carrie, then do yourself a favor and hang up and save your breath. I'm not calling you back. Have a great day!"

New outgoing message. Lovely.

I pretended the last part didn't exist and left a message.

"Stacy, hi. It's me…again. I know this is stupid, because you clearly don't want to talk to me. I'm not even sure if you're listening to these. But I want to talk to you…I *need* to talk to you. Please, please give me five minutes and a chance to explain. Jess wouldn't want us to, you know, be like *this*…please call me."

I stared at the phone for a second as if Stacy would suddenly change her mind and answer before I hung up, even though it didn't work that way.

I ran both hands through my hair, something Lucas often did, and traced the pattern of the carpet with my gaze to distract myself. It didn't work. My thoughts looped faster. Jessica was gone. Stacy wouldn't talk to me. Lucas was off clearing his own mind. I was going to go crazy in this room by myself.

My mind made up, I tossed my phone on the

bed, grabbed my purse, and left. When we'd arrived, I noticed a McDonald's across the street from our motel. The golden arches beckoned to my stomach, and my stomach responded with a growl. I could easily run over, get a sandwich, and be back before Lucas knew I had left.

The wonderful aroma of MickeyD's french fries greeted my nostrils as soon as I walked through the door. I moaned inwardly, then groaned when I saw the line of customers also craving grease and processed food. Oh well. The scent had already sold me.

Everyone knew the menu at McDonald's, and yet everyone read through it while in line, debating on their usual or something else. I was one of those people. Which was probably why I didn't notice the guy behind me until he slammed into my back. I lurched forward, catching myself before I hit the person in front of me.

"Excuse me," he said. "My apologies."

He tipped his ball cap at me, and something about the way his eyes bored into me made me queasy. Suddenly the salty scent of deep-fried french fries seemed to morph into fire and smoke.

"It's okay," I said, because it was the polite thing to say, and faced the counter. The line had inched up by one person, but I wasn't all that hungry anymore. The dark stare of the guy behind burned into my back.

I glanced up at the menu, ready to change my burger into a chicken sandwich, but the smell of sulfur overtook my senses. That and my nerves.

I slipped out of line and bolted for the door.

Once outside, the warm night air whipped around me, and for a second I could breathe, the breeze blowing away the nasty scent from inside.

Until the man from inside touched my shoulder.

"You all right? You look pale," he said.

I stepped away from him. "Fine. Thank you."

"I can walk you to your car if you want."

The news was filled with instances like these. I had so few options, and none of them worked their way into my brain. My eyes cut to the entrance, where a family of four walked out. They didn't even glance in my direction.

Should I scream?

The guy acted nice, but my creep-o-meter maxed out to bright, blinking red. Plus, the stink from the lobby had made its way outdoors and once again burned my nostrils. Regardless of this guy's intentions, if I couldn't get away from the smell, I was going to puke on his shoes.

"No, thanks. My…*dad*…is waiting for me."

The guy nodded, but the set of his jaw told me he didn't believe me. Dang, I wished I was a better liar.

I could run. But turning my back to him seemed like a stupid idea, especially since he studied me like a viper about to strike. Three escape routes finally filtered into my head. Unfortunately, logic told me they all ended up with me in the same situation: dead.

Another nice-looking family exited the building, and I considered jogging over to them and throwing my arms around the man's middle and calling him dad. Better to embarrass myself than end up in an alley dumpster. Just as I was about to go, a red sparkle stopped me mid-step. Dark red—

Blood red.

I froze in place, slowly locking with my attacker's pupils. Deep, blood-red pupils.

I shouldn't be able to see that. I swallowed hard, pushing down the vomit in my throat.

His pupils faded to black, and a coy grin stretched across his face.

"Now is when you run, Carrie."

I didn't hesitate. I tore through the parking lot, having no idea where to go. Definitely not to the motel. That would lead the demon to Lucas, and I'd die before I let that happen.

What did a demon want with me? Did he know I was here with Lucas?

Am I bait?

Villisca's previous necromancer once said that demons didn't target specific ghosts or people. Now she was dead. Dead for helping Lucas and me. And—

He said my name. The demon knew my freaking name!

I threw a look behind me, expecting to see him chase me. But he wasn't there. No one was there. I was running from nothing.

I slowed to a stop and hunched over my knees to catch my breath. The little boy hallucination, the silver mist of a ghost, the blood red pupils of a demon.

What a crazy day!

Delusional or not, I couldn't walk back to the motel. Not until I knew the demon was gone. I circled back to McDonald's, because why not? Maybe demons were like lightning and didn't strike in the same place twice?

I'd spent a good chunk of the day passed out. When had I eaten last? I hoped my hallucinations were the product of low blood sugar.

Inside the restaurant, only good scents filled my nostrils. Bonus: no line. I ordered chicken nuggets and fries and ate them in the dining room. Lucas would surely be finished with his shower and probably wondered where the heck I had gone. I should have left a note. Or brought my phone.

By the time I inhaled my food, the pinpricks on my skin had disappeared, and I felt normal again. No strange feelings. No nerves. No evil beings around.

On my way back to our room, I was sure this whole day must be the effect of me passing out earlier. My brain was finally sorting itself out.

Thanks, brain.

I slid the key card into the lock and opened the door. My heart plummeted. The blankets had been torn off the bed, the mattress on its side. Lamps lay in shards on the thin carpet. My clothes were strewn everywhere, and my suitcase laid in two pieces on either side of the room. The dresser no longer held drawers, and the television had a giant crack down the middle.

"I'm safe, Carrie. Don't give him anything," Lucas said inside my head.

"Tell who, what?" I answered back in my mind, but the words came out in a whisper.

"This doesn't have to be difficult, Carrie," a

familiar voice said from behind me.

I closed my eyes. Exhaled with a tremble that reached my bones.

"All I need is the book, and you and your ghost boy are free to go."

I faced the intruder, courage simmering to the surface of my skin. Strange how a little adrenaline could make you braver than normal. "You don't seem like the reading type."

"The book," he repeated.

"Doesn't Hell have a library? Why don't you check with them?"

"You realize how accidents happen, don't you, Carrie? This isn't your first encounter with us, but if you don't give me the book, I'll make sure it's your last."

I stuck my chin up in defiance.

"You have a plan, right?" I thought, praying Lucas was listening.

My spine stiffened when he didn't respond immediately.

New plan: stall. "I don't know what book you're talking about, but I think *Dante's Inferno* might be up your alley."

The demon glared at me, unamused by my sass. In my experience, demons lacked a sense of humor. "The witch gave you a book, a potions book."

"Must be important. Why do you want it?"

"I'm done waiting, Carrie Reese. Give me the book or die."

"I can't give you something I am not in possession of, so I guess we have a dilemma."

The demon chuckled. "I don't believe in

dilemmas." His arm shot out, and I flew against the wall, my feet dangling under me.

"Not creative," I rasped out, tearing at the invisible hand around my throat.

Then I dropped to the ground so fast I had no time to break the fall. My nose hit the floor with a deafening *whack.* Warmth trickled down my chin.

From the doorway, Megan rattled off her spell, and the demon vanished into the yellow bubble. She slammed it into the floor and the yellow light shattered, sending the demon back to Hell. "Gone one day and I've already had to save your asses."

Lucas appeared at my side and cradled me in his arms. "Oh, God, Carrie. What happened to you?"

"Sorry. I ran into a demon at McDonald's."

With Lucas's help, I wobbled to my feet. Blood dripped through my fingers and onto my shirt. I tipped my head up in an attempt to stop the flow from ruining my clothes.

"Yeah, asses who are in possession of a book you gave us. A book demons want," I muttered in response to Megan's comment.

Megan swooshed her palm over my face and clothes. "They're after a book?"

I peered down at my blood-free hands. "Thanks."

"Potions," Lucas answered her, his arm still wrapped around my waist to keep me steady.

Megan frowned. "Why?" she mumbled to herself. Then she locked onto me, "You didn't give it to him, did you?"

I glared at her. Hard. "Did you seriously just ask me that?"

"Yes. I mean, no, of course you didn't." She

picked up an overturned chair and sat down. "This is unprecedented, even for a demon."

"Asking for the book or ransacking the room?" I asked.

"Both." She looked at Lucas. "Where is the book?"

"In the Jeep with the rest."

"Good. Since the Jeep has hardcore protection spells, the book is safe."

"Or maybe it shouldn't be in there at all," I mumbled. "Good thing he didn't see it."

"Demons can't see through the enchantments," Lucas reminded me. Right.

"If it's important enough to target, they'll be back. At least right now it's a bargaining chip while we figure this out," Megan said.

"Bargaining for what? If we don't hand it over, we die."

In my time around supernaturals, I've learned to catch on to stuff. Little stuff, like expressions, a tilt of the head, squint of eyes, a purse of lips.

No one spoke for a full minute, the air thick and heavy around us. I held Lucas's stare, but he broke away too quickly. I recalled his reaction in the car when I'd asked about a potion in the book. That, plus now?

Hmmm…

"What's in the book?" I asked.

Megan hesitated. "Recipes for potions, but most of them aren't viable. They were the centuries-old dabblings of a madman. I have no clue why Hell would be interested."

I twisted to Lucas for any hint of inaudible

communication before returning to Megan. “What about the potion in the back? The last one?”

Megan shook her head, slow then faster. “It doesn’t work. Like I said, the dabbling of a madman.”

“Then why give us the book if the potions don’t work?”

“Because one of them might—the locator serum. I’ve tried it to find humans, cambions, and other witches, but I think…maybe…the potion doesn’t work on those with intact or dead souls.” She took in Lucas, almost apologetically. “I think it might work on lost souls.”

Chapter 7

Whoever said counting invisible sheep helped put a person to sleep was an idiot. After one thousand two hundred eighty-six, I quit and rolled onto my side. Megan magically repaired all damage and put protection spells around our room before Lucas teleported with her back to Villisca.

He hadn't returned yet.

I shoved the blankets off and paced the floor to let off some energy. Day one of our trip and already I'd passed out, hallucinated multiple times, been cornered by a demon, and was almost killed. Color me crazy, but I wasn't looking forward to tomorrow.

Sure, Megan had sent the demon back to Hell, but she warned us there'd be more. Whether we had the prize they sought or not, they *thought* we had it, and that was good enough for a diabolical search-and-attack mission. Demons simply didn't stop until they got what they wanted.

And the damn book was outside in the Jeep, less than twenty feet away.

Chills raced down my arms, and I spun around into Lucas's chest. "Couldn't sleep?" he asked.

"Not without you."

"I'm here now. Come on." He walked me back to the bed with my head snuggled up against his chest the whole way.

He began to tuck me in and prepared to lie on top of the duvet, but I stopped him. "I'm wearing Eskimo pajamas. Like, three layers of them. I need you closer."

Unbidden, moisture gathered in my eyes at Lucas's nearness. Today's events taught me one thing: we'd never be safe. Not as long as the demons could feel the power of Incenamus between us. Not as long as Lucas's spirit alone roamed the earth.

Facing me, Lucas slid under the blankets, cautious of cooling me too much. I wished he wouldn't worry about that. We wasted so many hours with a barrier between us when I didn't care about being cold. All I cared about was him, his smile, his touches, his kisses.

His thumbs caressed my face, catching the one tear I couldn't quite stop.

I leaned my cheek into him. "Why do I feel like this is the beginning of goodbye?"

"Goodbyes are just the crappy forerunners to new hellos. But I'm not saying goodbye, Carrie. No matter what happens, I will never say goodbye." Tender, his voice delved into my soul, and I wanted so badly to believe him.

"Can you promise that? After today, after everything we've been through?"

"It's for those very reasons I can promise you that. You are *not* my ending, and I will not be yours."

I studied his face while he did the same to me. I glided my fingers down his cheek, over his lips. They parted slightly for me and I moved in to kiss them. Icy breath mingled with mine. Wintery and sweet, he tasted like frozen peppermint. I deepened the kiss and didn't let go until I'd tucked his promise into the depths of my heart.

***

The crack of dawn arrived faster than it should have. Ugh, I hated mornings. Especially early ones.

Lucas breezed through our motel room door with a new suitcase and a giant Styrofoam cup. He was a morning person and had probably been awake for hours now.

"You look like you need some coffee." He handed me the cup, and it smelled freaking delish. Heaven in a biodegradable container.

I took a drink, not caring that the liquid burned my tongue. "That obvious?"

Lucas laughed at my half-asleep tone. My hair and smudged makeup too, I was sure. "I'll pack your stuff. Let me know when you're human again." He smirked.

"I like that plan."

By the time we loaded the Jeep—okay, Lucas loaded the Jeep—I'd downed the coffee and was flashing Lucas puppy-dog eyes for a refill.

"I take it you're not human yet."

I teeter-tottered the cup for emphasis. "One more cup, and I'll be as human as I can get. Pretty please?"

He obliged, and I smiled sweetly at him.

A full coffee later, we were back on the road. Lucas drove, because apparently I was bad luck behind the wheel, according to him.

"Funny how I got myself from Texas to Iowa without any problems," I pointed out.

"I agree: quite strange. An utter anomaly."

Like when we'd started this trip, I kicked off my shoes and tucked my legs under me. Lucas's gaze wandered over to my bare thighs, and I couldn't help feeling smug. I liked his all-too-human tendencies, including what my naked skin did to him. Too bad we couldn't get past second base without him losing concentration and fading out of existence. It frustrated the hell out of both of us. Talk about star-crossed lovers.

I grabbed his hand and placed it on my knee. He may have done it himself, given enough temptation, but I saw no harm in hurrying him up a little. Then, slowly, I slid it upward and inward, enjoying the coolness of his fingertips more than should be allowed.

Maybe if we skipped bases one and two…

"Don't tempt me, Carrie Reese," he said, his voice rough.

He pulled his hand away and I slumped in my seat.

"It's dangerous." His tone softened, like he too regretted the action.

"I know."

But that was the thing: everything was dangerous.

I peered out the window, watching Tennessee fade into North Carolina, Lucas's home. A boulder sank to the bottom of my stomach. The ache in my chest belonged to Lucas, but the boulder? The boulder belonged to me.

The scenery was beautiful, but I couldn't watch any more. It was here, in this place, Lucas would find his soul. I was sure of it. And neither of us knew what that would mean.

I twisted and picked up one of Megan's books from the back floorboard. Wings embossed in gold spread across the cover, and the title *Guardians* swirled in cursive over them. The spine crunched when I opened the book, making me doubt it had been read much. Megan's job as a witch was to protect the living and maintain peace among the dead. Angels didn't fit into either of those categories. They were their own entity, in their own separate world, doing their own thing.

Oddly, the text was in English. Wow, a book I could read? The first chapter outlined angel theories from all over the globe—where they came from and what they did. It was the latter that interested me. Lucas had seen them lined up over the trees yesterday, but he hadn't known why. Later, he'd theorized it was because of the accident.

There seemed to be three camps of thought regarding their activities on Earth. Some said they were God's messengers created to pass information from God to man. Others maintained they were the guardians of the human race, sent to protect, but not to interfere. The rest theorized they did God's will, including changing certain events in people's lives, even evading death.

What they all agreed on though was what Lucas said: they only concentrate their efforts on the living.

The next chapter contained history, the war between Heaven and Hell. I remembered the story from Sunday school. Some angels revolted against God to side with Lucifer, so God cast Lucifer and his angels into Hell, and thus they became demons, preying on humans and God's love…and the unclaimed souls on Earth went up for grabs.

It fit what Lucas once told me about demons and ghosts: a ghost's spirit was recruitable to Hell.

I thought about the golden glow Lucas saw yesterday. The angels lining up. The silver mist I thought I saw after Lucas disappeared.

"Lucas," I said, "where did you go yesterday? When you left the car at the accident?"

The veins in his hand bulged as he tightened his grip on the steering wheel. "The semi driver didn't make it. He died in the ambulance, and they couldn't resuscitate him."

"I'm sorry."

"His spirit fled his body, and that's when I noticed him." Lucas shook his head. "There was no angel there to ferry him to Heaven, no demon to take him to Hell…he was stuck. He did what I did: he bolted. So I went after him."

"Did you find him?"

Lucas nodded. "He wouldn't stop running, wouldn't listen. And when I saw the streak of red, I knew we'd been found." He looked at me, the beautiful green of his irises darkening. "I couldn't leave him."

"No," I whispered. "You couldn't."

"I couldn't convince him to come with me, either. I tried, Carrie. I tried so hard to save him." Lucas's voice cracked and he turned away from me. "The one demon grabbed him. I reached for him, but it was no use. The demon took him under, and I vanished before the second one could get me."

"You did everything you could," I murmured.

"It wasn't enough."

I thought about Jessica. About the vampire who killed her. "Sometimes everything isn't enough."

Lucas didn't respond. This marked Lucas's second attempt at saving a spirit from becoming demonic. He blamed himself for the first one, and it seemed he blamed himself for this one too.

I sank back into my own thoughts. Judging by Lucas's silence, he had too. So there had been a ghost in those woods last night. Was that what I'd seen? A ghost's silver aura?

Then what about the kid? He had no visible aura that I remembered.

But I had seen the red in the demon's pupils at McDonald's.

I guessed it was possible. I mean, I'd thought I saw demonic red before, when I first arrived in Villisca. Plus, there had been that time with Mike, after his football accident. I watched his spirit leave his body. I touched Lucas's skin at the time, so we attributed the power to Incenamus.

Is it Incenamus now?

Except, all those times yesterday Lucas hadn't been anywhere near me. Maybe our connection had strengthened even more?

I fingered the infinity necklace as I considered the possibilities. One time, Lucas allowed me to see inside his mind. Not simply thoughts, but scenes. Was it possible we shared other abilities too?

Chapter 8

We drove in silence, with only occasional remarks about the weather, a sign, or the scenery. Lucas's thoughts kept him occupied while the angel book held my attention. The closer we got to our destination, though, the heavier I felt in the pit of my stomach. That boulder seemed to have doubled in size.

I bit the inside of my cheek as a green interstate sign indicating that the next six exits belonged to Asheville, the closest large city to Lucas's hometown.

We'd had an uneventful second day so far, but that didn't mean much since the sun was still up. Nightfall would come soon enough, and the nerves already began to extend under my skin. Two hours ago, Megan texted Lucas that she had made contact with a local coven. A witch named Adelia would supposedly meet us in our room and enact the full gambit of protection and concealment spells.

"Take exit 50 now," the GPS lady said.

Lucas merged onto the exit ramp and ten minutes

later, the GPS lady found our hotel. I switched her off as Lucas pulled into the parking lot. He'd barely said a dozen words since we crossed the state line.

He cut the engine and leaned back against the seat. Then, he focused on something outside. All I saw was a line of hedges and the bank next door.

"You're home," I said. "Do you recognize anything?"

"You'd think I'd have some recollection of *something*, right? But there's nothing, from death *or* life."

"Give it time. Something around here is bound to trigger a memory."

He inhaled deeply, the alive part of him making me look away. It was easy to forget the truth about his existence, but then he went and did something so natural, so normal, like sighing, and it made me remember.

"We'd better check in and text Megan our room number," I said.

Lucas opened his door. "Yeah." The distance in his voice had him somewhere else entirely.

He keyed out Room 532 to Megan once we got to our room. He'd requested the top floor. To be closer to the stars, he said, and I secretly hoped we'd be making some late night roof trips.

I shoved my suitcase in the closet and plopped down on the mattress. Lucas joined me. We sat there, our thighs barely touching, staring at the wall in silence. The place we thought would bring us freedom, so far, had only brought tension. What seemed like hours dragged on until Lucas's voice sounded in my head.

"I'm putting you in danger."

"I accept the responsibility for my own actions."

"That's what I was afraid you'd say."

"You should know me by now. I laugh in the face of danger," I said out loud, laughing afterward to prove my point.

Lucas smirked, but then the tiny grin vanished. "Danger isn't funny."

I nudged him in the side. "Oh really? I met a demon at McDonald's. *McDonald's!* Who knew demons had a thing for Big Macs, right? You have to admit that's kinda funny."

"Maybe a little."

I straddled him, linking my ankles behind his back as if that would keep him there. "See? Danger and funny can be synonymous."

"Danger is the difference between life and death."

"So are McDonald's french fries, but they are oh so delish and keep people coming back for more." I pecked his lips in hopes of eliciting a chuckle.

He awarded me with half of one. "I'm serious, Carrie."

"So am I." I cupped his face like he always did with me and gazed into those emeralds I fell in love with a million times a day. "When people get married, they vow for better or for worse. I realize we're not married, and I realize we don't have much of the 'better' and a whole lot of 'worse,' but I don't care. If the universe has decided that me loving you means danger is our new best friend, then so be it. I'll take whatever gets thrown at us, because no matter what, we're better together than we are apart."

"I'm not going to win this, am I?"

I shook my head. "Win what? It's a done deal. And besides, if you sent me back to Villisca, you wouldn't have anyone to kiss."

Lucas combed his fingers sweetly through my hair. "That's the best point you've made."

Then he kissed me. Sweet and wonderful, like I was the most precious thing in the whole world.

When he pulled away, my heart stuttered at the absence of his touch. "I'm staying," I said.

Lucas nodded. "I need you with me. But I also need you to be inside this hotel after dark. No going out alone. Not even for McDonald's french fries."

"McDonald's french fries are da bomb, baby. Even demons know it."

Lucas tucked a strand of hair behind my ear. "We need to be careful. Now more than ever, as it seems we're being targeted."

"I get that. But stop brooding."

"Brooding, huh?"

"Total brooding. Not attractive."

"Because my end goal is to be attractive." Now, *now* he laughed. Silly ghost.

A knock on the door made me jump.

"I didn't order room service," I said.

Lucas unhooked my legs and nudged me off his lap. I followed him.

He peered through the peephole. "I think it's her," he said, then opened the door. "Adelia?"

The woman standing on the other side had to be pushing seventy. She reminded me of a dark-haired version of my great aunt Helen. Had her salt and pepper hair been down, the braid wrapped around her head might have dragged on the floor.

"Hello, Lucas." Her small brown eyes shifted to me. She studied me hard, her gaze boring into me as if she could see my soul. Then she smiled, her cheek bones prominent under thick, black eyelashes. "You must be Carrie. It's a pleasure."

"Likewise," I said, stepping behind Lucas. Being a witch, she must be sporting a green aura visible to Lucas alone. Even so, the way she undressed my insides made me uncomfortable.

"Miss Megan said you are in need of assistance," she said.

"Yes, ma'am," Lucas replied. "First, we need enchantments around the room. Everything you've got."

"Of course. Step inside, please," she said, backing into the empty hallway. She held both of her hands out in front of her and muttered words I'd heard Megan recite. When she finished, she dug into her bag and pulled out a piece of chalk. She dropped to her knees at the threshold of our door and drew on the carpet.

"What is she doing?" I murmured to Lucas.

"It's ancient magic. Some witches and warlocks prefer the old ways along with the new as a precaution."

Precautions were good. The more the better.

When Adelia stood up, I watched as the white chalk slowly faded into the carpet until it disappeared completely. She continued drawing symbols and words around the doorway and the door itself. They soaked into the wall and wood like water in a sponge.

Satisfied, she let herself into our room. "Now the window."

She repeated what she'd done outside our door around the window and inner doorframe. She drew around the vents and on the air conditioner and cast spells toward the ceiling.

So thorough.

"That should keep out any unwanteds," she announced, facing us. "Sit. Both of you."

We did, and Adelia pulled out the desk chair. Her legs dangled off the edge, her tiny, slippered feet hovering over the floor.

"Now. Miss Megan said you have a demon problem. Tell me what happened. Leave no detail out." Her stare hung on me as if she already knew what happened and all my secrets were out too. The ones I hadn't told Lucas, for instance, about seeing red. I still wasn't sure if that part was real.

I squirmed and reached to Lucas for support. Then, clutching onto him, I told her about the demon, except the parts I hallucinated. I also left out the events that led up to our unfortunate meeting at McDonald's.

"It knew your name, you say?" Adelia asked.

"Yes."

"Did anyone say your name in front of the demon, and he could have heard?"

"No, no one there knew me."

"Have you seen this demon before? Was he familiar to you?"

"Not at all. I've never seen him before in my life." I paused. "Do you think he followed us from

Villisca?"

"Demons don't stray far from their entrance into this world. The one they come from is the one they must use to leave, and demons cannot survive in daylight. If he did come from Villisca, then he has been watching you for a while now. Maybe passing and receiving information along the redlines."

"Redlines?"

"Demon communication system through Hell."

"What do you suggest we do?" Lucas asked.

"First, you stay out of the dark. Second, you research. Yes, they want this book, but that is not what you need to research."

I shifted a little, uncomfortable at how Adelia considered me. "Okay…so what do we research?"

She pointed at me. "The question is why do they know you? You are not spirit, or body, or soul. You are all three, one piece. Yet"—her finger waggled—"they know you. They should not know you, dear."

Now, I studied her as she studied me. This woman with dark, beady eyes knew more than she let on. My gut said she knew why the demons wanted me…and the book.

"Okay, so why then?" I asked.

She grinned, again wiggling her finger at me. "You, my dear, must learn that on your own. It's very important that you do so."

My discomfort over Adelia began to ease into intrigue. "But *you* know."

"Miss Carrie, I am an old woman. I have seen many things, heard many things, know many things." She closed her eyes and inhaled deeply. When she opened them, charcoal pupils dilated and bored into me. Her voice changed too. *"One will come who can save them all. An Otherworldly connection will grow her, and when she is strong, evil will pursue her. A choice will be before her, and the decision must be hers: to live or die. Only one will bring life to those without."*

What the hell was that?

Adelia blinked, and her pupils returned to normal. She looked at Lucas, who had gone still. Like statue still. His focus pinned, unmoving, at me, but he didn't see me.

"Lucas?" I asked, waving a hand in front of him. Nothing.

I faced Adelia. "What did you do to him?"

Adelia slipped off the chair and walked toward the door, not answering me. After she opened it, she turned around.

"Salvation is not without sacrifice, Miss Carrie." She nodded toward Lucas, snapped her fingers, and left. The door slammed closed behind her.

A second later, Lucas came back to life. He shook his head, dazed. "Where's Adelia?" he asked. "What happened?"

I stared at the door. "I have no idea."

Chapter 9

I found Megan's number and hit send. Adelia's visit had shaken me. I needed answers, and I needed them ten minutes ago.

"Hello?" Megan asked as if she didn't know it was me.

I wasn't in the mood for meaningless introductions. "Who is Adelia?"

"Did she not show?"

"Oh, she showed all right," I said. "What is she?" Emphasis on the what.

Megan seemed confused. "She's a witch, Carrie, like me. Lucas can see her aura, and—"

"That's not what I'm asking. What kind of witch?"

She met my question with silence, but I could hear her sigh on the other end.

"What *kind*, Megan?" I repeated.

"She's an oracle. The *only* of her kind."

"So like a precog, like Jessica?"

"No, she can't predict the future. She's the keeper, protector, and speaker of prophecies."

Megan's voice lowered. "Why are we having this conversation? What happened?"

"You said she speaks prophecies. How would I know if she spoke one?" I asked.

"Uhh…I've never heard her speak one before. Prophecies can only be told to the person they are about."

With my back against the wall, I slid down to the floor. Wow. Adelia's prophecy was about me.

"Carrie, are you there?" Megan asked.

"Yeah, um, that happened."

"What happened? Adelia prophesied?"

My gaze flitted up to Lucas. Between Incenamus and his better-than-human hearing, I didn't have to tell him Megan's side of the conversation—he already knew.

"Yes," I answered. "And I think she did something to Lucas while she spoke it." I hadn't asked him about it, but I was pretty sure I was right.

"Wait, the prophecy was about *you*?"

"By what you've explained, I guess so."

"Well shit," Megan sighed out. "A prophecy on top of a demon problem, a soul to find, and my mom. Lucas, why the hell did you have to come into my life?"

"Destiny," he said, half-laughing from across the room.

"Yeah, well, tell Destiny she's a bitch."

"She knows."

"So what did Adelia do to Lucas? It's like he froze," I asked Megan.

"Essentially, that's what she did. As I said earlier, prophecies are only meant for those they regard," Megan answered. "Now that it's been spoken, it's yours, and you can do whatever you want with it."

"Okay," I said, standing up and joining Lucas at the window. "If it's mine and I can do whatever I want with it, then I want to tell you. Because I have no idea what it means."

Somehow I remembered it word for word. After hearing it one time, it already ingrained itself in my brain. When I finished, Lucas's brows furrowed. Megan repeated it softly to herself before she blew air into the receiver.

She hummed. "I think we can be certain of only a few things. One, the 'her' is you. Two, the connection is Incenamus. And three, Incenamus has made you strong, meaning you're ready."

"Ready for what?" I asked.

"The fulfillment of the prophecy."

***

"You should get some sleep," Lucas said, though we both knew they were just words. The sun would be up in less than an hour.

"What do you think the choice is?" I asked the only question I'd thought about since I lay down.

"I don't know." He pulled me against him.

"It sounds like a life or death choice. I don't want that kind of power."

Lucas kissed the top of my head, and we lay in silence until my alarm rung One Republic. I hit snooze and we cuddled for another ten minutes.

"Can we stay in bed all day?" I asked, nuzzling

his neck. “I don’t want to let go.”

I slipped my hand under his shirt. Cool, perfectly smooth skin greeted me. Even so, heat pooled in my abdomen, and already my breath quickened.

I was so freaking tired of thinking. Demons, souls, prophecies—I wanted, for a few wonderful minutes, to pretend none of it existed. I wanted the world to stop spinning and the only things left to be Lucas and me.

I tilted my head up and pressed gentle kisses along his jaw line. His eyelids fell closed, his lips parted. As if alive, his chest expanded with unnecessary breaths.

By the time my mouth reached his, I’d worked his shirt up. He lifted his arms to the headboard, and I finished the job and threw the white cotton onto the floor. After all this time, his flawlessness still amazed me. No scars. No moles. No signs of his death. Just beautiful skin that belonged to me.

Lucas’s tongue massaged mine, and my body instantly responded. He started slow, as he usually did, then increased his intensity. He gripped my hips and sat me on top of him. I tugged off my own shirt and tossed it behind me. The feel of my breasts brushing over his chest sent shivers down my spine.

Carefully, he rocked me against him. My heat turned to fire.

I wasn’t ready for this to end. I wanted more, always more. But how tightly he held me—

Concentration creased his brow. He moaned into my mouth, working to hold himself together.

“Carrie,” he murmured.

“Stay with me,” I whispered, lightly biting his

lip. “Please.”

His eyelids fluttered open, a mixture of pain and desire filling them, which was how I knew.

“No,” I breathed.

Apologetic eyes met mine. “I can’t.”

And then he faded into vaporous mist under me. My knees, my palms now touched only the mattress.

“I’m sorry,” he murmured in my head.

“Yeah.” I tossed off the blankets, fighting to contain my frustration. It wasn’t his fault. It wasn’t. I shouldn’t blame him. But…

I grabbed my shirt from the floor. “I’m gonna take a shower. Then we can go.”

Chapter 10

I'd never used microfiche before. The ancient device came from the prehistoric era, and the librarian helping me probably also helped the cave people. She seemed unnerved. She muttered things like, "Funding cuts for library classes," and "What do they teach in schools nowadays?"

How did people live without computers?

Lucas wanted to know as much about his life as possible, so we went back 35 years. Reid, a cambion and Lucas's best friend before he died, had given us enough information on Lucas's past to know what to search for in the old newspapers.

I scanned through the pages, skimming the headlines for anything that might be useful. I checked the obituaries, the sports sections, the student papers. Anything with Lucas's last name I read.

"Check this out," I said, pointing to a headline that read **"Brother Honors Brother with Basketball Scholarship."** Under it was a picture of two boys in basketball jerseys. The younger one I recognized immediately.

"Reid?" Lucas took a few seconds to skim the article. "That's Parker, his older brother. He's the one who received the scholarship for a summer camp in Raleigh that he forfeited to Reid. I don't remember why."

"That was nice," I said.

Lucas squinted at the picture. "I don't recall anything more about Parker. And he gave up his life for me."

I caressed his arm. "It's okay. We'll keep looking."

Hours later, we'd found a ton of articles on "Reynolds." We searched most of them and xeroxed the relevant ones into a pile to sort through later. We also found more on Reid and Parker, mostly the older brother though. Articles on Parker's death and Reid's disappearance were easy to find—front page news.

We gathered our new homework, packed up, and made it back to the hotel before dark.

Lucas ordered in Chinese for me, and as I ate, he toyed with an egg roll. Holding cabbage between his fingers, he stared at it for a second before he glanced up at me and snickered.

I wiped my mouth, worried. "What? Do I have something on my face?"

"No, I just remembered something." He shook his head a little, like his memory seemed silly to him. "I was a kid, seven maybe. Anyway, we had a dog. A little one, I guess, who'd sit under the table at my feet when we ate. I used to feed him, her, whatever, my egg rolls because…I don't know why.

Stupid thing to remember, huh?"

I smiled at the thought of Lucas as a kid. Briefly, I wondered if he had freckles, wore braces or glasses, played T-ball. "No memory is stupid." I moved to sit beside him and ran my fingers through his hair. "Plus, it's a memory. There will be more."

"Funny how I don't remember the dog's name. Only feeding him egg rolls."

"It'll come."

I expected a sigh from him, but it didn't come. Instead, his posture straightened as he turned toward the open window. A glint flickered in his eye, worry lines spreading over his forehead.

"What's out there?" I asked, peering out, but seeing nothing out of the ordinary.

"Angels. A bunch of them."

"Lined up like last time?"

"Lined up in front of our hotel."

Another glimpse out the window and I caught a faint sparkle of gold before it vanished. I closed my eyes for a second, then reopened them, hoping to refocus. An elderly man helping his wife in the parking lot was all I saw now.

"What are they doing?" I asked about the angels.

"Standing."

"That's all?"

"Yeah."

I crossed the room and dug the angel book out of my bag. The chapters I'd read didn't mention anything like this, so I dug into my reading again. By the time sleep caught up with me, the only new thing I learned was that angels only had wings in Heaven.

***

He watched her sleep. He loved how her hair hung over her face in wisps on her cheeks. Her lips always parted after she entered deep sleep, like they were now. Beautifully pink and full, they teased him. He often succumbed to the temptation to kiss them. Sometimes she stirred, but not tonight.

He may not remember his life, but he remembered every second of his death. The years before her, God they were a mess. Empty with nothing to live for, nothing to die for. Simply an existence, and a shitty one at that.

But then there she was. A chance meeting and everything changed. From the moment he first saw her, he felt life explode inside him. He wanted to hold her, protect her, wipe away the sadness in those gorgeous chocolate irises of hers. With one look, this girl stole every reason he had to be in that town.

He'd followed her, watched her, biding his time before he appeared to her. The first time was supposed to be an experiment to see if what his gut said was right. And then she touched him. The shock she elicited against his skin rocked him and almost made him lose concentration. He hung on to his body—barely. But the meeting proved he'd been right: she completed him.

And there he was, with a part of his soul resting inside of her, the part that concerned him so much. Today had been a good day—no seizures—but it wouldn't last. They seemed to worsen with each episode. On their ride here, she'd been unconscious for eight hours. How much more could she endure?

The demons and the prophecy made him want to call the whole thing off, go with her to Texas and live the rest of his existence by her side, trailing his fingertips over her skin and kissing her lips.

Too late for that dream.

His new dream was simple: ensure that Carrie had a long, happy life no matter the cost.

A ray of hope hit him that if Megan could figure out the potion soon, he and Carrie might have a shot at a real future together.

Something was happening, he was sure of it. He'd been watching the stars and the planets over the last few weeks. He wished he knew what the alignment meant. All he knew was that, between the prophecy, the angels, the demons—something huge was about to go down. Whatever it was centered on Carrie.

He needed to protect her, but how could he when he didn't know what was coming?

He caressed her face. She moaned quietly but didn't wake. He smoothed her hair from her cheek and kissed her. He didn't want to leave her, but Megan would be calling any minute, and Carrie needed to sleep. She'd be safe in the hotel room.

With one last look at her, he grabbed his phone and disappeared.

In the Jeep, his phone rang. Megan's number lit up the screen.

"Are you alone?" she asked before he could say hello.

"Yeah, she's asleep up in our room."

"Good. Because this is a goddamn nightmare!"

In a muffled voice she added, "Sorry, Mom. I meant damn nightmare—it's a regular damn nightmare."

"How is Vanessa?" he asked.

"Getting weaker every day."

"Angels are following us, Megan. They show up in droves and form a front line, like they're getting ready for battle."

"Are you serious? Where?"

"First, I saw them at the semi accident site. I thought they were there for the driver. But the driver went spirit and the angels didn't pursue."

"The two demons after you, were either of them the same one that cornered Carrie?"

"No, they were different. Low rankers."

"And the other one?"

"He had years on him. Captain, maybe?"

Megan always clicked her tongue when she was thinking. "If we interpret the evil in Carrie's prophecy as demonic, we have a connection."

"Evil is a broad term. It could refer to anything."

"True, but demons don't target—and yet they are."

"Because of the book. The evil pursuing her could be something else entirely."

"Ugh," Megan grunted. "I hate prophecies."

A flash of gold skimmed by the Jeep, jolting him from the phone call. Angels stood shoulder to shoulder in front of the building, chins held high and shoulders back as if awaiting battle. He hadn't counted before, but their numbers had grown. Now, they almost formed a full circle around the hotel.

He stared at them, their golden auras making it

difficult to see them plainly. Holiness wasn't meant to be seen by the unholy.

"Lucas, did you hear what I said?" Megan asked.

"No," he answered, forcing his attention away from the angels.

"What do you want to do? We have few options and even less time."

He ran a hand through his hair, an act that came so naturally to him. It must be a habit from his life.

"Where are you on the new potion?" he asked.

"Closer," she answered. "A few more tweaks, and it should be ready for testing. Maybe by the end of the week."

He gazed out the window to study the angels. They were like an army gearing up for a war he knew had to involve them. Why else would be they be here?

He couldn't save Carrie in his current state. The potion was their best shot.

"Do it," he said. "Contact me when it's ready."

"How will we administer it with Carrie there?"

"Leave that to me."

"And in the meantime?"

"Carrie is researching angels. We have leads on my family."

"The angels are the least of our worries," she said. "We can't do anything about them anyway."

"Good. Carrie doesn't need to worry about anything else."

"Lucas," Megan sighed, filling a small gap of time after saying his name. "You realize the odds of any of this working out in our favor are less

than—"

"I know. It doesn't matter. Nothing can happen to her."

He hung up before Megan could respond. Of course he knew their chances were slim. He'd known from the beginning.

And he hated it.

Chapter 11

The Incenamus connection blew my mind. Sometimes I could break into Lucas's thoughts the way he always did mine, and sometimes I couldn't. Sometimes I could feel his emotions running beside my own, and sometimes I couldn't. And sometimes the dreams I had of him were real events, but other times?

Well, some were too strange to be real, like the ones where Lucas turned into a demon or Megan called the moon and stars into the palm of her hand and stuffed them into her pocket. Obviously, those things didn't happen.

Ones like last night though, ones that seemed ordinary, but the conversations weren't clear? Those scared me the most, because they were likely real.

So far, Lucas didn't mention having a private conversation with Megan. I decided not to probe. Maybe the dream was just a dream. We had a lot to do, and I could always bring it up later.

"Hungry?" Lucas asked when someone knocked

on the door.

"Did you order room service?"

"It's the best way to have breakfast. In bed."

I giggled. "You spoil me."

"You're welcome."

A minute later, Lucas had a tray of steaming scrambled eggs, perfectly cooked bacon, and a stack of pancakes on my lap.

"The hotel has better cooks than me," he said, his dimple sinking into his cheek.

"I loved that you tried."

I filled my fork with a king's helping of fluffy, buttermilk pancakes and stuffed them in my socket, as Grandpa would say. I let the amazingness sit on my tongue for a second before I began to chew.

"Ohmygod," I said with my mouth full. "These are so good."

Lucas laughed at the face I made. "I'm glad you approve."

He lay down beside me, his head propped up as he watched me eat.

"Want some?" I offered.

"They're for you."

"That's not what I asked."

Gingerly, he wiped the corner of my mouth with his thumb.

The shadow in his gaze rather than his touch gave me pause. I recognized the trepidation in his expression and knew it shouldn't be allowed to fester.

"Open up, and close your eyes." I added the last part, because Lucas couldn't feel or taste like I did. If I took away his ability to see, perhaps his other senses would heighten. Worth a shot, right?

He did as I asked, and I placed a syrup-coated piece of pancake on his tongue.

"Now savor it," I instructed.

Lucas's jaw worked as he chewed. He swallowed, waited a second, then peered up at me.

"Good?" I asked, hoping.

"Better than I imagined."

I smiled at his attempt to humor me.

The entire universe separated us—life and death. Yet how could I not love him? Every look, every touch, every kiss and caress belonged to him. *I* belonged to him. To the end of the world, the end of my life, I would love him.

Halfway through the plate, I gave up. "I'm so full," I said, dragging out the last word. "I think I'll just lie down and die from delicious-food overdose."

Lucas's eyebrows lifted. "I don't think that's a thing."

"Ugh," I said, rubbing my belly. "Then I'll make it a thing. Scientists can name it after me and I'll be famous. They'll make public service announcements and the whole world will be aware of the dangers of Carrie-Reese-itis, and June will become National Carrie-Reese-itis Awareness Month."

"You have big plans for your make-believe disease."

I fell back against the pillows. "I do. I've thought long and hard about this. They will create foundations and give out grants in an effort to combat this worldwide phenomenon. The ribbon color will be burnt orange, because 'go Longhorns.'"

Lucas chuckled. "Longhorns and Carrie-Reese-itis. I can't wait."

"Yes. And all the laboratory work to find a cure will be located at UT. And then some super-smart grad student will come along, mix up some great concoction, and boom! The cure."

Lucas kissed me. "Well, I'm glad there's gonna be a cure, but there's one big flaw in your plan."

"Yeah? What's that?"

"For Carrie-Reese-itis to be discovered, you have to die, and I'm not going to let that happen."

"That does put a kink in my plan." I puckered my lips in fake thought.

He kissed me again. And again.

And again.

"I have a new plan," he said against my mouth.

"Hmmm?"

"You stay alive until you're one hundred years old. Eat pancakes with maple syrup every morning in bed. Make up with Stacy and your dad. Go to college at UT and buy a whole wardrobe of burnt orange shirts and scarves and whatever other girly stuff they have."

"Nail polish?" I asked, wiggling my unpainted fingers and ignoring the sneaky part about Griffin he threw in there.

"Of course nail polish. What was I thinking?"

I laughed.

"Marry a man who loves you more than life and who you love more than life. Have a bunch of babies. See Paris. Have a bunch of grandbabies.

Then die in the arms of the man you love."

"Are you prepared for all that?" I whispered. "Because that man is and always will be you."

"It will be the best life anyone has ever lived, and I'll be with you. Forever."

***

We spent the next few days in our hotel room, sorting through the copies of articles we collected from the library. We read each one word for word, highlighting important information and taking notes. The events of the night Carver beat Lucas and kidnapped Reid and Parker lined up exactly how Reid had explained.

Based on the newspaper report of Lucas's car accident, Reid's story proved correct as well—without all the first-hand details. Not that we doubted him, but the non-biased confirmation added to his credibility. He was a cambion after all.

We read high school sports articles with mention of anyone whose names we recognized—Lucas, Reid, Parker, and Rachel. Sheriff's reports. Honorary mentions. The article about Mrs. Reynolds' book drive for the local library, and Mr. Reynolds' letter to the editor regarding a stop sign close to one of the middle schools.

Lucas skimmed over his father's letter again. The corner of his mouth tugged up. "How bothered do you have to be to write one of these?"

I glanced at the date, did the math in my head, and shrugged. "You were six when he wrote it. I guess he was already concerned for your safety."

“Overprotective?”

“I think that’s usually a mother’s role. Dads are more of the ‘suck it up!’ type,” I said in a husky voice.

Lucas quirked a brow. “Maybe Mom wrote it and signed with Dad’s name.”

I picked up an article featuring Mrs. Reynolds at the historical society and showed it to him. “She does seem more the type.” I flipped the newspaper and examined the picture. Like her son, Mrs. Reynolds had dark hair and a dimple in her left cheek. They shared the same high forehead too, but Mrs. Reynolds covered hers with long, feathery bangs. “She was really pretty, your mom.”

Lucas didn’t reply. Instead he went back to shuffling through his stack. It had been five days and nothing we found had triggered memories that could link Lucas to his soul.

The potion in the book the demons wanted, the one Megan thought was a locator serum, had ingredients that were difficult to procure. She was working on locating them. In the meantime, all we had were non-existent memories as guides.

Bits and pieces of other things came back, though. He remembered that he used to have a brown hamster named Regal, and that Rachel’s white hamster, Mouse, ate him. He recalled summers when he and Reid would spend their afternoons at the park shooting hoops. The time Rachel hit him with a baseball bat right where it counted, and as payback, he stole her diary and gave it to her sixth grade crush.

Oh, and he finally recalled the name of his dog:

Marty.

Tying together someone's past was more difficult than television shows depicted. Though every piece was important, not all would lead us to his soul. Our new game, "Fill in the Gaps," had my head spinning with confusion.

We might as well have been searching for an ounce of humility in a vampire.

Lucas seemed to feel the same way, because he crumpled up the copies in frustration and threw them across the room with a grunt.

His hard gaze settled on me, his lips pulled tight.

"I want to visit my parents' house."

Chapter 12

Like the awesome sleuths we were, the next morning we parked on the street and watched the little yellow house with white shutters. For a while the only movement on their property belonged to a middle-aged woman walking her dog down the sidewalk and a gray cat that lovingly took its bathroom break amongst Mrs. Reynolds' tulips.

"Maybe they're retired and sleeping in this morning?" I suggested.

Lucas honed in on the lunette window above the door. "That doesn't sound right."

"You remember something?"

"No. But considering what we've read about them, they don't seem the type to be retired at their age and sleeping in."

"Maybe…" The rest of the sentence lodged in my throat. I didn't even want to think it, yet the thought couldn't be stopped. *"Your death changed who they used to be."*

"Only one way to find out." He scanned the sidewalks and surrounding homes before his gaze landed on me. “Stay here. I’ll be right back.”

Not again.

“Lucas—”

But he’d already disappeared.

“Seriously?” I grumbled.

No way was I sitting in the Jeep while he scoped things out. I wasn’t here to be his sidekick while he went off alone.

I reached for the handle and opened the door.

“Where are you going?”

Lucas’s voice startled me. I swung to face him. His eyebrows perched high on his head.

“I said I’d be right back.”

“Yeah, and I’ve heard that line before. Two hours and you were still MIA.”

“I ran into a little problem that time. This time, I didn’t.” He pulled a house key out from his pocket. “No one’s home. Let’s go.”

“Where did you find a key?”

“They used to have one buried in the dirt of the blue flower pot. Mom’s idea.”

I smiled at his newest memory and followed him up the sidewalk to the front door.

“What if the neighbors see us breaking in?” I asked.

“I already checked. They’re not home either. Besides—key.” He held it up again, in case I didn’t see it the first time.

“I don’t know, Lucas. This feels wrong.” Lucas could simply disappear into thin air if we got caught. Crazily enough, I couldn’t.

“This is my home. It’s not called breaking and entering if you live there.”

"*Lived.* Past tense."

Ignoring me, he pulled out the key and twisted the knob. The door opened. "Coming?"

I threw a glance behind me to be sure no one saw us. "Lead the way."

I followed Lucas inside and quickly closed the door behind me. We stood in a living room with dark hardwood floors. Mrs. Reynolds seemed to be a good housekeeper; the place was immaculate. White, white walls. White furniture. White fireplace mantel. White area rug.

Fluffy purple decorative pillows.

Heavenly.

I swallowed the thought.

"Your mom likes white," I said.

Lucas's brows knit together as he concentrated on the white sofa. He shook his head. "She used to hate white. Said it got dirty too easy." He closed his eyes, concentrating. "The furniture used to be black in here. We had carpet. The walls were this blue-grey color." He paused for a second. "I hit my head on the corner of the coffee table—not this one. It bled all over my clothes and dripped onto the carpet. Marty licked it off my hand. Mom came with a washcloth and pressed it to my head. I got three stitches."

His eyes opened. "That wasn't this room."

He walked over to the fireplace. Hanging in the center was a black and white family portrait of the four of them. Lucas didn't look older than me now.

Below it, a dozen pictures in silver frames fanned out along the mantel. He picked up the one on the end, of a round-faced baby with wispy black hair. The baby's toothless laughter and wide green irises danced off the photo.

Lucas put it back and reached for the next one. The baby had grown into a toddler, with spaghetti sauce in his hair and smeared over his cheeks. One by one, he went down the row. The final picture, in the middle of the mantel, had two people. The baby boy had grown into a man and a beautiful girl with dark hair and the same green eyes stood at his side.

Lucas's sister.

The rest of the row belonged to her, ending in a baby picture much like Lucas's. Lucas took it off the shelf and sat down. My heart sank at his expression. Mouth curved down and his brows lowered.

"Rachel," Lucas said, tracing her little face with his fingertip. "We fought all the time, her and I. Over stupid things too. A toy or who got the last cupcake. Who called shotgun first. Who got dibs on the pool table that Saturday night. But when it counted, she was there for me."

"That's what sisters are for," I murmured, even though I had no experience of my own. Jessica and her sister were like that though.

Lucas sat in silence, studying the picture. As he did, I allowed my gaze to travel around the room. Outside the obvious focal point of photos, I noticed smaller frames littered around the room. On end tables. On shelves. On the piano.

And beside them all rested glass angel figurines.

Goosebumps sprouted along my arms, and I had to look away from them.

Finally Lucas stood up and returned the picture

of Rachel to the mantel. He moved through the spotless kitchen, decorated in white like the living room. Off the kitchen was an office with a mahogany desk and floor-to-ceiling bookshelves covering one wall. There were a few books, but mostly the shelves held pictures and children's artwork.

Family snapshots of vacations, camping trips, and sporting events stood like trophies in a place of honor. Lucas's high school graduation had a whole shelf dedicated to it. The color in his face, the tan of his skin…wow. However it was possible, he'd been even more gorgeous when he was alive.

Lucas paused in front of each framed snapshot of his life. All these little moments separate events, but together they filled in the missing pieces of who he used to be.

I lowered myself to the floor to scope out the bottom shelf. The books, I noticed, weren't ones you'd expect to see in an office. I pulled *The Cat In the Hat* off the shelf and opened it.

To my first nephew,
Never be afraid to try new things.
Love,
Aunt Lauren

I smiled as I flitted through the pages, most with crayon marks on them. Little Lucas apparently enjoyed coloring.

Next, I picked up a tattered copy of *Treasure Island* that looked as if it had been read a million times, and I wondered if it had been Lucas's favorite book. My heart stuttered as I removed the next one from the shelf. *Love You Forever* had been my favorite bedtime story, and every night my dad would tuck me in and read it to me. Until now, I'd forgotten he did that.

I crossed my legs and opened the book. My dad's voice echoed in my head, soft and tender and steady. I cuddled up to him, and every time he read that the little boy would always be his momma's baby, he smiled. Sometimes he tapped the tip of my nose.

Emotion rose into my throat, but I swallowed it down.

Memories. They had a nasty habit of making you feel things you didn't want to feel.

Before I closed the book, I checked the inside cover.

My Lucas baby,
I will love you forever and always.
As long as I'm living, my precious son you will be.
Until always ends,
Momma

I fisted my hand and held it against my mouth to choke back a sob. Until always ends. I bet she never thought *always* would be merely twenty short years.

"Carrie," Lucas said, startling me.

I wiped the extra moisture from my eyelashes and stood up.

"Check this out."

He held out a picture. The girl was clearly his

sister. And the boy with his arms wrapped around her? Reid.

"They seem happy," I said, because they did. *In-love*-happy.

"I took this picture. In the backyard." He went quiet for a moment, then added, "There's a bunch of photos of them together."

Sure enough, like Lucas's graduation shelf, Rachel had one too, and most had Reid in them. He had a healthy glow in life, a little pale, but he obviously had all three parts of him—spirit, body, soul—intact and alive. He'd been happy. Rachel had been happy with him. And then one day all of that was taken away when Carver killed Parker and turned Reid evil. Seeing his pictures made me feel for him.

A life stolen.

"She was so nervous when she told me he asked her out. She thought I'd be mad." Lucas chuckled at the memory. "She used the word 'forbid.' That I'd forbid her to go." He focused on the picture he held. "Reid asked my permission first, and I told him if he ever screwed with my sister's heart, I'd rip his throat out of his ass. I made sure he knew the risks of dating Rachel." His Adam's apple bobbed as he swallowed. "But I think he'd loved her since the first grade."

He placed the frame back on the shelf and threaded my fingers with his. Then he squeezed them.

When we first met, there was distance in those gorgeous greens. Even in our happiest moments, hints of it remained. Over time, it diminished, but right now, in the house he grew up in, with snapshots of a past he couldn't remember, that same look consumed his irises again. Sadness. Guilt. Remorse. Uncertainty. All wrapped into a stare that broke my heart.

Lost in his own thoughts, he led me out of the room. We walked down the hall. Pictures of Lucas lined the left-hand side while pictures of Rachel lined the right. It was another timeline, from birth to probably the last picture the Reynolds' had of their children.

Lucas pointed to the one where he stood next to a red Mustang. "Guy had good taste in rides."

"I bet red was his favorite color."

"Likely."

"You don't remember?"

Lucas shook his head. "No." He opened the closed door at the end of the hall. "I bet this one was mine."

I swallowed, suddenly nervous. It was only a bedroom—a room with a bed and other stuff. But—

My gaze pinned on Lucas's back as I walked in behind him. The gray carpet had been recently vacuumed. I thought about how my flip-flops would ruin the perfectly spaced tread marks. Something about it felt off.

Lucas's bedroom now was this neat, and I wondered if he'd always kept it like that. The walls, painted light blue, had posters of Duke basketball hung over them. White shelves neatly displayed trophies, ribbons, plaques and other awards, and a bookcase stood in the corner, photos resting on the top. Strange that Mrs. Reynolds kept his room as if he'd never left.

He moved to the glass desk on the other side of the bed. I went for the bookshelf, to the photos. One specifically caught my eye. A girl, one who wasn't Mrs. Reynolds or Rachel. With long blonde hair, glossy pink lips, and a seductive grin, posing at the beach. Suddenly, I noticed she appeared in all these pictures. In some she was alone. Other snapshots were of Lucas and her together. In one, he had her in a dip, their mouths mortared together.

Girlfriend, my traitor brain thought.

"Who's this?" I barely got the words out before I swallowed the jealous lump in my throat. It didn't go down.

Lucas twisted, his eyes moving from me to the pictures. He showed no emotion as he scanned over them. "I don't know."

My gut said to believe him. I had no reason not to. I still couldn't rummage through the rest of the room with him. He opened all his dresser drawers, went through the clothing hanging in the closet, books, and shuffled the items under his bed.

But I was mesmerized by the girl, the one who was clearly mesmerized by Lucas. The only thing I could think about was how *warmth* radiated from him when she touched him. How his heart must have pounded against her ear. How he could feel her when they kissed.

He could make love to her without disappearing.

She got Lucas's life, while I…

I turned away from the bookshelf so her face was at my back. One more thought like that and I'd break.

He closed the doors to the closet. "I found a few things."

"Great," I said with forced enthusiasm. I cleared my throat to cut some of the growing tension. "Let's go see what's behind door number two, shall we?" The fake excitement made the words sound stupid.

Lucas led the way out. Emotions I couldn't sort out stirred in my chest. The girl, this house, the *life* of the man I loved. The air around me thickened. My lungs hardened to glass, and I had to work to fill them. If this was how this place affected me, Lucas must have been ready to implode. However he felt, he'd somehow severed our connection so my feelings were my own.

"Nothing," he answered my thought.

"How is that possible? I mean, after seeing all this, you don't feel…anything?"

"I don't. That guy on the wall?" He points to the last photograph of himself. "He's a stranger to me. This whole house, the memories, the people, they don't belong to me."

The lack of care in his voice made me ache inside.

Before I closed Lucas's bedroom door, I took one final look over my shoulder.

With the curtains drawn, the sun barely cast in any beams. The room darkened and finger-like shadows crept along the floor.

On the ceiling, though? Glow-in-the-dark stars sparkled against the grey. To an amateur, they seemed to be haphazardly placed, but I recognized the patterns. This was the night sky during summer solstice.

“Lucas,” I murmured, my head tipped upward. “Above us.” He tilted his head back too. When he said nothing, I whispered, “Still feel nothing?”

A second passed before he murmured, “Whoever he was, he knew his astronomy.”

Then he turned and left.

Chapter 13

Rachel's room reminded me of a mix between Stacy's and Jessica's. Not overly girly or overly sporty. She must've played basketball too, because, like in Lucas's bedroom, she had shelves decorated with basketball trophies and medals.

Pom-poms hung from the posts of her headboard, and turquoise lamp shades covered the black iron lamps on her white nightstands. Strands of lantern lights looped over the two curtain rods, and strips of snapshots clung to the edges of her vanity mirror.

This room, like Lucas's room, had been left untouched over the years, as if the Reynolds' expected their children home any day. I thought about the redecorated living room, the photos of Lucas and Rachel scattered everywhere…the angel figurines watching over them—

This wasn't a house. It was a shrine.

The walls felt like they were squeezing inward. My lungs wouldn't fill, and I heaved in my next breath.

I tried to focus. I squinted to make out Rachel and Reid in the pictures on her vanity. At least, I thought it was Reid. My vision blurred and I couldn't make out their faces.

My eyelids weighed down like I had piled ten pounds of mascara on them. I needed air. Fresh air, outside this house that had suddenly become too small.

I turned toward the hallway. Took a step forward and had to grab onto the wall to keep from falling. Black dots faded in and out of my vision, blinking sleepily at me.

I understood what was happening a moment too late. Pain roared behind my ribs and I dropped to my knees, clutching my heart. An agonized gasp forced its way out of my mouth. The last thing I wanted was to cut Lucas's trip down memory lane short. He didn't need to deal with the fire erupting inside me right now.

But before I could finish a deep inhale, he crouched and gathered me into his arms.

"It's happening again," he said against my temple.

It had been almost a week since the last episode, and I'd secretly hoped that whatever it was had left me alone.

I curled into a ball. The smaller I made myself, the less the pain ripped through my body, I thought.

The waves of pain swelled, pressing pressure against my ribs. How I wanted to pass out like last time! I couldn't. This I had to endure.

"Lucas," I moaned out, wincing.

There was nothing he could do except watch

from the sidelines while the person who held his very soul fought against pain that wouldn't ease. Being helpless, his own grief was probably as great as mine.

"Hold on to me," he murmured.

My limbs trembling, I did as he asked. Then all breath flowed from my lungs, and my muscles tightened as they became one with my bones.

A moment later, I sucked in air as if I'd been without for minutes instead of mere seconds. The pain in my body tapered off, but I couldn't open my eyes. Judging by the smell, though, I was back in our hotel room.

Soft cotton brushed against my cheek. Cool arms released me, then settled me into bed. Too weak to speak, my words fumbled through my mind instead. *"Go back without me. Something's taped under her vanity."*

Sleep claimed me before he could respond.

***

I hugged the top of the duvet to my chest and rolled on my side. Immediately, my stomach growled.

I tried to ignore the hunger and drift back into unconsciousness, but my tummy would have none of it.

I expected Lucas to be at my side. Maybe lying beside me, but no coolness wafted over me.

Because he's not here.

I bolted upright at the realization. Other than me and a silver tray on the desk, the room was empty.

Soft blues and pale pinks peeked in through the curtain, and I went to the window to confirm my thoughts. Twilight.

I slept all day?

I wore the same clothes as this morning, minus the flip-flops. Those were on the floor beside the bed. The clock on the nightstand read a quarter till nine, so yes. I'd slept all day. No wonder I was starving.

My stomach growled again when my gaze hit the tray. I walked over and removed the lid. A cheeseburger, fries with ketchup, a side salad—

And a note.

I'll be back before dark. I love you.—Lucas.

The lack of explanation shouldn't have surprised me, yet the least he could have done was let me know where he ran off to. Or flew off to—whatever.

I grabbed a french fry, dipped it in the glob of ketchup, and ate it. After inhaling half the cheeseburger, I fisted up a handful of fries and peered out the window again. The sun now grazed the tip of the horizon. Nightfall would be here soon.

Cars buzzed by on the road, and patrons walked in and out of the hotel. I'd finished off the fries and was about to grab for more when something bright caught my attention. From the corner of my eye, it glimmered like golden dust in the morning light. I snapped in that direction, but saw only a man in a suit, carrying his briefcase inside.

Maybe the light is reflecting off a latch?

I almost convinced myself when another sparkle flashed in my peripheral. Again, I looked. Again nothing seemed to have caused it. Just the outdoor pool, filled with happy children.

The sun sank under the scope. Only hues of yellow, blue, and pink remained in the sky. I rubbed my temples. I didn't have a headache, but maybe it would relieve hallucinations.

It didn't. Oh, hell no, it didn't. In fact, it only made them worse.

They appeared. Angels. At least sixty of them. Sixty golden heads tipped skyward. Toward the building.

Toward me.

Golden auras blurred their images so I couldn't make out facial features, but their beauty had me torn between hiding from them and basking in the glory they exuded. Their hands thrust out at their sides in a low V. Like an accordion of very beautiful paper people.

"Carrie. You're awake."

A relieved voice breathed out the words, and I jumped and screamed at the sound.

"Ohmygod, Lucas," I spit out, clutching my chest.

Concern knit his brows. He pulled me against him.

"You okay?" he asked.

I shook my head in small, quick movements into his shirt. "No."

He released me just enough to cup my face and search my eyes. I don't know what he saw in mine, but in his I saw fear.

"What happened?"

"I…don't know." Really, I had no clue what was going on.

"Come here," he said, leading me to the bed. "You're shaking."

I nodded toward the window. "Those angels you told me about. Are they there now?"

"Yeah, they're there." His thumb caressed my jaw. "Why?"

Saying it would sound crazy. Bat-shit crazy. Cat-lady, bat-shit crazy. Humans weren't supposed to see the supernatural world. Not even witches could see the auras of beings if they weren't corporeal. I had no explanation, except that I'd passed out and slept all day. It seemed to be a common theme to my hallucinations.

Lucas isn't a hallucination…

"No reason," I said. I sank into his embrace. "I guess I'm tired and hungry and worried."

"Worried?" The other two items he apparently believed.

"About you. Where did you go?"

He blinked, his irises darkening to forest green. "Villisca. To talk with Megan."

My relaxed posture reversed, and I moved to face him. "You couldn't call her?"

"It was just as easy to go there." He shifted on the bed, leaning on a hip to dig into his pocket. "You were right. I found this taped under Rachel's desk."

Lucas dropped a silver ring into my palm. Small diamonds circled a large center gemstone.

"An engagement ring?"

"That's my guess. Reid conveniently left that part out."

My gaze locked on his as a thought entered my mind. "What if it isn't Reid's?"

"What makes you say that? Reid was all over her bedroom. His pictures, I mean."

"Because she hid it. Because no one has found it until now, including Reid. Wouldn't he have searched for it if he'd given it to her?"

Lucas rubbed two fingertips over his chin. "Hopefully we'll find out soon. Megan used the ring to do a tracking spell. Reid—or someone—will have answers."

"Did you find anything else there?"

"Not much." He opened the top drawer of the nightstand. "A pocket book about constellations, a family picture, and this thing—I think it's a good luck charm of some sort."

"It's an arrowhead," I told him. "They're kinda special."

"I kept it for some reason."

"What about Rachel?"

"Just the ring. No diary or journal."

"Maybe we should go back tomorrow."

"Nah. There's nothing there." A sad glint passed through his eyes, but it faded away when he smiled. "Now that we have the worry part out of the way." Lucas got up and retrieved my half-eaten dinner. "Let's take care of the hungry part. Microwave?"

"Pfft. Microwaves are for sissies. It'll be fine."

I scooted up on the bed until my back rested against the headboard. I crossed my legs in front of me, and Lucas sat the tray on my lap. I finished off my cheeseburger.

"So, worry, check. Hunger, check. Tired, huh?" he asked, mimicking my position on the bed. "How is that possible? You've been asleep for three days."

I choked on my last bite. "What?"

Three days? As in, one, two…*three*?

How was that even possible?

"These episodes are lasting longer. The episodes themselves and the recovery."

"I'm fine," I assured him, because physically, I was. "I'm a little shocked is all."

He held a vial filled with seaweed green liquid between his thumb and index finger. Already, I knew whatever plan he had sucked.

"A potion," I deadpanned.

"It won't stop the episodes—"

"Stop calling them episodes," I said.

He ignored me. "It won't stop the episodes, but it should lessen the pain."

"What if I don't want the pain lessened?" I said, surprising him. "Look, if we're on to something, and the pain is this half"—I patted my chest—"calling out to the other half, then I need the pain. What if the stronger it is, the closer we are to your soul?"

"Carrie, we weren't close to anything at my parents' house. There's nothing there, yet it was like you were having a heart attack. If your theory is correct, then I don't want to know what an episode will do if we really *do* get close."

"I'll be fine," I murmured, caressing his face. The coolness of his skin mingled with the warmth of mine, and I eased his lips to me. "We're here to find your soul, Lucas, and that's what we're going to do."

He placed the vial in my palm and closed my fingers around it. "I'm not taking any chances."

Reluctantly, I accepted it and put it on the nightstand. Whatever made him happy.

"How do you think it works?" I asked, slowly returning to him.

"The potion?"

"No. Your soul. What will happen to me if you get your soul back?"

"Nothing will happen to you," he said, his brow softening. "The part of my soul in you now belongs to you. It's a part of you."

"Like an organ transplant?" I half-joked.

"Exactly like that. It's how Incenamus works. There're no returns."

"I don't plan on returning it. Your soul is stuck with me forever."

He smiled, his dimple sinking deep. "It's where it belongs."

I scooted closer to him, satisfied for now. "TV tonight?" I suggested. "You know, to pretend we're normal."

He draped an arm around my shoulders. "Sit-com or drama?"

"Sit-com. I've had enough drama."

We found something easily, but even as we watched, my curiosity drew me back to the window. I'd been awake for a while now, and I had a full stomach. Maybe that was all I needed.

Maybe I'm not crazy after all.

Even so, a nervous shiver shot up my spine. No matter how I justified the auras, my gut told me they were here to stay. What I really needed was research.

I peeled back the curtains, closing my eyes as I did. I inhaled, then let the air out onto the glass, creating a circle of fog. Slowly, I opened my eyes.

The angels were gone.

Chapter 14

Two days later, Megan still hadn't called about the tracking spell she'd cast on the ring. Lucas spent his time pacing a hole into the hotel carpet. It was bizarre too, because the hole seemed to grow on its own. Threads wore down, but nothing looked to cause it. If I tipped my head to the side just right, the hole actually made the carpet design interesting. His stir-craziness was driving me crazy, which wasn't good, since I was probably on the verge of it already.

With each lap, I wondered how much more either of us could take.

Gah! I needed answers.

I wish Stacy was here.

It wasn't the first time I'd thought it. The Three Musketeers dropped to two, and those two hadn't spoken in months. Not very Musketeer-y.

"Lucas," I said, peering up from the angel book I'd stopped reading twenty minutes ago. A cool breeze brushed past my bare toes at the foot of the bed.

"Yeah?" His voice rang out in my head.

"I can't see you."

A white t-shirt, ripped blue jeans, and pale arms appeared beside the window. The rest of him materialized soon after, his normally radiant irises dulled with apprehension. "Sorry, I must have faded—"

"I know," I interrupted. "I think I'm gonna go down to the lounge for a while. Grab a Pepsi and clear my head."

"I'll go with you," he offered too quickly, reaching for a nicer shirt he threw off earlier.

I held a hand up to stop him. "I don't think that's a good idea. A person being there, then suddenly only half there, then not there at all might be too strange for most people to handle." In different circumstances, it would be a stupid excuse to get some alone time. He'd never faded away like that before, but considering his pacing and fading the last couple of days, it made sense. "Might be best to, you know, check out of corporeal-form for a bit. You could use a mental break too."

He raked through his hair. Studied me for a moment. "Sunset is in an hour."

"I'll be back by then. I'm done with demon run-ins." I laughed even though it wasn't funny.

I stuffed the room key in my back pocket, along with some cash. I kissed Lucas long and hard, something to remind myself why we continued on this path.

"I love you," I murmured.

"I love you more."

I smiled instead of spouting off a cheesy

argument about why I loved him more. The time for cutesy had long passed.

I took the elevator down to the ground floor. Walked through the massive foyer, decorated in greenery and floral arrangements. At the center ran a large waterfall overflowing from the fifth floor that ended in a wishing well.

Why not?

I dug out a penny and made a wish, pressing the copper between my palms as if in prayer.

I wish for a happy ending.

It was simple and I offered no explanation. I just hoped that whoever granted these things heard me and understood.

I didn't know how this worked, so for extra luck, I kissed the coin before I flipped it into the pool.

"Do your thing," I said once the penny hit the bottom.

The lounge was through a set of French doors in the corner of the foyer. A baseball game played on the big screen over the bar, and a few guys with tumblers of whiskey at their fingertips chatted about the score. I walked up and ordered a Pepsi.

After the barista gave me the glass, I sat down at one of the small tables and pulled out my phone.

I swiped the pad of my finger across the screen until my used-to-be best friend's face grinned back at me. I hadn't tried Stacy in over a week. She probably thought I'd given up, but I was stubborn, which she should know about me. In fact, my stubbornness rivaled hers.

Her message hadn't changed from last time. Good sign.

"I'm in over my head, Stacy. And I'm scared. Listen, you were right: Jess and I should have told you. We didn't because we thought we were protecting you. I'm sorry for that. But please call me. I could use someone to talk to."

I let the last words hang in the air before I hung up. Best friends since pre-school. She'd call back.

I tapped my text message icon and scrolled down to Mike's name. Our last text conversation had been about schoolwork and an old movie he finally ordered off Amazon. The dork even took a picture of the e-receipt as proof.

Carrie: About what I said at the party…I didn't mean it.

Then I deleted it. I *had* meant what I said.

I tried again. I finally settled on something the third try.

Carrie: I'm sorry I hurt you. I never meant to.

And hit send.

A minute later, my phone buzzed.

Mike: I know.

Relief lodged in my throat. What I wouldn't give to have him sitting here with me now. I wouldn't care if he had disdain written all over his face. He'd still let me rattle on about everything. Probably volunteer to help.

He'd risk his damn life, because he was in love

with me. It was why I couldn't confide in him. He almost died helping us defeat Carver, and I wasn't going to let him do it again.

Carrie: How's farming going?

Small talk was better than no talk. Plus, Mike's life was normal. Awesome, actually. Like my Pepsi, and I needed more of that right now.

Except ten minutes later, my phone remained deadly silent. No call from Stacy. No text-back from Mike.

A man sauntered in after I got my refill. He nodded in my direction and plopped down on an empty stool with the others at the bar. The game must be a good one, because their voices rose into cheers. I didn't twist to see.

I could make a bunch of excuses over my silent phone: Stacy's working, Mike didn't hear the new text buzz. But what was the point? Excuses were only lies you told yourself to make yourself feel better.

I looked up from my cell when the man who had walked in pulled out the chair across from me.

"Can I buy you a drink?" he asked instead of the typical pick-up line.

He wore a business suit, resembled a clean-cut accountant, but I wanted to gag. The smell, like rotting fish, filled my nostrils.

My eyes flicked out the window. How did I not notice the sun went down?

They found me.

My gaze locked on his as I slowly scooted my

chair away from the table. I fought to not search for an escape. My back to a demon wouldn't end in my favor.

"Come on, Carrie," he said sweetly. "I'm not here to hurt you."

"Right. You came to purchase rum and coke for a minor. How nice of you."

He rotated his wrist, and a tumbler of what I guessed was rum and coke appeared on the table in front of me. "It's nice to see your boyfriend let you out of that overprotected dungeon. You must feel trapped." He nodded at the drink. "You came down here to clear your mind, so clear it."

"I'm not drinking anything you offer."

"It's not poisonous," he urged.

I said nothing. He had my answer.

"Your loss." The demon snapped, and the drink vanished. "But like I said, I'm not here to hurt you."

Out of the corner of my eye, I noticed silver mist at the entrance to the bar. Incenamus told me it was Lucas. I stiffened in my seat, staying focused on the evil in front of me as to not allude to Lucas's presence.

"I'm fine. Don't come any closer," I warned him. The demon said he wasn't here to hurt me, but he'd make a grab for Lucas given the chance.

"Then why are you here?" I asked the demon.

The corner of his lips curved up in a sly grin. "I want to offer a deal."

"I don't make deals with demons."

"You might want to listen to the deal before you make such statements."

"You want a book I don't have. I don't see a deal

to be made."

The demon chuckled. "The witch has taught you well. Wise for such a young girl."

"Are we done?"

He leaned forward on his elbows. "I want the book. You have one week to deliver it. If you don't meet the deadline, that smart-ass friend of yours—Mike, I believe—will no longer be able to answer your text messages."

He might as well have slit my throat because I couldn't breathe.

He has Mike.

The demon rose from his chair. "Seven days. I'll be in contact."

I watched his back as he left. As soon as he rounded the corner, I sucked in a breath and grabbed my phone. I shot out a text to Mike faster than projectile vomit.

Carrie: 911: Are you okay? Where are you?

Lucas materialized in the seat the demon had occupied mere seconds before. "Are you all right?"

"Where's the book, Lucas?" My voice scared me, how it shook.

"We have seven days," he answered softly.

"They could do *anything* to him in seven days!" I may not be part of the supernatural world, but I knew better than to trust a demon.

My phone buzzed. It took me two swipe attempts with trembling hands to unlock it.

Mike: I'm fine. At home.

I read Mike's text twice. He was fine. At home. How was that possible?

"They're not going to kidnap him right away. That would alert the authorities and draw attention. But it does mean that they know his habits, know where he lives, and have taken precautions so that a new slew of protection spells won't work against them," Lucas clarified, reading my thoughts.

"Seven days, Lucas," I repeated. "Seven days to—"

"It's not about Mike. Demons are jerks, doling out their time frames. They do it to break you mentally, soften you up for the trade off."

I bowed my head into my palms. "I put him danger."

"He chose danger. We all did."

I swallowed the lump in my throat before I met his stare. "We have to give the demon what he wants, Lucas. No one else can die."

"No one will."

***

Back in our room, Lucas got me calmed down and made me a cup of tea.

"This wasn't part of the plan," I said, absently swirling the amber within the cup.

"We don't seem to stick to the plan very well, do we?"

"We should work on that."

I breathed out something that sounded like a laugh. "Yeah. Next time."

Lucas threaded his fingers with mine and pressed

them against his lips. I thought he'd say something, but he didn't.

The silence made me uneasy. Like one of those times where you have so much to say, so much to discuss, that you can't bring yourself to say anything. Because if you do, the small respite where only you know your thoughts will come to an end and nothing will be the same.

Deep down I knew we had to break the silence.

"Say it," I murmured.

Lucas faced me, his jaw clenching. "I have to go for a while."

"You mean leave?"

He nodded.

"For how long?"

"I don't know. A few days," he said.

Cool palms found their way to my face, fingers weaving into my hair. "I don't want to, Carrie, but I have to."

"No, you don't," I challenged. He made this choice by himself, and it didn't include me.

"Yes, I do." He closed the distance between us until only a whisper of breath separated us. His voice lowered. "Megan called. She found Reid."

I straightened in defiance. "Reid won't hurt me. Take me with you."

"When Reid left, his cycles were fast and strong. God knows what they are now. He could be a full-fledged cambion by now. I won't risk taking you with me."

"But you'll risk leaving me here? With demons after me?" It was a dumb argument considering the slew of spells on the room. According to Adelia, our room was the safest place on earth. And of course there was no danger during sunlight hours.

His thumb caressed the side of my face. “We have seven days before they expect payment. Megan contacted Adelia, and she’ll be keeping an eye on you. Plus, there won’t be a risk if you stay in this room after sunset.”

I didn’t speak for a moment. Why was he so hell-bent on going alone? Sure, there was the Reid being evil thing, but when did evil beings ever stop us?

“What aren’t you telling me?” I asked, lowering my voice to match his. “Why don’t you want me with you?”

Lucas leaned in until our foreheads touched. “This isn’t about me not wanting you with me. I’m doing everything in my power to protect you. We’ve come this far, and with the prophecy, and the book, and you blacking out, I think you’re safer here. Adelia—”

“Will be babysitting me. Yeah, I know.”

“Not babysitting. Chances are you won’t even see her.”

I sighed, giving in. “Where is he?”

“Canada.”

“Did she find him from the ring?”

“Yeah. A sliver of his essence was embedded on it, which strengthens the tracking spell.”

“So the ring *is* his. For Rachel,” I thought out loud. Odd, because I’d really thought it was someone else’s.

“Seems like it.”

I reached behind me until I skimmed the silver

ring on the nightstand. I picked it up then held it out to Lucas. "You'd better take this with you."

Gingerly, he folded my fingers inward until the tips hit skin. "No. It stays here with you, where it's safe."

"Safe? It's just a ring, Lucas. And technically, it belongs to Reid."

"It belongs to Rachel."

I tilted my head to the side in sympathy. "She's gone."

"You mean dead," he said as if the harsh reality of the word meant something different. "So am I. So is Reid." He traced the outline of my jaw, moving in slow, even strokes over my face. "Hold on to it for me, please."

Then, slowly, he uncurled my fingers, and for a second I thought he'd changed his mind about taking the ring with him. Instead, he slipped the band onto my finger. The fourth one. On my left hand.

His gaze floated up to me. "Consider it a place holder for the real thing."

Any lingering frustration I had disappeared like that. Poof.

I nodded, because I didn't know what to say. A tear leaked out, making the corner of Lucas's mouth curve up into a half-grin before he reached up and dabbed the droplet onto the pad of his finger. How did it sit there, so perfectly shaped?

He held my tear close to my lips. "Make a wish."

"I think that's supposed to be with an eyelash," I murmured.

"Hmm, well. That's because they're easier to

acquire. Wishes made by blowing away a teardrop have special powers. They always come true."

"You made that up."

"Only one way to find out." He leaned in, his cheek brushing against mine, and whispered in my ear, "Make a wish, Carrie."

I closed my eyes. The wishing well in the atrium had nothing on Lucas.

I wish Lucas could always be mine. Forever.

I puckered up, repeated my wish in my head, and blew.

Cool breath flowed over my neck like silk as Lucas left a trail of kisses from one side of my throat to the other. He moved slow, creating a new wave of heat under my skin. I lolled my head to the other side to give him better access. I moaned when he finally reached my ear.

With his teeth, he tugged lightly on my earlobe in a final kiss.

"Wish granted."

Chapter 15

When I opened my eyes, Lucas was gone, and I was alone. I honed in on the closed curtains, wondering, but quickly decided I didn't care. Honestly, they were angels. Big deal. They existed to protect humans, so what did I have to worry about?

What I should worry about was that I had a freaking demon who'd be contacting me in seven days. A best friend the demon was stalking. A prophecy I hadn't figured out. Half a soul aching in my chest for completion. A mysterious ring. A lost cambion. And a boyfriend whose soul continued to elude us.

If I really wanted to depress myself I could add Vanessa's illness, my father's upcoming wedding, and my deteriorating relationships with Mike and Stacy. Oh, and let's not forget about those college acceptance letters I hadn't responded to.

Thinking about it would push me over the edge, so I passed over the angel book and opted for fiction. I needed a break from my own issues, my own world, and this claustrophobic hotel room. I didn't bother changing into pajamas or brushing my teeth. I fluffed my pillow, pulled the blankets over me, and sank myself into someone else's life until I drifted off.

***

"This is the new formula?" Lucas asked, holding up the vial of clear liquid to the light.

"Newest and greatest," Megan assured him.

"What did you use as the missing ingredient?"

"Oil of Tarasmith. It's a flower that's nearly been wiped out of existence. Pain in the ass to find. The Ancients used it to stimulate cell regeneration. It makes sense, but since all I have to go on is the first letter, I won't know if this is what we're missing until we try it."

Lucas scanned the page. The final ingredient had been cut out, leaving only the letter O to go on. Not much of a hint, as there were hundreds of substances it could be.

"You ready?" he asked, satisfied with his analysis of the potion.

Megan nodded toward the far corner of the room. "Chair's over there."

Lucas frowned. "That's not what I meant."

"I know."

She motioned again for Lucas to take a seat, and he complied. He sank down on the arm chair, stretching his legs out on the ottoman. Vial still in his grip, he tipped it up in a salute, then downed it in one gulp.

He leaned back against the backrest, his eyelids falling closed, his body relaxing into the cushions.

Megan studied him like a chemist waiting for a reaction. Methodical and calculating, she placed two fingers against the pressure point of his wrist while staring at the clock.

"Come on," she muttered.

She chewed on her lip, nodding as the second hand ticked off another round.

Then Lucas started to convulse. His chest and hips jerked up while he dug his head backward into the cushion. He grit his teeth to suppress the pain and thrashed his head back and forth.

"I've got a heartbeat," Megan said. Her tone was clinical, because they'd done this many times before. "Fight, Lucas."

He twisted onto his side, yanking away from Megan's grasp. Feral sounds tore from his throat.

"It's almost over," Megan encouraged. Steely eyes set on his writhing form.

Finally, Lucas's body relaxed. The spasms tapered off, and he opened his eyes and sucked in air like he'd never tasted it before. His skin, no longer pale, shone healthy under the dim light.

He sat up and faced Megan. "It worked?"

She cocked her head to the side in a side-nod. Then she clicked on the stopwatch she'd grabbed from her workstation. "Last time you got ten minutes. Anything over that would be an improvement."

"If this Oil of Tarasmith is correct, the improvement might be permanent."

"Lucas," Megan breathed out. "Don't get your

hopes up too high."

"Let's get my check-up over with."

Megan murmured out perfect vitals and drew three vials of blood. "You're as healthy as you were the last time I brought you back to life. Try not to die this time."

"Yeah. Did you make me food?"

"What is it with guys and food?" she said, writing dates and times on the blood samples. "I did order you a couple of tenderloins from the diner, though. Give me a sec."

"I might not have a sec."

"Good point." She put the test tubes down. "I'll be right back."

When she returned, Lucas's pupils dilated at the food she carried. "I can smell that, holy shit!"

Megan mouthed the words along with him as if it were routine. She gave him the food and returned to her work. "You say the exact same thing every time."

"You've never gotten me a tenderloin before. It's usually burgers or pizza." He ripped a bite off and closed his eyes as he chewed. "God!"

"He says, 'You're welcome,'" Megan said dryly.

She filled a syringe with Lucas's blood, then pushed drops into a bubbled tray.

"You talk with Mike?" Lucas asked, his voice muffled by the food.

"I did."

"How'd he take the demon news?"

Megan shrugged. "Refused the memory charm, so I guess good."

"Him keeping the memories won't save him."

"True. But sometimes it's nice to not know what's killing you."

Lucas paused. "Depends which side of the veil you wake up on."

"Mike is in no danger of staying here." She filled a new syringe with clear liquid and squirted a couple of drops into each bubble of blood. "I checked out his house, his car. The only place he'd be safe is inside Robert and Renae's house."

"Are those spells still holding from before?"

"Barely. I recast."

Lucas gave her a small nod. "Does he know that?"

"He does. Said he's not going to stop living his life and cower in a corner. If his time is up, it's up."

"Brave of him." Lucas swallowed his last bite of the first sandwich and dug into the second. "Any more thoughts on this prophecy?"

"Not any more than what I told you."

"How about your mom?"

"No improvement. I even gave her some of the Oil of Tarasmith. Seems whatever is ailing her has nothing to do with her physical being."

"It has to be soul or spirit related, then," Lucas mused.

"You'd think. Except neither part is dying. They're—" Megan stopped her tests and leaned forward on her knuckles. "It's like they're disappearing. They're moving on without the collapse of her body. Without a necromancer here, the spirits seeking her out for help will eventually drain her until there's nothing left. And then her body will die."

Lucas stopped eating, his shoulders falling in condolence. "I'm sorry, Megan."

"I don't know what else to do." She wiped a tear from her eyelash as she averted her attention back to her work.

Lucas picked up the stopwatch that had been ticking since his first breath—nine minutes and fourteen seconds. Last time, he'd gotten ten minutes. Life really was but a moment in time.

He placed the empty plate on the floor and walked over to Megan's workstation. "Give me something to do. I'm not going to sit around and wait to die," he said.

She huffed out a small laugh. Handed him a test tube of blood and containers of chemicals. "Centrifuge, please."

"Yes, ma'am."

"Call me 'ma'am' again, and I'll re-kill you myself."

He slid the tube into the machine, evened out the opposite side, and flipped the switch. A sensation of lightheadedness caught him off guard, and he swayed.

No. Not again.

Inhaling deeply, he concentrated on the hum of the centrifuge until the nausea left.

He waited for more signs—weakness, blurred vision, loss of hearing. None came, and tentative relief trickled in. He chuckled to himself; he'd lived past ten minutes.

He sucked in a lungful of air—he'd never take that for granted again—and rejoined Megan on the other side of the table. Her gaze met his, and, proud, she offered a celebratory smile. Then, with a small pump of her chin, she pushed a tray of blood samples in front of him.

"We need slides," she said, giving Lucas a stack of rectangular glass pieces. "Make sure they're labeled properly."

Epic or not, Megan always stayed calm during research. That trait of hers had brought him back to life.

At fifteen minutes, her smile grew. "Feeling okay?"

"So far," he said. He felt great!

"All right. Let's check your vitals again."

She examined his pupils, took his heart rate, blood pressure, and drew another three vials of blood. She wiggled the tube in front of him. "Everything looks spectacular, better than the average twenty-year-old. You've been alive for almost twenty minutes now, double the time of the last formula."

"So, am I cured, Doc?" he teased.

"Ha! You stay alive for another fifty years and I might confirm it. Until then, consider yourself in remission from death." She flicked the glass with her finger before putting a label on it. "But I think it would be wise if you stayed here tonight. You know, like a twenty-four hour thing."

"I need to find Reid."

"I agree. Tomorrow. Doctor's orders." She set the new sample next to the first ones and continued with her slides. "Besides, twenty minutes alive hardly gives you clearance to travel halfway across the United States, let alone cross the border." She

nodded toward the centrifuge. "It's done. Get to work, deadbeat."

"Witch," he muttered, his dimple poking inward with his grin.

She returned his smile. "Watch it."

Lucas stood up, but as soon as he did, dizziness set in. His vision blurred, sending the world around him into a tailspin. The room twisted, and he collapsed onto the floor.

"Lucas!"

That voice, he knew it. But she called to him from so far away, he couldn't make out the rest.

He clutched his chest, the newly beating heart failing him again. Beating in spurts, in non-rhythms that made no sense.

Thump. Thump-thump.

Thump-thump-thump. Tha-thump.

Tha...

Ummp.

Sharp pain sprang out from his chest. He heaved in a breath, wheezing with the intake.

He knew. He understood what this meant: the potion didn't work. He was dying.

Megan's frown met him. His palm laid in hers, but he couldn't feel her warmth. No, all he felt was cold.

Her mouth moved like she was talking to him. He couldn't hear that, either.

He let his eyelids fall, imagining the only face he wanted to see. It was the one he saw every time he died. Beautiful chocolate irises, silky-smooth brown hair that framed a perfectly-shaped face. God, he loved her. She was his reason for everything.

In his mind, he saw her lean into him. Her lips met his, and he could feel them, really *feel them against him. Soft, amazing. Language had no words to express the sensation.*

He'd failed her.

The thought hurt more than dying.

Concentrating on his hand, the one he hoped was still in Megan's, he forced himself to squeeze before he let go.

Chapter 16

During the day, I almost did the housekeeper's job because I was so bored. But last night I'd had the strangest dream. It was so real, so vivid, like the ones I used to have of Lucas. Except this one didn't actually happen. Like demons playing mini-golf.

The dream was part nightmare, having to suffer through Lucas's death. I woke up with a sob I couldn't swallow burning in my throat. I'd grabbed for my phone and shot Lucas off a quick text. So far today, I hadn't heard from him.

I clicked off the TV, tired of watching reality show re-runs. There were only so many times I could roll my eyes at stupidity. Stacy, though? Man, she loved these shows. And by loved, I mean *loved.* My best friend was a superfan.

The thought of Stacy had me reaching for my phone again. My incoming call log remained empty. No calls from her, no calls from Lucas or Megan, and unsurprisingly, none from Mike.

I exhaled loudly, deciding whether or not I wanted to try Stacy now. I'd only called a million times, what was one more?

Oh, what the hell.

I hit send. Let it ring until voicemail answered.

"Leave a message. You're going to anyway," she said as if giving me attitude for not taking her advice about my hair color. No doubt about it, this changed message was for me. It kinda made me laugh.

Beep.

"You know me well, Stacy. But I'm serious. I need you to call me. I could really use a friend, you know? Okay, well, until next time." I sounded like a song whose chorus replayed so many times it got annoying. Whatever. I was stubborn.

I ordered cheese sticks and a salad from room service, then texted Mike a message that went unanswered. I ate, thinking of how the demon was right. This must be what prison felt like. Too much longer cooped up in here and I'd…I didn't know what I'd do.

I decided to visit St. Paul's Cemetery the next day. Lucas and I would end up there eventually, but so far, he avoided the trip. I understood that. Lucas was gone though, and I needed something to do. Maybe I'd find some kind of clue there.

That night, I drifted off to sleep without my phone going off once.

A heavy need for sleep had Megan's eyelids dropping. Then, as if her task raced back to her memory, they snapped open wide. She blinked and rubbed her palms over them before squinting at her work.

She yawned, her gaze lifting tiredly to the clock. Sighing, she continued with another round of blood samples.

Minutes later, Lucas's voice interrupted her. Her head jerked toward the empty chair in the corner. Vapor swirled to fill out a transparent body.

"That sucked more than last time," he said, his voice low and raspy.

"These potions seem to be taking more of a toll on you."

His figure materialized, his brow scrunched in concentration. Back in corporeal form, he lay on the armchair with his feet on the ottoman. His skin was paler than usual and his irises barely displayed their green color. He looked as though he'd donated every last drop of blood.

"It's always hard watching you die," she said.

"It's hard dying."

She grabbed a chair and scooted it beside him. "How do you feel now?"

His chest didn't move; he took in no oxygen. The small, needless act required more energy than he had. When he told the witch that this time had been more difficult, he understated it. This time had been absolute hell. Dead had never felt this...dead. It surprised him that he managed to materialize again already the next day.

The idea of giving up and fading into nonexistence enticed him more than ever. It would have been so easy to do. Close to the veil, the temptations to leave were promises, and they sounded so damn good.

He almost said yes, almost let go. But then an

ache in his chest urged him to close his eyes and reconsider. It was then that he envisioned Carrie again. Her smile, her laugh. The way she tucked her hair behind her ear even when no hair had escaped its place. He couldn't leave her.

The thought of Carrie brought him back.

He pushed a hand through his hair, too exhausted to answer Megan's question about how he felt.

A small shake of his head was the only answer he could muster. And it sucked too, because he had to find Reid. Unfortunately, that was impossible in this state.

Then he disappeared.

***

The drive to St. Paul's Cemetery took close to an hour. The place was beautiful. Green and lush, it resembled a park featured in some magazine. Except this park had headstones lining the sidewalks, and instead of instilling joy and delight, it boasted solemn introspection and tears. Since I had no idea where Lucas and Rachel were buried, I pulled over on the edge of the drive and decided to walk.

The Jeep beeped as I locked it. The air was warm and thick, and my hair stuck to the back of my neck. In the shade of the trees, though, a light breeze brought relief from the Southern humidity.

I walked down the sidewalks, carefully scanning the stones on both sides. Some I could easily write off, like the ones in heart shapes and those that had room for two people—two married people. I also skimmed over ones that pillared up or resembled objects, such as benches or flowers.

That only left me with…most of the cemetery.

Finally, his last name caught my eyes. ***Reynolds*** was splayed in large letters across the silver tombstone. The name wasn't an unusual one, and I assumed I'd come across many I wasn't searching for. But the heaviness in my gut prompted me toward it.

I stood in place, staring at the surname on the granite. It was silly of me, because why else had I come? What else had I expected to find? I swallowed to calm my beating heart, but it only beat faster.

I could turn around, go back to the hotel room, and pretend this moment away. Gloss over it in my mind and replace it with something happy. But Lucas's journey ended here.

I stepped onto the grass. The tips tickled my toes as I crossed over the lawn. My eyes fixated on the engraved characters. I didn't dare look at the smaller stones beside it. Last names I could handle. It was the first name that scared me.

Two clumps of lilacs decorated the metal vases on either side. They were nice, like someone came here often and took care of them. I didn't know if that made me glad or if I wanted to cry.

I discerned the first names the closer I got. Maxwell and Rose. Grandparents, I guessed. Died thirteen and three years ago, one day from the anniversary of the other.

Two identical, smaller stones rested beside

theirs. I worked on the lump in my throat, trying to force it down. Again, the urge to walk away tugged at my heart. Did I really want to see this?

No.

I peered toward them. They had flowers too, and I wondered why I hadn't thought to bring any. I should have. I should have brought…

Why didn't I bring flowers?

I bit my lips together to keep a sob from escaping.

I had nothing to fear. Soon, I'd be back in Lucas's arms, and this—all of this—would be part of a past that didn't belong to me. There, I could convince myself this place didn't exist.

I opened my eyes. Focused on the name in front of me.

Emotion welled in my belly. Crazy how a slab of rock could pierce you through the heart with nothing but a name engraved on the front.

They say the value of life becomes clearer at a cemetery. That you realize how short life really is. How, in an instant, that fragile little thing we take for granted can be torn away from us and left to rot, alone.

They were right.

Lucas J. Reynolds.

I died again, facing the granite of the truth I never wanted to believe. Six feet below me rested Lucas's body. *My* Lucas's body. His flesh, his bones, his dust.

I choked on the sob that finally broke loose. I

couldn't do this.

I scrambled to my feet, wiped the tears from my face, and ran back to the Jeep.

Chapter 17

"Give it one more day, Lucas. You're not ready," Megan urged.

Lucas slid an arm through a leather jacket. His pale skin gleamed under the fluorescent bulbs, but it no longer seemed ghostly. Color had returned to his irises, brightening to their characteristic shade. He zipped up the coat.

"I don't have one more day, Megan. I've been here for four days. Mike has three left, and God knows how long it will take to find Reid and get the information I need." He folded up the locator map and thrust it into his inner pocket. "I can't afford one more day of rest."

"The trip alone will drain you," she said, more for his information than to convince him to stay.

"I know."

"Well, that makes me feel better."

Lucas chuckled. "We need to figure out why the demons want the book and are willing to go to extremes to get it."

"Regardless, we're gonna have to give them the

book. I can't risk a life on this."

"I agree. But the 'why' may be useful. In the meantime, you need to get Mike to safety at Rob and Renae's."

"That might require a straightjacket.

"Do you have one?"

Megan laughed. "Maybe in the attic."

"You have my permission."

"I'm sure that will go over well."

"It's better than dying."

"So what about the potion?" She held his gaze, unblinking.

Lucas sighed. "I don't want to give up yet."

"I was afraid you'd say that. When does it end?"

"This is the last option I have left."

"No, it's not," Megan murmured low, her focus shifting off him.

"The only one that keeps me on Earth with Carrie." He pressed a kiss to her cheek. "Thank you for everything, Megan."

Then he vanished.

I stretched on the mattress, woozy with sleep. These dreams! They were beginning to make sense, but could they be real?

If so, Lucas lied to me. I hated that almost as much as I hated demons.

Gah, I wished he would just answer his damn phone. Or text back. I mean, come on. How long could it take to type out, "I'm okay. Be there Tuesday."

So far during his absence, I'd watched television until my brain went numb, finished a three-book series, gone to the cemetery, and surfed the internet. Which most of the time started off noble, researching any connection to Lucas I could think of, but I always ended up on YouTube, clicking on cat videos.

As Lucas said, I hadn't seen my babysitter. I knew she was keeping tabs on me though, because when I got back from the cemetery, there was a note on my bed from her, reminding me of my curfew…which was humorous, considering I returned at three in the afternoon.

At least I hadn't had an "episode." I thought back to when they occurred: discussions about leaving Villisca, on the trip to North Carolina, and at Lucas's old house. They seemed to be triggered by something Lucas-related, like the closer we got to answers, the stronger they hit me. Odd, then, that nothing happened at the cemetery.

The largest one, though, happened in Rachel's room when I'd spotted the ring.

The ring…

I twisted it around my finger. The ring had to mean something, because why else had I seized at that exact moment? I examined the gem under the light. It sparkled like a diamond, but it wasn't clear like a diamond. Stacy would know what it was.

My phone was on the nightstand, and I considered calling her again. The track record of her answering though was like zero to gazillion. I probably had a better chance of one of the Seven Sisters picking up for me. Besides, it wasn't like she could examine the jewel via phone.

I tapped my nails against my teeth and allowed

my mind to wander again. I thought about Jessica's unsolved vision, the number 314 she kept seeing. To my knowledge, that number hadn't popped up anywhere yet. I assumed I'd see it eventually, but so far, nothing.

Something as simple as a number could lead to anything: a house, a hotel room, coordinates, a time, a location, a locker at the train station. Unfortunately that was all we had to go on. She hadn't seen more.

Unless...

My best friend had kept the fact she'd seen her own death from me. Also, she used to see visions in short clips or pictures. Maybe she saw more but didn't connect the images as being from the same event.

I swiped my phone open, bit the inside of my cheek, and called Stacy.

"Leave a message. You will anyway."

Beep.

"I need a favor, and it's super important. Please, Stacy, please call me back. It's about Jessica."

I hung up and let my brain burn cells until I finally fell asleep.

Lucas lay on a motel room bed. The ugly yellow floral pattern of the duvet made him seem more flushed than before, if that was possible. He pushed a hand through his dark hair before he tucked both of them behind his head.

He'd arrived in Blainville, Quebec exhausted and weak, but a few hours of rest fueled his determination. The locator map had Reid here, and as soon as he came out of hiding, Lucas would find him, incubus or not.

Like most cambions, incubi preferred prowling for victims after sunset, which was two hours away. He would be putting himself at risk being out at that time, but to his knowledge there were no rifts to Hell close by. It still wasn't safe, of course. He'd have to be careful.

He'd search the pubs and local taverns for Reid first. Drunk victims were easier targets than sober ones. After that, he'd head to the hospital, Reid's old stomping grounds, and the one place Lucas loathed more than any other.

He had a plan. Until then, he'd rest.

***

A knock on the door broke him from his sleep. He shot a hurried glance at the alarm clock to find it was almost midnight. He'd wasted half the evening!

Cursing to himself, he walked to the door and peered out the peephole. Flaming red hair atop a familiar freckled face gave him an annoyed expression.

"Gonna open up, dude?" he asked.

"Yeah. Hang on." Lucas slid the chain lock off the door.

It shouldn't be a surprise to see Reid here. Months ago, the same thing happened when he showed up in Lucas's living room. Word among cambions traveled fast, and locator spells weren't known for their anonymity.

Lucas opened the door. Dressed in jeans and a long-sleeved black shirt, his childhood friend was wide awake at this late hour. Not only that, but he was fully human too.

"Heard you were in the neighborhood," Reid said.

"Can't deny that I am." He widened the door and motioned for Reid to enter.

"You look like death, more than usual."

"It's been a long day."

"Got anything to drink?" Reid asked, walking in.

"There might be some bottled water in the mini-fridge."

Reid puffed out a laugh. "Typical. You were always boring like that."

"I can't argue, seeing as you have more memories of me than I do."

Reid leaned up against the dresser, his legs crossed in front of him. "We get to the point early, I see."

Lucas plopped down on the bed. "I'm not here for my *memories. I'm here for yours. More specifically, yours with Rachel."*

Reid straightened at the mention of her name. "I told you the details. I have nothing else to add."

"Really? Nothing about a ring?"

Reid laughed, his head tilting to the side before he refocused on Lucas. "How do you know about the ring? Dude, 'cause if you've got some memories back, I'd love it if you shared."

Lucas frowned "You didn't give it to her?"

Reid rubbed the back of his neck. "No, man. I

didn't give her the ring."

Chapter 18

I woke up to a text message ringtone. Considering last night's dream, I made myself a deal. If it was Lucas saying he'd be back today, I'd kick his ass, because that meant the dreams over the last week had all been real, and he had a lot of explaining to do.

If it belonged to Mike or Stacy, I would order ice cream for breakfast, because Hell had clearly frozen over.

As I reached for my phone, I crossed my fingers for some good ol' mint chip. The hotel had to carry that flavor, right? Mint chip had to be, like, the third most popular flavor after chocolate and vanilla. My mouth salivated at the thought.

My mental deflection only half-worked until Lucas's face appeared on my screen. And the message?

Lucas: Be at the hotel by noon today. I'm bringing Reid with me.

Forget the ass kicking. I was going to kill him. Plus, now he had cost me an ice cream breakfast.

I had a few hours before they'd arrive, and I had nothing to do. I finished reading the angel book two days ago, and the only new thing I learned was that they didn't actually have halos. Real helpful.

I moved on to demons. Internet demon lore varied from country to country, culture to culture, and person to person, making it difficult to sort out truth from fiction. Everyone seemed to have an opinion, but their opinions spanned from close-but-no-dice to whacked-out-government-space-alien-cover-up-theories. From my experience, demons didn't care about crop circles or human implants. Though the few sites that mentioned demons controlling corrupt politicians, or *being* corrupt politicians might have some merit.

I giggled to myself at that. Sometimes I was funny.

Witch reference books seemed to be the most accurate; however the only book Megan left us regarding demons was, of course, written in Latin. I began typing the first paragraph into Google Translate, but stopped when I realized how long it would take to do a six hundred page book.

The thought reminded me of my prophecy. Another thing I didn't understand, and that *was* in English. I leaned back against the chair and crossed my arms.

One will come to save them all. Me, okay, but I had a hard time thinking of myself as "the chosen one." Seemed too George-Lucas to me. And save whom from what?

The next line I'd pretty much figured out. *An otherworldly connection will grow her, and when she is strong, evil will pursue her.* Incenamus, the otherworldly connection I shared with Lucas, would grow me. I'm not sure how much I'd grown, but whatevs. And I'd had demons on my tail since I left Villisca. Didn't get more evil than that.

The rest spoke of choices and life and death, and those decisions were bigger than me. Who had the right to choose who lived and died? No person should, and definitely not me.

I held my hand up to examine the ring, watching the center jewel sparkle in the sunlight. It was beautiful, whatever it was.

The setting too. The large gem in the middle, surrounded by smaller ones in a spiral down to the polished silver band. Had Rachel ever worn this?

My gaze drifted over to her picture that Lucas borrowed from his parents' house. It was of the four of them at Lucas's high school graduation. He wore a blue oversized robe, like the one I wore a couple of weeks ago. The coincidence made my heart ache.

The sound of the door made me look up from the photograph. Lucas walked in, and even though he wasn't an intruder, I debated on ramming the chair into his legs for being gone so long without a note of communication. But then I looked at him—really looked. I took in the pale skin, even whiter than normal. Heavy eyelids that half concealed weak irises. Disheveled dark hair that he ruffled as soon as he entered.

If he were alive, he'd probably collapse.

I pushed away the concern, because he did this to

himself, to me, *without* me. Without me knowing a damn thing.

"You've had an eventful week," I said, narrowing my eyes into a glare.

His chest expanded with an inhale. "I didn't block enough, did I?"

"Oh-em-gee, Lucas! *That's* your answer?" Anger flushed my cheeks. How could he do what he did and be okay with it? I felt my nostrils flare.

"Hey, old married couple." From the hallway outside our room, Reid waved his arms like he was directing airplanes down the runway. "Can y'all do this later? Seems like we have less than twenty-four hours before you gotta meet up with a demon."

"Welcome back," I said dryly, giving him a onceover. The sensations that had ripped through me when he was in cambion mode were absent now. I gave him a chin up. "Human?"

"Like your boyfriend would let me near you if I wasn't. If I remember right, though, I only got half a show last time." He winked, a smirk pulling up the corner of his mouth.

"I guess that memory will have to hold you over for eternity, 'cause that's all you'll ever get."

He chuckled. "Good to see you too, Carrie."

"We should get to work," Lucas said, his voice husky. He blinked out of existence before returning.

"You should lie down," I suggested. I caressed the side of his face, worry overriding my frustration. When my fingers trailed over his lips, he kissed them as they brushed by.

"I'm sorry," he murmured, and his gaze finished the apology for him. He held me there, a mixture of remorse and sadness passing from him to me.

"Rest," I choked out, then cleared my throat of his feelings. "I need you, so please. Rest."

He did as I asked and lay on the bed. I propped pillows under him and watched as his head lulled to the side in relaxation.

"Excuse me, lovebirds." Reid sounded annoyed from where he still stood in the hallway.

"You're not a vampire. No invitation needed, right?" I said.

"If only. I can't come in," he said, nodding toward the invisible writing around the door frame. "The symbols keep out *all* evil creatures."

"You're not evil right now, are you?"

"Whoever put these up did a damn fine job. Didn't miss a thing." He roamed over the frame as if he could see the symbols. Maybe he could. "Impressive work."

I glanced at Lucas, hoping he would be lucid enough to figure out this issue. Part of his reasoning for me not going with him was because of Reid, and now, here Reid was. But Lucas faded into silver mist, his eyes closed, resting like I asked.

"I don't know how to remove them," I said to Reid.

"Well, who put 'em on?" He thrust his hands out like the answer should be obvious.

"A witch here in town."

"Great. Get her on the phone."

With Lucas asleep, now completely invisible, I wasn't sure how wise it would be of me to be trapped inside this room with Reid by myself. He was human at the moment, yeah, but I had personal experience on how quickly that could change. His incubus charms had me half-naked once; no way would I chance that happening again.

"We can hear each other. Talk from there." I grabbed a chair and plopped down, facing him, a safe distance away. Not that he could cross the barrier anyway.

His eyebrows arched high on his forehead. "You can't be serious. You want me disclose highly sensitive information *from the hotel hallway*?" His voice rose at his last words. "Why don't I just write an article and publish it in *Demons Weekly*?"

I studied him. As an incubus, this guy might be the world's best liar, but as a human, he proved himself trustworthy. Another peek at the empty bed and I sighed.

The soft click of Reid tapping the face of his watch drew my attention back to the cambion. He was right. We were running out of time. *Mike* was running out of time. I had to find a way to keep him safe.

"Fine," I said. "I'll make the call."

"Good choice." Reid pushed off the doorframe. "Have Luke call me when this witch finishes up. I'm going downstairs for a drink."

I closed the door as soon as he left. I didn't actually have Adelia's number, so I called Megan for it.

"What's up, Carrie?" Megan answered.

"I need to get a hold of Adelia. It's important."

"Why? What happened? Lucas there?" Her string of questions hit me as odd, but time didn't care about human inquiries, and I had very little at my disposal.

"Yeah, all's great. I need some of these protection spells removed."

She went silent for a second. "For Reid?"

"You…know he's here." I didn't ask, because of course she knew. Lucas had gone to her first.

"Lucas called me. My flight arrives in Asheville in an hour, and I'll take care of it."

She's coming here*?*

Anxiety stole the breath from my lungs. "What about Mike? The demons will be after him soon, and we don't have—"

"The demons won't hurt Mike, because one, he's safe at Rob and Renae's, and two, they'll have what they want by midnight tonight."

***

Megan must have spotted Reid in the lounge, because when she knocked, he stood behind her. She wheeled her luggage inside, leaving Reid in the hallway again.

"Adelia did a phenomenal job," Megan said to me, sighing.

"So I've heard."

"I can't remove anything," she admitted. "I called her. She'll be here soon."

Reid held up his tumbler in a cheers motion, then downed the rest of the liquor in one gulp. "I guess I'll wait here."

"Sorry, Reid," Megan said nonchalantly before she turned to me. "Where's Lucas?"

I nodded toward the bed. "Sleeping."

"Good," she said, staring at nothing on the bed.

I rested my hands on my hips, wondering if she'd elaborate. Ghosts didn't require much rest, and we both knew that. Yet he'd been out for a couple hours.

"Oh, before I forget." Megan tossed me a white envelope. "From Mike."

"Did he forget how to use a phone?"

She shrugged. "Don't shoot the messenger."

"You said he was at my grandparents'?"

"Yes. Rob and Renae's had enchantments around it from before. I re-cast them last week. They should hold as long as Mike stays within the boundaries."

"Good," I said, relieved.

I folded the note up and pocketed it for later. He kept me waiting this long, he could wait too.

I moved in closer to Megan and lowered my voice. "Is he gonna be, you know, okay?" I ticked my eyes toward Reid.

"Lucas wouldn't have brought him back here if he wasn't. He's been taking the potion I made. Doesn't stop the cycles, but they're at least manageable. He should be fine."

"I'll be fantastic," Reid said from the doorway. "Thanks for asking."

I swung to him. "Sorry. I thought…"

"Yeah." He dropped his chin toward the floor. "Got room service here? I could use another drink."

"Sure thing." I ordered what he wanted and slid my back down the wall beside him. "Might as well sit."

"I feel like an ass out here," he said, lowering

himself to the carpet in the hallway.

I laughed. “Mind reading skills would be useful right now.”

As soon as I said it, a man walked past. He had a difficult time keeping his eyes to himself.

Reid made a face. When the man moved out of earshot, Reid cocked his head at him. “That dude? Thinks we’re all on drugs.”

Megan sat across from me. “Nah. Probably thinks you locked yourself out.”

“Damn. I’m talented since the door is open.”

I giggled, absently twisting Rachel’s ring around my knuckle. I peered up to find Reid staring at it with his eyebrows lowered.

I cleared my throat and tucked my hands behind my back. “Hey, your drink’s here,” I said nodding to the server behind him.

“Jack and Coke?” the server asked.

“I should have ordered two,” Reid mumbled, digging out his ID.

Satisfied, the room service guy gave it back along with the drink. “Thank you, sir.”

“Charge it to the room.”

“Of course, sir.”

We sat in silence. Megan tapped her nails on the wall behind her, the only noise I could decipher. Patrons walked down the hall, most ignoring us. Others though quirked their brows and whispered to each other.

“They clearly have boring lives,” Reid said as I watched a pair of the second variety saunter down the hall.

“Normal, you mean.” I didn’t realize I spoke out

loud until Reid's stare hit mine.

I bit my lips together to keep quiet. I had a great life, really. One with more love in it than most people. I guess normal was overrated.

"Ah, you must be Miss Megan, yes?" a familiar voice asked. Adelia stopped behind Reid, though she stood only a head taller than him with him seated. Hair wrapped in a braid around her head, she smiled at the witch rising to her feet.

Megan stretched out her hand. "Adelia. Thank you for coming."

"Is my pleasure, dear." Dark irises the color of coal shifted to me. "Miss Carrie. I trust you are well?"

"I'm not dead," I answered, standing.

Reid rose at the same time, towering over the oracle. Her chin lifted as her head tilted backward. Studying him, her posture stiffened. "There is great evil about you." She closed her eyes and touched his arm. He didn't flinch. "Yet…there is ambition. Loyalty." Her eyes flashed open. "Love."

Reid said nothing. He simply peered down at her like he was used to people analyzing him.

Adelia patted his arm. "Hmmm, yes. Your story, Incubus, has yet to end. You will find what it is you so seek."

Reid's Adam's apple bobbed as he swallowed. "What is it that I seek?"

Adelia released him. "You need no confirmation from me." She turned to Megan and me. "Now, you need symbols removed, yes? For his entrance."

"Yes, please," Megan answered. "We'd also appreciate it if you had time to stay. We have, um, some issues to discuss."

Adelia nodded knowingly. "The demons. Yes. I know about this. I shall stay."

"Thank you."

"I assume you want to grant only *this* incubus entrance?"

"Correct."

Adelia turned to Reid. "I shall need a drop of blood."

Reid held out his arm. "That's what they all want."

As Adelia started to work, I went back inside. I lay down on the bed, facing where Lucas fell asleep. I extended my hand into the air until the temperature dropped and coolness inched over my skin. It used to bother me more, the coolness of him. Now, though, it was one of the things I loved, because sometimes, my touch warmed him, and my warmth became his.

"Lucas," I murmured, caressing what I thought to be his face. "Everyone is here. Adelia's working on the symbols."

No response.

I sucked in a deep breath, my eyelids falling on the exhale. I made my shoulders relax, my muscles following their example until my whole body felt like it was floating on top of the duvet. The veil that separated us moved in my mind, flowing like silk in the wind. I'd torn it down before, reached Lucas beyond it.

This time, it fell on its own.

Lucas, my love. Come back to me.

In my mind, I saw Lucas emerge from the other

side. He wore white, like an angel. Barefoot, he walked toward me, each step soft and gentle over an invisible floor. The shimmering jade of his eyes found me, and a perfect smile spread over perfect lips.

He was beautiful. So, perfectly beautiful.

"I missed you," he said in my thoughts. *"I promised forever, and I never want to miss you again."*

Coolness brushed the side of my face, and a thumb glided over my mouth, bringing me out of my own head and back into the hotel room. I didn't open my eyes though, wanting to memorize this moment and lock it away into the recesses of my mind. Those types of memories weren't meant to be shared; they were meant to be cherished in private.

Fingers combed into my hair, and I felt the air of my exhale against my lips. This, right here, was pure, pristine happiness.

It was love.

Finally, I opened my eyes to see Lucas's green ones, bright and full of life. His pale skin was no longer as pale, and I could have sworn his heart beat beneath his ribs. Of course that was impossible.

"If this is the last memory I'll ever get, I could die happy," Lucas said, leaning in until our foreheads touched.

"I'll make you even happier if you stay alive," I murmured, our breath mingling in the space between us.

"Get a room already," Reid groaned from inside our room.

Lucas got up and gave him a man hug. Yep, man

hug. With exactly two back pats each.

"You look better, man," Reid said.

"I feel better." He chin-upped Megan. "Thanks for making the trip."

"Let's get this figured out. I need to get back to Mom," she said, hopping up on the desk and crossing her legs.

The scene reminded me of another talk, back in Lucas's house. A slight change in attendees and agenda.

"We gotta stop meeting like this," I joked once everyone found a seat.

"Let's make this the last time," Reid said.

And no one dies.

Judging by Lucas, Megan, and Reid's expressions, I assumed they thought the same thing. At least we were all on the same page.

"The demon said he'd contact me in seven days. Tonight, after sunset, my time is up," I said. "We have no choice; we have to give him the book."

"She's right," Megan said, pulling the prize from her bag and dropping it in the middle of the bed. "We can't lose human life over this."

"Oh my," Adelia murmured when Megan left it there. "That is one powerful book. The only in existence."

"What's so special about it?" Reid asked, grabbing it and thumbing through the pages. "Just a spell book."

"No, no." Adelia tick-tocked her index finger at him. "Not *just* a spell book. This book contains potions by a man whom some would call mad. He played with dark magic. He believed that if darkness mixed with light, the light would be powerful enough to extinguish the dark."

"Makes sense," Megan said. "Good is stronger than evil."

"*Love* is stronger than evil, Miss Megan. Not good. See, the power of good and evil, they are equal in strength. Many times, evil outpowers good. You have heard the saying that great evil is done with the best of intentions, yes?"

I bobbed my head along with Megan. Not long ago we tested that saying ourselves, using good intentions to vanquish evil. To the extent of using evil to *kill* evil. And the outcome? Jessica died.

As if reading my thoughts, Adelia continued. "So it is with this world. But love, my dear, love is different. Love casts out all evil. It is selfless, pure, true. Love is the only thing in this world that is truly good. It is the only thing that defeats darkness."

Megan motioned to Reid for the book. She smoothed over the cover. "You're saying these potions in here, their power can go either way? Good or evil."

"That is correct. The potions themselves do not contain love, thus cannot keep out dark magic within the spell."

"Okay, but I still don't understand why the demons want this book. They do enough evil on their own, and if they use the potions, wouldn't they run the risk of possibly doing some good?" I asked, beckoning to Megan for the book. She gave it to me, her gaze flicking to Lucas as if asking his permission first. I started going through it with new interest. It was written in Latin, except the English notes in the back.

I flipped to the spell with the notes. There was something about it…

"Maybe they want to, I don't know, take out the good and toss in more evil?" Reid said. "Create more beings like me or something."

Adelia chuckled. "No, no, Incubus. Demons, they have thousands of potentials at their disposal." She nodded at Lucas. "Ghosts—the bodiless—are ripe and plentiful for the picking. Remember, ghosts have no ties to Heaven, or Hell, or Earth. They belong nowhere."

As they talked about ghost recruitment to Hell, I opened my laptop and signed into the hotel's Wi-Fi. Thank God for Google. I adjusted the settings to translate Latin into English and typed in the potion's title: *Restitue animam ad inferos deducentur*.

The answer…

I stared, unbelieving, at the screen. The voices around me disappeared.

No. This couldn't be right.

I blinked, making sure I read the output correctly.

Is it possible?

My heart stopped at the translation—

Restore life to the dead.

Chapter 19

It wasn't just me; the room really had gone silent. I pursed my lips to keep the emotion contained and closed my laptop. I put it aside, focusing on my own movements.

A cool arm hooked around my waist. Cooler breath wafted over my neck. "Are you okay?"

I blew out an exhale, keeping my gaze trained on the floor as the clues fell into place. The potion Lucas and Megan had been experimenting with. Changing dosage amounts and searching for the missing ingredient…?

I needed to talk with Lucas alone.

"I thought you said there was no potion that could bring the dead back to life," I whispered.

"There's not," Megan answered. "Not really. You see, in twelfth century France, there was an apothecary—a potions master—"

"A witch?" I asked.

"Madman," Adelia corrected.

"A warlock," Megan said. "Matthias Jaquemound. The legend is his wife was murdered in their bed while he was away. Upon his return, strange things began happening: candle lights flickering, floorboards creaking, papers scattered across the room. This continued for a fortnight, almost driving Matthias from his home. And then she appeared to him in a mist. Stuck on this side of the veil, she hadn't learned how to communicate with the living yet. So Matthias went to work to come up with a potion to bring her back to life."

"He succeeded, didn't he? This"—I pointed to the potion recipe—"is his work."

"Yes. After years of tinkering, he was able to bring his wife back long enough for her to voice the name of her killer."

I perked up with hope. "Then, you're saying it can be done. That there's a way to unite Lucas's spirit, body, and soul. He can live again."

Adelia locked on me. Facial features hardened, she shook her head.

Other than her eyes roaming over the pages of the book, Megan sat motionless. She dragged her fingertip over her own handwritten notes and sighed. "No, Carrie. Death is death, and Death doesn't give back life."

"But you said—"

"Matthias Jaquemound brought his wife back, yes, for thirty seconds. And then he had to watch his beloved wife die in his arms all over again. The second time, she crossed over." She paused, her focus meeting mine. "You see, Death doesn't take survivors. He takes what belongs to him, and he doesn't let go."

Lucas took my hand and squeezed. My heart

thudded, the beats making no sense. I twisted to see Lucas but had to look away from the pain in his eyes.

"Let me get this straight," Reid said, pushing off the windowsill. "The potion works, but for, like, a minute, right?"

Megan nodded. "Correct."

"So imagine if this potion actually worked? If somehow, someone was able to manipulate the ingredients as to bring ghosts back from the dead? Now put that kind of power in the hands of a necromancer…" He nodded toward Lucas. "See where I'm going?"

Lucas smirked to himself, shaking his head like the answer was obvious. "And you cut Hell's supply of demons in half."

"At *least* half. Maybe completely."

Megan groaned, throwing her head back in a puff of laughter. "That's why they want it. That's why they want the book."

"How did they know of its existence?" Reid asked.

"Until now, the book has been no more than a myth." Adelia turned from Lucas to Megan to me to Reid as if one of us held the answer to her unasked question.

"I found it," Megan said. "Locked in a trunk in the attic. Under a bunch of old family heirlooms."

"Pouvoir family heirlooms, yes? Your mother's family."

Megan shrugged. "Yeah."

Adelia tilted her head. "Pouvoir, it is a French name, is it not?"

Understanding lit Megan's face. "Matthias Jaquemound. He's my ancestor."

"The Pouvoirs are a very powerful magical family. You are clairvoyant, but you also know your way with potions. You never traced a family history?"

"No, but that doesn't explain how Hell figured out I have it."

"Hell watches those with power," Adelia said. "It watches *very* closely." Her stare moved to me.

"Are you saying they knew because Lucas and I have been experimenting with it?"

Adelia nodded once.

Silence dropped over us, creating a web of tension that made me jump at the sound of my phone ringing.

Lucas reached for it on the nightstand. "Private number," he said, his tone husky.

I swallowed, taking the phone from him. It could only be one person. "Hello?"

"Carrie Reese," the demon answered, half laughing. "Lovely to hear your voice again."

"Can't say the same."

"We have a date this evening, you and I alone. Reservations are at ten-fifteen at Cardell's. The black dress you brought with you should do nicely. Come alone and don't forget the book. You know what's at stake."

Click.

I didn't get a chance to ask how he knew about my wardrobe. Or decline his stupid reservation. Going to dinner with him hadn't been part of the deal, but what choice did I have? If the date was the price for Mike to keep breathing, so be it.

"See you then," I murmured into the dead line.

Lucas touched my shoulder. "Nothing is going to happen to Mike or you."

"What time?" Megan asked.

I rattled off the details, leaving out the dress request.

"I'll escort her," Reid offered.

"No!" I snapped back. "I have to go alone. I have to do what he said."

"The demon is delusional if he thinks I'm going let you meet him by yourself," Lucas said. "Adelia, is there a way to conceal one of us?"

"There isn't, but do not believe *he* will come alone. You must follow his orders, and you must have a plan."

"We planned for a drop-off, not a date in public," I said.

Reid checked his watch. "Six hours. Not much time to come up with a plan B."

"I just texted Mike to make sure he's at the Reese farm by nightfall," Megan said. "It's the best we can do, and it was all he would agree to."

"So it's the four of us and what? Two demons? Two dozen?"

Adelia pushed up from her chair. "No, my dears. Not four—three. This is a battle Destiny has given to *you*. And *you* must fight it."

"You're not helping?" I asked, the dread in my stomach growing.

"No, Miss Carrie. I cannot." She smiled at me, the wrinkles spreading at the corners of her eyes. "Remember the prophecy. That is all the help I can offer."

I did a quick scan of the others in the room, hoping one of them would somehow convince her to stay. Reid had his arms crossed. Megan bowed her head, already in thought. And Lucas, my Lucas, had worry lines stretched across his forehead. Deep down, I knew that whatever we came up with, Lucas would have a secret plan B if things went south.

Then I realized that no one had moved, not even to blink, and I understood that Adelia had frozen them.

My focus flitted back to her, and she pointed a stubby finger at me. "Remember, my dear."

The room unfroze, and Reid's shoulders relaxed. Megan tipped her head up, and Lucas hugged me to his side.

Adelia walked toward the door. "Good luck. You will need it."

Chapter 20

We spent the rest of the time we had piecing together a plan none of us liked. The three supernaturals worked out the details on their end while I showered, put on makeup, and curled my hair. This was *not* the reason I'd packed this dress. The freaking demon had to pick one of the city's most upscale five-star restaurants as a trade-off location.

I slid my arm into the dress's one sleeve and adjusted the neckline that dipped under my armpit, leaving my other arm bare. The special bra I had to buy dug into my side boob, but a few pulls and yanks of the fabric, and it no longer bothered me. In that regard, anyway. The fact I was showing off this form-fitting number to a demon instead of Lucas made a wave of nausea rush through me.

I'd burn the dress after tonight.

I strapped on the too-high black pumps and examined myself in the mirror. I looked hot as hell, but all things considered, I didn't think that was what I should have been going for. Still.

Let's do this.

I opened the bathroom door and stepped out, interrupting the discussion. Lucas's reaction was the only one I cared about, and it was everything I'd hoped for. Lips parted in a gasp. Irises darkened into a lustful shade of green that traveled the length of my body.

I squeezed my thighs together at his obvious approval.

Reid whistled, eyes wide in appreciation. "Hot damn, Carrie."

Lucas immediately swung to his best friend, shooting him a death glare. "Keep the incubus under control, dude, or I won't be the only dead person in this room."

He put his hands up in surrender. "I won't touch, I swear."

"Don't even look."

"Sorry, man. That can't be helped."

Megan grabbed Reid's arm. "How about we give them a little privacy?" She motioned toward Lucas and me. "Meet you in the lobby in five."

I nodded, keeping my eyes on the love of my life. As soon as the door clicked shut behind them, I slipped into Lucas's arms and nuzzled my face into his chest.

"I don't want to do this," I said.

"I don't want you to either. It should be me."

I puffed out a laugh. "None of it makes sense. I mean, why did the demon request *this* dress?"

"The dress is the only thing I *do* understand." Gently, he leaned me back to examine me again. His eyes lingered on my cleavage. "Damn, Care. If we live through this, I promise to have that dress on the floor as soon as we get back."

I blushed. Fire should have ripped through my body at the anticipation of his promise. Except it didn't. The damned caveat hung like a flashing light in my brain: *if* we lived through this.

I'd been up against demons too many times, and I'd seen what they were capable of.

Lucas must've been in my head, because his flirtatious smirk slowly slid into something more serious. He brushed loose strands of hair away from my face, watching his own motions instead of me. His gaze dropped to mine and he held it for a moment before he kissed me.

"I won't let anything bad happen, Care. I swear to you."

He'd *try*, I knew he would. The thought didn't make me feel better. Success was me walking out of Cardell's to Lucas untaken to hell and Mike alive.

The lives of at least two people hinged on my actions tonight, and I was no diplomat. Making deals with demons—*how had we gotten to this point?*

"The potion you took from Megan, to bring you back to life?" I said, changing the subject. "A few months ago, when you were pale and sick…you weren't fading away. You were dying."

The coolness of his palm settled on my cheek, and he nodded. "I had died, yes."

"Because you were experimenting with this potion, and it didn't work?"

"Yeah."

I shuffled my feet on the floor, debating if I

wanted an answer to my next question. I swallowed the emotion rising in my throat. "How many times have you died?"

He tipped my face up to his. "Fifteen."

That emotion raced back up, and a tear fell onto my cheek. With his thumb, Lucas wiped it away.

Fifteen.

"I'd die a million more times if it brought me a step closer to you hearing my heartbeat. We might be here to search for my soul, but I'm not giving up on us."

I caressed his face, memorizing the smoothness of his skin, how his dark eyelashes accentuated the color of his irises, how tiny laugh lines appeared at the corners of his eyes when he smiled. And that lone dimple. He knew how to work his half-grin so that it appeared just enough to make my heart forget to beat.

Yes, my broken soulmate belonged to me, and I to him.

"I love you," I whispered. "Remember that, okay?"

"Forever."

The numbers on the clock flashed in my periphery. "We're two minutes late."

Lucas wrapped in me in close. "Come on, then, beautiful. It's date night."

***

One of the many faults in this plan was my team's dependence on me keeping Incenamus open for communication. Most of the time, Lucas heard me clearly. Me getting into his head was the problem.

I dropped off my protection team six blocks from the restaurant as to not draw attention.

I pulled the Compass up to the valet and dropped a ten-dollar-bill and a set of keys into his palm. I kept a second set in my purse. Reid had a third, and Megan a fourth. I straightened my skirt, sucked in a deep breath, and nodded at the gentleman holding the restaurant door for me.

"Good evening, ma'am," the hostess greeted. "Do you have reservations?"

"Yes, ten-fifteen. Um…" The demon hadn't given me a name, so I guessed. "Reese. Carrie."

With a nail, she trailed down her notes. "The rest of your party is already here, Miss Reese. Please follow me."

I did, making sure to take in as much of the dining room layout as I could in case I needed to make a fast getaway.

The hostess led me to a private room in the far back corner of the building. Great. Privacy. The one thing I didn't want at the moment.

I caught sight of my date, his back facing me, but of course he knew I'd entered. He sat with perfect posture, his head held high. Black hair gelled upward, it shone under the dim light. His broad shoulders reminded me of a member of the Secret Service, but his silk suit screamed Hollywood. He stood up and pulled a chair out for me, then watched with lustful intent as I crossed the room. None of the other tables were occupied in here. Seemed Mr. Demon had paid big bucks for a very private dinner with me.

"Thank you, Corinne," the demon said to the hostess. First-name basis with the staff. That couldn't bode well.

I sat, and he slid my chair forward. The scent of month-old fish covered up with too much cologne wafted off him.

"I'm glad you could make it, Carrie," he said. "You truly are a breathtaking sight."

"And you smell like sewage."

The demon snickered. "Good to see your senses are improving. How's the eyesight lately?"

"None of your business."

"Ah, Carrie. Don't be like that. Tell me, have you seen anything strange? Colorful, perhaps?"

That caught me off guard, and for a moment, I lost my poker face. I frowned. No way could he know…right?

Regaining my composure, I crossed my arms. I wasn't giving him any information.

He tapped the pads of his fingers against his wine glass, the devilish smirk on his face growing. Then he signaled for a server.

"Do you see me for who I really am right now?" he asked, keeping to the subject I had no intention of succumbing to.

"I see a supernatural asshole. Is that what you're asking?"

The server showed up. "What can I get for you, Mr. Marax?"

"The girl will have a glass of Château Carfeal Margaux," he said.

"As you wish, sir." She did a little bow before

she walked away.

“I didn’t ask for a drink,” I said.

“And I didn’t ask you if you wanted one.”

“Let’s make the trade and get out of each other’s lives, shall we?” Even as I said it, I knew the suggestion was naïve. For all I knew, I was a plaything for this demon’s amusement. He held the power, control, everything, and all I had was a stupid book, which he could pry from my dead grip if it came to that.

“I hope you’re not this rude on all your dates. And no, that’s not how tonight will work.”

The server put the glass in front of…what had she called him? Marax? “Merlot for the lady,” she said.

With a nod of his head, he pushed the glass toward me. “It’s the finest Merlot in the history of the world.” He swirled the dark liquid in his own glass.

“Great.” I pushed the wine he’d offered further away from me. “So, your name is Marax?”

“I have others, but you may use that one if you’d like.” He motioned to my glass. “Drink.”

“I’m not thirsty.”

“I didn’t ask if you were thirsty. Drink.”

I jutted my chin out in defiance. “No thank you.”

Marax leaned forward over the table, his stare piercing into me. “Look around the room, Carrie, and tell me whom you see.”

I did a quick scan without turning my head. “No one.”

“And whom do you think will come to your rescue if I snapped your neck?”

I swallowed, hoping my team could hear. My voice came out smaller than the first time. "No one."

"That's right. Now, wouldn't it be a shame to die over a glass of wine?"

I reached for my glass, forcing myself to do it. My muscles acted fine; the rest of me screamed in protest.

Slowly, I lifted to drink, my eyes not wavering off Marax. Whatever game he was playing—and no doubt, this *was* a game—I wanted to be prepared for it as much as possible.

I tipped the glass back and allowed a drop of liquid to pass through my lips.

"More," Marax said, studying me.

I felt myself twitch at his command. Trapped. Like a freaking puppet on a string.

I swallowed more of the wine and set my glass down, praying to God he would be satisfied. The wine tasted divine, but on principle, I vowed to not have more. Ever.

Marax watched me, expectantly awaiting my verdict.

"As dark as your soul," I said.

He chuckled. "Well, you know what they say: the darker it is, the better it tastes."

I remained silent, my skin crawling. Sexual innuendos from a demon were worse than those from an incubus.

"So, where were we before you so rudely resorted to name-calling? A supernatural asshole, was it?"

Again, he expected me to answer his stupid

question. Nope, no way. I blinked, keeping my mouth shut.

Marax held his arms out to his sides in a wide V. "What do you see?"

My opinion hadn't changed in the last twenty minutes, but if I wanted to make this trade—the book for Mike's life—I needed to move this evening along. I took a few seconds to scrutinize him, taking him in as if I took his question seriously.

"A demon disguised as a man, wearing a tailored suit and silk tie with a diamond pin. Gemstone cuff links. Black hair, large nose with hairs that could use a trim, beady eyes, and ears too small for your head. I see manipulation, evil, greed—all wrapped up in a pretty narcissistic package. How's that for you?"

The corner of his mouth lifted in a sly grin. "Accurate, but not what I was asking."

"Then what are you asking?"

"To delve deeper. See what's on the inside."

I scrunched my nose in disgust, wishing I'd asked the server for ice water or sweet tea. The Merlot couldn't wash down the loathing sticking to my throat.

"I know what's inside," I said, my voice steady. "Nothing."

Marax squared his shoulders, unamused by my words. He reached for a cell phone in the middle of the table, switched it on, and typed something in. "And here I thought you'd be more cooperative. I have to be honest, I'm disappointed." He held the screen in front of his face. "Akouk, our girl here needs some help remembering why she's here."

"Yes, sir," a voice answered, and my heart dropped into my stomach.

No…

Marax flipped the phone around so I could see the live feed. The screen showed Akouk carrying his phone across a yard. He opened a set of rickety, paint-peeled cellar doors and descended the cement steps into the dark.

The doors I recognized. They were at the Moore House in Villisca.

I held my breath, clasping my hands so tightly my nails bit into my palms. It was like watching one of Mike's horror classics, where the fear of what came next was so compelling you had to watch no matter how horrifying you knew it would be.

Only this moment was worse than that. So. Much. Worse.

Terror gripped my insides and squeezed at the sound of a drawstring light clicking on. There, directly under the light, sat Mike. Wrists tied above his head, secured to the ceiling by a thick rope. His body just hung there, legs too weak to hold his full weight. Splatters and streams of dried blood stuck to his bare chest, and bruised sections covered his stomach. Head hung low, his face darkened by shadows.

I gasped, biting on my fist to stifle more noise. How had they gotten to him? The last thing I wanted was for Mike to get hurt. And now?

Akouk grabbed Mike's hair and jerked his head up toward the light. Then he jabbed his knee into Mike's stomach.

"No!" I cried. "Stop, please stop!"

Mike grunted, and when Akouk let go of him, his head fell back down to his chest.

"Carrie…" my best friend rasped, his voice barely audible.

"I'm so sorry, Mike. I'm so sorry," I sobbed.

"Carrie," he repeated. Slowly, he lifted his face to the camera. Black circles framed his eyes, and gashes bled from in his cheeks and lips. Mike had already been through hell. Probably while I dressed up for this atrocious date.

"Don't make…a deal," he panted.

I reached out to touch his face on the screen. "What deal?"

Marax pulled the phone away before I made contact. "You get the point. I expect cooperation from here on out."

"You son of a bitch!" I spat, breaking down. "This wasn't part of the deal! He wasn't to be hurt!"

"Our *arrangement*, Carrie, was that Mike would be released when you gave me the book. We have yet to make good on that arrangement."

I tugged the book out of the bag and thrust it at Marax. "Here. Arrangement is over. Now let Mike go."

Marax calmly pushed the book back at me. "We make the trade when I'm ready to make the trade. We haven't eaten dinner yet." He *tsked*. "Manners."

I wanted to scream screw him and his manners, but Marax held all the cards. Every word, every action would result in one of two things: Marax's approval or Marax's disapproval. And Marax's disapproval equaled pain for Mike.

I sucked in a deep breath, and when I exhaled, my courage, my strength, my resolve went with it. If I wanted Mike to walk out of that basement alive, I had to be a good girl. Obedient. I could no longer be me.

"Your eyes are red," I said flatly.

Marax beamed at my sudden cooperation. "Have they been since you arrived?"

"Yes."

"Good. Very good." He snapped his fingers and the server rushed in. "What color are my eyes?" he asked her.

"Dark brown, sir," she answered as if the question was one she got all the time.

"You may bring our meals," he said.

"Right away, sir."

She left and Marax settled on me again. "Anything else identifying me?"

I shook my head. "That and the smell. Otherwise you resemble humans."

"Your powers are growing, but they have not matured. It'll be soon though." He nodded to himself like his own assessment made him happy.

"I don't have any powers," I said.

"Oh, but you do, Carrie, you do."

I watched him tap a thick finger against the stem of his wine glass. Apparently my purpose here was to answer his questions, not ask my own. His comment still intrigued me.

"What powers?"

"I think you know, and unfortunately, if I want them to mature, I cannot tell you. Some things you must learn on your own."

His words sounded too much like Adelia's when I'd asked about the prophecy. Wait.

Is that what this is about? The prophecy?

I let the thought simmer in my mind. Marax must have seen me contemplating something, because he sat in silence until our meals arrived. It was the best minute of the evening.

"I took the liberty of ordering for you," he said, pulling a knife from the rolled-up napkin. "I hope you enjoy lamb. It is one of my favorites."

I poked at the meat with my fork. Honestly, I'd never eaten lamb before, and if Marax liked it, I didn't want to.

"Eat," he said. "And drink your wine."

I sipped the Merlot and stuck to the asparagus on my plate. The desperation in Mike's face hadn't left my mind. When would we make the trade?

"I have a proposition for you, Carrie," Marax said, savoring another bite of lamb.

"I think we should finalize the first one before we jump into another," I suggested politely.

"Under normal circumstances, I'd agree. However, something tells me that as soon as the book is in my possession, you will be out that door"—he tilted his head toward the exit—"and I won't have time for another proposal."

He was a demon; he'd make the time. And it would probably include a death threat.

He went on without waiting for my reply. "The world is changing, Carrie. I think you sense that it is. A force will soon come into play that could dump the supernatural world on its head. The outcome could be disastrous."

"For you? Or for everyone else?"

"For everyone," he answered.

"How?"

"By disrupting the balance. As you know, the world turns, producing both good and evil, love and hate. Humanity feeds off this balance." He held out his hands, palms up. "Too much evil in the world creates cruelty, disease, poverty, and death." He tipped up one palm while the other went down. "Too much good and humanity becomes self-serving, self-righteous narcissists." He tipped the scale the other way. "Supernaturals work in the same way, except with overlap into mankind. If the balance is disrupted, it won't only be supernaturals—or demons—who suffer."

"I don't see what this has to do with me," I said.

Marax leaned forward. "You, Carrie, you have the power to stop it from unbalancing."

"I have no power," I insisted.

"I thought we already established that you do," he said, sitting back against his seat to examine me. "You are a human girl. Not a witch, cambion, or angelic being. Yet. You can see me for what I am. You see past the guise, and I'm sure I'm not mistaken in saying it's not just me you can see." He paused, staring expectantly at me.

I sat up a little taller and pinned my gaze on him. Unblinking, I lied. "No. Only you."

"Is that so?"

"Seems to be a demonic thing with me, I guess."

"Well," he said, his lips curving into a smile. "Give it some time. I am not wrong on this."

"And if you are?"

Marax laughed—a dismissal. "My proposal: denounce your power and live happily ever after with your ghost boy."

I blinked. "That's your proposal? Denounce a power I don't have and do what I planned on doing anyway?"

Marax lifted his glass with a nod. "I'm not such a bad guy."

Yeah, right.

"Maybe I wasn't clear. Live happily ever after with your *alive* ghost boy."

My heart lurched. "Alive? You can do that?"

"I don't make deals I can't keep."

"*Don't make a deal,*" Mike's voice rang in my head.

The questions rolled in. This demon, in essence, offered Lucas and me his blessing. Something was seriously wrong with that.

My mother used to tell me that if something sounded too good to be true, it probably was.

"I'll think about it," I said.

"Good. Now, let's finish our meal."

Marax hummed with each bite while I picked at the lamb. I ate to appease the demon, but I stopped with a third of the food still left on my plate.

"Delicious stuff," Marax moaned.

"Yeah, it was great." I nodded in agreement. Great because dinner was finished, and now we'd trade.

Marax signaled for the server again. "I hope you've left room for dessert."

Not great. Torture.

I faked charm. "Of course."

Please don't ruin ice cream for me.

The server picked up our plates and replaced them with Dutch apple pie a la mode. I could have died.

"It's your favorite, correct? Your grandmother always bakes it for you."

"How do you know that?" Anxiety flittered through my veins. This demon knew way too much about me.

"We've kept close tabs on you, Carrie."

"*We*?"

"I command many legions of demons. You'd be surprised."

"I doubt it." I swallowed, remembering my place in this game. "I mean, you seem pretty powerful. Like a manager of Hell or something."

Marax snickered. "*Something*."

"Why have you been spying on me?"

"I've already told you. Weren't you listening?"

"The…balance thing?"

He nodded.

I shivered, and not from the cold. Fear stretched its deathly fingers around me and squeezed. If he'd been watching me, he'd also been watching my grandparents, maybe my parents too. Maybe my friends. He knew exactly where to gut me.

I finished my dessert, hating myself with each delicious bite. Damnit.

The server came and collected the plates.

"Check," Marax said.

"Right away, sir."

How kind of him to pay for dinner.

"At least I chose well with the dessert," he

prided himself.

"Spectacular."

He made a little show of clearing his throat and smoothing out the cloth napkin he placed on the table. "All right, now, Carrie. The moment you've been dying for. The book?"

"Yes, right here," I said, passing it to him. "And since we're being civil, may I ask why you want it?"

Marax caressed the cover with a lustful glint in his eye. "Again, I have already told you."

"Right." I bit the inside of my cheek. "And your part of the deal?"

Marax took his time thumbing through the pages before he answered me. "As I said before: I always make good on my deals."

He picked up his phone and spoke to the screen. "Akouk, you may leave the prisoner."

"Leave? What about release?" I asked, panic rising in my voice.

Marax turned the phone for me to see the light click off and Mike disappear into the darkness. The screen showed the cement steps, and then Akouk closed the cellar doors.

"My legions of demons have been instructed to stay away from Mike. I cannot, however, speak for legions I do not command. I'd say he has about ten minutes before they come for him."

"That wasn't our deal," I ground out, standing to leave.

"Yes, Carrie, it was. You only made the deal with *me*. And speaking of deals, have you considered my latest proposal?"

"If I decline?"

"You die."

"Well, then," I said, holding my chin high and walking backward toward the exit, "I guess that simplifies things…"

"So we have a deal?"

Get out of there! Lucas's voice screamed into my head.

I held Marax in a stare-down, tension filling the gap between us. "I don't make deals with the devil," I said.

And then I got the hell out of there.

Chapter 21

Somehow I made it to the front door of Cardell's alive. As soon as I hit the sidewalk, Reid honked the car horn. He slammed on the brakes and threw open the passenger side door for me. I jumped in, shutting the door while Reid stepped on the gas.

"That was fun," I said, buckling my seatbelt.

Reid checked the rearview mirror. "Yeah, we got company."

"Marax wants me dead."

"No shit."

Reid weaved through traffic, heading toward downtown. Toward more people, I guessed.

"Where's Lucas?" I asked.

"He went for Mike."

The fear that had gripped me in the restaurant tightened its hold. The Moore House contained a rift to Hell and it was well after dark. If demons went after Mike, they'd definitely go after Lucas too.

"They'll be fine," Reid reassured me as if reading my mind. He probably just masked his fear better than me.

I twisted in my seat to look out the back. I regretted it immediately. The blood-red auras of no less than six demons followed behind us. Two of them were only streaks of red mist soaring through the sky. The four in corporeal form drove two separate vehicles, speeding after us.

My heart rate sped up, and I squeezed my eyes shut, hoping to unsee what I saw. But when I opened them, the demons were still there, auras visible.

I turned back around and tugged on the seatbelt. Human Reid might have mad driving skills, but that didn't mean I wouldn't spill out of this vehicle unscathed. He wasn't as careful as Lucas.

"Red light, Reid!" I yelled, pointing in front of me.

"That's nice," he said, dodging an oncoming car as he ran it.

"We're going to be on the news," I muttered.

"Megan will take care of it."

Reid threw the Jeep in a hard left, and I slammed into the passenger door. The tires squealed, and the poor drivers around us blared on their horns. I couldn't blame them.

"Hang on," Reid said, halfway through the turn.

"A little late for the warning, you think?"

He straightened the Jeep on the road and threw a glance over his shoulder. "Better late than never. Do me a favor and let me know when you see a black Charger on our ass, okay?"

"We're gonna have black *and white* Chargers with flashing lights on our ass soon if you don't drive in the right lane!" I growled.

"Cops I can deal with. Demons are a bit more difficult to lose."

I gripped the door and watched the reflection in the side mirror. The airborne demons flew behind us, but the two cars following us seemed to have disappeared. Probably because demons worked to not draw attention to themselves. They preferred private torture of human souls, and Reid wouldn't be driving into a deserted alley or parking lot anytime soon.

Creating car accidents, however, they excelled at.

Headlights behind us seemed to be gaining speed. I squinted through the gleam of downtown lights to confirm a make and model of the cars before alerting Reid. Before I could, the blood red pupils of the driver shown like lasers through the windshield. No mistaking their identity now.

"Two car lengths back," I said to Reid.

"Only one?"

"Yeah."

"This'll be fun."

I couldn't tell if that was sarcasm or not. The small grin playing on his lips made me think it wasn't.

I twisted in my seat again. Their auras lit up the inside of the vehicle, and the sight alone made my stomach churn. I couldn't chalk this up to imagination or craziness.

"Shit!" Reid yelled, throwing the Jeep to the right and almost sideswiping the minivan beside us. As I lurched to the side, I caught a clear view of why Reid swerved. A solid black Charger swooped in from the opposite direction and veered into our lane. "Found the second one."

My phone rang, Stacy's favorite Cold Play song filling the car.

Great timing.

"Hey!" I answered, half excited about her call and half…well, the demon thing.

"Carrie, what the hell is going on?" Stacy yelled through the phone. "You call me a thousand times, babbling on about some secret shit and danger and explanations. This had better be good."

"I'm glad you listened to my messages."

"All sixty-three of them."

"Now might not be the best time for girl talk," Reid said, maneuvering the car around a semi.

"Yeah, um. Sorry, Stace, but can I call you back?" My voice rose in imaginary hope.

"Excuse me?" She drew out the words. She had all the time in the world. "No, Carrie. If you want to talk, it's now. You have less than two minutes."

Oh, Stacy. So dramatic.

"I kinda have a demon on my tail," I said, shouldering the phone and clinging onto the door as Reid weaved around what was probably a bachelorette party crossing the street. The one in the white veil flipped us off.

"That isn't funny," Stacy said.

"I agree one hundred percent." I checked the side mirror again. "Reid, they're both behind us now."

"Reid? Who's Reid?" Stacy asked. "Never mind, I don't care."

"You're a minute too late on that assessment, copilot," Reid said. "I could really use a second set of eyes here."

"Stacy, listen to me," I rushed. "Jess's death was an accident, caused by a vampire and demons. Jessica was a witch, Lucas is dead, and Reid is an incubus, who is currently driving like a maniac through Asheville to ditch some demons. It's crazy, I know, but I'm not making this stuff up. Now, I need your help. I need you to go to Jessica's bedroom and see if you can find a diary or a notebook or *something* that might resemble research on lost souls. Specifically on a ring and the number 314."

Stacy didn't respond, but she didn't hang up either; I could hear her breathing.

Finally, she laughed. "Yeah, Carrie. You're right. You're crazy. Don't call me again."

Click.

"Stacy! Stace!" I yelled, even though it was pointless. I chucked the phone into the backseat. That was not how I'd envisioned that conversation, and I probably just blew the ashes of the burned bridge into the wind.

"You gotta focus, here, Carrie," Reid said. "We need to find a place called Gabriella's Herbs and Oils. There'll be a dead end alleyway beside the store. That's where we're headed."

"Oh, privacy. Great idea, Reid."

"Megan's there. Or she should be anyway."

"And if she's not?"

"We improvise."

Our great plan at work.

I peered out the windows, frantically searching

the storefronts. The ones decked out in flashing lights and bright colors were easy to see, but they drowned out the darkened fronts of the other buildings. Plus, Reid refused to drive in a straight line.

My eyes darted in every direction. Passengers within vehicles and pedestrians out for the night life glared at us, gaping at the audacity of Reid's driving. A few times I waved, muttering "sorry" as I did.

"What's with all the people tonight?" I asked, not that I was complaining. It was the reason we headed downtown.

"Karaoke night at Duke's Palace. We should go some time."

"Maybe next week. I have plans to not die tonight."

Then I spotted it. A sign written in golden letters: ***'Gabriella's Herbs and Oils,'*** set against green paint.

"We passed it," I said, jerking my head as the store blurred by.

"Damnit, Carrie," Reid groaned, throwing me a scowl. Half a second later, and without slowing down, he pulled a U-turn in the middle of the intersection. A horn blasted at us, and a man stuck his head out a window and screamed obscenities. I must have done a complete one-eighty when Reid did, because I no longer cared.

"Half a block," I instructed, pointing to the store.

The two black Chargers sped up. They must have seen the commotion we caused and would probably attempt to block our turn into the alley.

"Reid," I warned.

"I see 'em."

He pounded on the gas and went for the alley entrance at an angle, causing a couple of vehicles to fan out in avoidance. The tires screeched into the alley, and Reid slammed on the brakes moments before we rammed into the brick wall.

"Get down!" he demanded, pushing my head under the console.

I was about to protest when the Jeep lit up with flashes of green light coming from every direction. I knew that light—a spell to trap a demon and send them back to Hell. Megan and her mother had used it to save Lucas and me. I ducked down further.

After the lights faded, a palm smacked twice against the window. "We gotta move before they send more!" Megan yelled.

I sat up as Reid unlocked the doors. Outside, cloaked figures moved back into the shadows. Megan slid into the backseat.

"Hotel. Go!"

Reid peeled out of the alley, barely missing a semi. Yep, headlining story on the news, right here. Hopefully Megan could change license plate numbers with the swipe of a hand.

"Who were they?" I asked, referring to the people in the alley.

Megan held onto the back of my seat. "A local coven. The one hosting Adelia."

"Hosting? You mean that's not her coven?"

"Oracles go where they're needed. What, did you think it coincidence she was in the exact same town as you to deliver the prophecy?"

I blew out a breath. "I guess I never thought about it."

"She'll move on to another coven when her work with you is finished."

"When will that be?"

"Only fate knows the answer to that," Megan said, releasing my seat and leaning into the backseat.

Reid did a slightly better job obeying traffic laws on our trip to the hotel. He still ran every red light, and somehow the police in town didn't take notice. It was either Megan's doing, the coven's, or the city of Asheville was seriously understaffed.

When Reid pulled into the hotel's parking lot, bright rays of light almost blinded me. When I refocused, I puffed out a gasp. The number of angels surrounding the building had doubled. Golden glows emitted radiant beams that stretched skyward in a sea of magnificence.

Amongst the gold, I caught a glimpse of silver, and my heart sped up.

Lucas is here!

Without thinking, I shoved open the door. I ran, kicking off my heels in the first two steps, and flung myself into his arms.

"You're okay!" I wanted to cry, but the weight of the emotions rising inside me was too much. No person had the ability to feel them all at once. I pushed most of it down and only let out my relief.

Lucas threaded his fingers through my hair, holding my head against his chest. "Oh, God, Carrie. You're safe. You're here."

"Of course I'm here," I murmured, breathing him

in. After everything, his scent continued to remind me of lilacs and springtime. Fresh, airy, and beautiful. "I hate demons."

Lucas's chest rumbled in a chuckle. He kissed my head, keeping his lips there and speaking against me. "That makes two of us, baby."

Megan jogged up to us and held out my shoes. "We can't linger out here."

Reid parked, jumped out, and tossed Lucas the keys. "Not a scratch on her."

Lucas gently pushed me away from him to examine me.

"The car, dude," Reid clarified. "Any scratches on the girl were *not* from me."

"Maybe from your driving," I said.

Angelic movement had me twisting to see behind me. In one graceful yet commanding motion, they all swung to face south. They raised their hands over their heads, tipping their chins upward too, as if in battle mode.

Being a witch, Megan wasn't able to see angels when they were incorporeal, but she must have sensed them…or whatever *they* sensed. She backed up against us and held her hands up, matching the angels' stance. "Get her upstairs, Lucas. We have another round coming in!"

In an instant, Lucas gathered me against him and the earth squeezed in on me. I gripped Lucas's shirt until the world fell away again, and I relaxed. I'd never get used to being transported this way. My bare feet grazed the thin carpet of our hotel room.

"Adelia's symbols will hold," Lucas assured me, his gaze roaming over me like he had in the parking lot.

"I'm fine," I said. "Nothing hurt me. Did you get Mike out?"

"Yeah, I got Mike out. He's pretty beat up, though."

"You didn't bring him here?"

"He refused, so Megan set him up in a safe house for now."

I shuffled my feet. "Did he say anything to you?"

"He asked if you made the deal."

"What did you tell him?" I asked, worried how my decision would affect Lucas.

"I said I didn't know. I left before you gave your answer." Concern lined his brow, and his Adam's apple bobbed in his throat. He heard the offered deal though: I denounce my power and then I get to live happily ever after with him.

Lucas would be alive and our forever could begin without demons or danger or anything of this hell. It was the deal dreams were made of.

He touched my face, his coolness seeping into my skin and reminding me of what I'd have to live without.

Because of me, Lucas would remain dead.

Slowly, I shook my head. "I'm sorry. I didn't make the deal."

Chapter 22

Lucas exhaled, his chin lowering to his chest. I disappointed him. Hell, I disappointed myself. What was I thinking? All my *no* did was make our situation worse, because not only was Lucas still dead, but now we had legions of demons after us too. I wondered if I could summon Marax and accept his offer.

Lucas wrapped me in his arms. Nuzzling my neck, he whispered, "Thank God, Carrie. Thank God."

I held him, sinking into his embrace and finally allowing my body to relax. My muscles released their tension, and the anxiety drained out of me.

"You're…happy?" I asked, still unsure.

He unhooked my shoes from my fingers and dropped them onto the floor. A glint in his expression, his gaze traveled over my body. He bit his lip as his hands glided over the curve of my hips. "So happy," he murmured.

"But I lost our chance to—"

"Be in debt to Hell," he finished for me. "There

is one deal, though, I expect you to pay up on." He worked his way up the side of my dress until he found the zipper.

Goosebumps spread along my skin as I remembered his promise. Regardless of how many times we attempted to make this work and failed, my body always reacted the same way—with hope and unbridled anticipation.

"Man, it's such a steep price too." I lifted my arm a little to give him better access.

He kissed the underside of my arm, leaving a trail of cool breath while he lowered the zipper. I watched eagerly. Lucas never made promises he couldn't keep, and this one? This one I was dying for him to fulfill.

Maybe this time...

The door to our hotel room banged against the wall. "I freaking hate demons!" Megan growled.

"At least those angels took care of the last ones," Reid replied. "Mighty kind of them."

Megan stopped when she saw me break away from Lucas and frantically tug at my zipper. Her brows perked up. "Are we interrupting something?"

"No," I said at the same time Lucas responded with "yes."

"Right." Megan plopped down on the bed, sighing out her exhaustion. "We've got major issues here."

"Thank you," Reid said, swinging the desk chair around to sit. "No one has come to that conclusion on their own."

Lucas pulled me down on his lap. "Can we discuss them tomorrow? It's three in the morning, and Carrie's had a long night."

"Her night isn't the only thing that's long," Reid muttered under his breath, then fake coughed. I didn't miss the slight nod of approval he shot Lucas's way either.

"My flight leaves in a few hours, so whatever we need to talk about, we need to do it now," Megan said. "Along with my mom, I have Mike to oversee too. You guys will be on your own."

That didn't sound good. Her magic came in handy.

"Fine," I said, resigning myself to another boring summit instead of Lucas's promise. This night couldn't get any crappier. "At least let me change my clothes."

I sent Lucas a frown before I gathered up a pair of yoga pants and a t-shirt and headed to the bathroom. I didn't hurry. I mean, my night was already ruined, I might as well enjoy the routine. Through the door, I heard the others small talking and giving kudos to a plan that actually worked out. They tossed the word "miracle" around.

But all I could think about as I splashed cold water on my face was how clearly I saw the demons' auras and deep red pupils and how Marax seemed to know that I could. With Lucas, I could wave it away as being an Incenamus perk. The demons and the angels though? I had no explanation for.

I gathered my dress clothes. If Lucas had heard most of the conversation with Marax, I wondered what he told Megan and Reid. Did they know I could see demons?

I opened the door and walked out, but I wasn't prepared for what greeted me. The three of them talked, yes, except they were different. Silver misted Lucas, a slight black haze surrounded Reid, and Megan's green glow wafted off her like a glowstick under a black light. I dropped my clothes on the floor.

Lucas bored into me at my reaction.

"Carrie?" Megan asked. "What's wrong?"

"Um…" I closed my eyes, wishing for the colors to disappear. It had worked before. But when I opened them again, the auras remained. I grabbed my hair and pulled. "I'm seeing shit! Shit I'm not supposed to see!" I half laughed, sounding like a maniac even to myself.

Megan stood up and cautiously walked toward me. "What are you seeing?"

I pointed at her and she stopped. "Green glow." I swung to Reid. "Black." Then Lucas. "Silver. And outside is a whole horde of angels." I returned to Reid. "And the demons chasing us? I saw those too. I'm…I'm…"

Hyperventilating.

Lucas appeared in front of me, hands cupping my face. "Carrie, breathe. In. Out." He nodded as he instructed me. "In. Out. Good girl."

I kept my focus locked on him, doing what he said until my breathing began to slow to normal. I didn't concentrate on his silver aura, only on those gorgeous greens I loved so much. They knew me, understood me, and in them, I'd found myself many times before. Now, I found myself again.

"Better?" he murmured.

I nodded.

He led me back to the bed. He turned down the duvet, but I stopped him. "I don't want to lie down. I'm fine," I insisted. "Really," I added at his quick intake of air.

Lucas relented, flipping the blanket back up over the pillow and tugging me down beside him. Everyone's expectant eyes dug into me.

I crossed my legs to give myself an extra few seconds before I spoke. "Marax, I think, knows about the prophecy. At least something about it," I said, my voice coming out small. "He knew I could see his aura. And I think…" I paused, because the thought had only come to me during Lucas's breathing exercise. "I think that's what the prophecy is about."

"Back up, Carrie," Megan said softly, as if a change in volume might set me off again. "You saw the demons chasing you tonight?"

I nodded.

She motioned to the window. "And the angels outside?"

I nodded again.

"And just now, you saw us. What else have you seen?"

"On the way here, to North Carolina, I saw angels too. And another ghost. And the demon when he cornered me at McDonald's."

"So this is a recent thing?"

"Yes," I said, then paused. I thought back to when I first arrived in Villisca. I'd seen flashes of red, and I saw Mike's spirit leave his body during the football game. I changed my answer. "No. I've caught glimpses here and there for a year. Lately, it's gotten stronger.

"At first I thought that it was my imagination. Then I thought it was Incenamus. But now…now, I'm not sure it's either of those things. Not after what Marax said."

Megan shifted to Lucas. "What did Marax say?"

"You didn't tell them?" I asked, glad he hadn't.

"I wanted to talk to you about it first," he said to me.

I bit the inside of my cheek and motioned toward the others. "Go ahead. If we're going to figure this out, we'll need help."

He proceeded to fill in Megan and Reid, while I cuddled up closer to him. I desperately needed his nearness right now, the comfort of him around me.

"So the deal, then, was that Carrie would give up her ability to see supernatural beings?" Megan asked. She rolled her nails over the pad of her thumb as she thought it out. "A human with this power…how does that create unbalance?"

"Mike knew about the deal before Marax made it," Reid pointed out. "How did Mike know Marax would make a deal with her?"

"The other demon, um—what was his name?—Akouk—must have told him." It was the most logical answer I'd come up with.

"You think a lackey would have that kind of information?" Reid asked, shaking his head to answer himself. "Nah. It was something else."

"Maybe he didn't know about a new deal. Maybe he was talking about the one I already made to trade his life for the book?"

"I don't think so," Lucas answered. "Because Mike asked me if you made the deal. If it was about the book, he'd know the answer because he's still alive."

I dug out my phone and texted Mike. He was probably asleep at wherever the safe house was, but he'd see it in the morning. Maybe he'd even call me.

"Carrie," Megan finally spoke up. "Can you repeat the prophecy?"

"One will come to save them all. An otherworldly connection will grow her, and when she is strong, evil will pursue her. A choice will be before her, and the decision must be hers: to live or die. Only one will bring life to those without," I rattled off easily.

Megan's shoulders sank. "All this is connected somehow. Fate's a bitch like that. The book, the prophecy, Carrie's power—I'm missing something."

"Have I already made the choice in the prophecy?" I asked. "I said *no* to Marax, which means Lucas stays dead."

"Marax's deal was *a* way; it isn't necessarily the *only* way." Megan began to pace.

"Are you talking about the potion?" Lucas asked. "Because it didn't work and now the formula is in Marax's possession."

"The soul locator spell with it," I muttered. We were still one ingredient down.

"You Xeroxed it, right?" Reid asked, making me think, "Duh."

Megan answered Reid first. "No. There are

enchantments on the pages that make them impossible to duplicate. I do, however, have some of each formula back in my lab." Then she turned to Lucas. "True. But that doesn't mean it *won't* work. Just that so far it hasn't. If we could figure out what the O stands for, we might be able to finish it."

"If we finish it, then Carrie has another life or death choice, right?"

"I don't know, Lucas. Prophecies are always vague."

"So, you're saying that all that's left on the page is the letter O?" Reid repeated.

"Yeah, the page was ripped at the bottom."

Reid smiled, his gaze stopping on each of us before he started to laugh. Like, hysterically busting a gut laughing.

"Dude, you all right?" Lucas asked, holding me closer, probably in case he cycled into incubus mode.

Reid lifted his head, his laughter morphing into a chuckle. "Yeah, man, I'm great." He crossed the room toward us and snatched the ring off the nightstand.

"Hey!" I yelped.

Reid ignored me. Back at the desk, he spun around and held the ring up like a trophy. "Rachel's ring. You're not looking for an ingredient, y'all. You're looking for this—a gem. The Opal of Veritas. I knew that Matthias guy's name sounded familiar."

"I'm lost," I said.

"Me too," Megan agreed. "From the beginning, please?"

"Okay, so Lucas, I didn't tell you about the ring because I didn't know about it back in Villisca. When we parted ways, I came back here. I needed closure, to visit Rachel, tell her again how sorry I am. At the cemetery, the guilt of what I did consumed me, so I went to her bedroom to feel close to her again. I lay on her bed. If I concentrated hard enough, I could still smell her on the blankets. I turned my head and that's when I saw something catch a beam of light."

Reid turned the ring over in his palm like its existence confused him. "She had it taped under her desk, not in a box or anything. Resembles an engagement ring, doesn't it?" He held it up before us, then he shook his head. "Damn, the thoughts that ran through my mind. But Rachel would never cheat on me. We talked about marriage, so I wondered if she'd gone out and bought her own ring. Stupid, right? She worked at the bowling alley; no way she had the cash for a rock this big."

"Okay," I said, drawing out the word. "Then how did she get it?"

"I did some research. Took it to a few jewelry stores, and the gem baffled them all. No one knew what it was, which I thought was freaking crazy, because there's only so many gems, right?" he said. "Strange that no jeweler could place it. That's when I began to wonder if it was something magical.

"The ring stayed safe under the desk for years, so I put it back—and went under the grid. Talked to other cambions, showed them a picture of it I'd taken and edited, and acted as if I were on a search mission. Weeks went by with no luck, until one day

I hit the half-court shot. A vampire, an old one, recognized the gem immediately. Said it was the Opal of Veritas, Matthias Jaquemound's most prized possession. But he also said it was useless without the elixir, and that Jaquemound took the recipe to the grave."

Megan let out a small snort. "Good to know *that* community is clueless. If they understood what this is—what it's capable of…it's not an engagement ring. It's a life crystal."

"Wait. You're saying that even with the book, Marax can't do anything, right? Not without the gem," I asked.

"Right. And I'm going to guess that he doesn't know that, because all he asked for was the book."

"The potion won't work without the crystal and vice versa," I said. "He doesn't want to use it; he just wants the option to be out of play. We have no problem."

"Marax is a demon, Carrie. He won't leave something as precious as the Opal of Veritas to chance."

"I wonder how my sister got a hold of the ring in the first place," Lucas said. "Or if she knew what it was."

"I wondered the same thing, dude. The possibilities scared the shit out of me. That question is what took me to Canada—to a coven. One of the witches, a blind old woman, said she'd be able to see the ring's past, but only if she had the actual ring."

"A recog," Megan clarified.

"Yeah, but then Lucas showed up in Canada.

Told me I needed to come back down here. Perfect timing." He closed his fingers around the ring and stuffed it in his pocket.

"Wait, why do you get to take it?" I asked, suspicious.

"Because I have the contact. I'm not running off with it, but we need to be smart. We need to know everything there is to know, and more importantly, how in the hell Rachel got her hands on it. Prophecies, demons, freaking angels outside. This is a war!" Reid's voice rose and he pointed toward the window. "Megan's right: fate doesn't deal in coincidences. I don't know who's pulling the strings, but I'm ready to cut them. This ends."

"I agree with Reid," Megan said quietly. "Nothing that's happened over the last year has happened by chance. I think the only way this ends is to fulfill the prophecy."

I frowned. "You think all this is because of me?"

"I didn't say that." Megan's stare landed on me. "I'm saying this all ends with you."

Weight settled on my shoulders. Slowly, as the realization sank in, the pressure burrowed deep in under my skin until it clawed at my being. Pain shot out from my chest, and my vision blurred. Then I toppled over onto the duvet. I barely heard Lucas's voice. The coolness of his touch didn't register.

Only the pain.

I couldn't fight it. I tried before, and it didn't work. My gaze floated to the potion Megan made me to numb the sting. But no. I couldn't do it. My gut told me I needed to endure.

All I could do was allow it to devour me,

overtake my spirit, my body, and my soul.

My head went into a tailspin, going down, down. Gravity could be a cruel beast, but I relaxed my muscles and allowed the pressure to expand within them.

Somehow I knew I had to bear this pain, this weight pushing down on me. This was the line that separated life and death. I had to experience both, because you couldn't have one without the other.

I forced open one eye to see Lucas peering down at me, his face pained. I lifted my hand and caressed his cheek.

And then blackness engulfed me.

Chapter 23

"How long this time?" I asked when I awoke. I knew the drill by now.

Lucas sat beside me, my head on his lap and stroking my hair. Best way to wake up. "A week," he said.

"Figures," I muttered, my stomach rumbling.

Lucas breathed out his relief at the sound. "I ordered room service when you started to stir. Should be here soon."

"How is it even possible for me to be passed out for so long without food or water or…um, use of the bathroom?"

"I wondered that too, so I called Megan a few days ago. Her best guess was that since Incenamus links you to me, you somehow get what you need from me.

I'm just happy when you finally wake up."

"What did you do while I was unconscious?" I asked, because I hadn't dreamed of him. In fact, I hadn't dreamt at all.

"Watched over you and waited for Reid to return

from Canada."

"That sounds boring."

Lucas grinned. "Nah. Being with you is never boring."

I returned the smile, humming out my delight at his words. "So Reid went to see the recog witch?"

"Yeah."

"What did she say?"

Lucas moistened his lips, studying his own fingers as they slid down a lock of my hair. "Nothing. She couldn't get a read on it."

I blinked. "Nothing at all?"

"Nothing we don't already know. Everything before the ring came to Rachel had been erased."

"Like, *by* someone?"

Lucas nodded. "By whomever gave it to her, I assume."

Freaky.

"Okay, then what happened after Rachel got it?"

"She taped it under her desk and left it there."

"Immediately? Without anything else?" This kept getting stranger. Had she been told to hide it? Was she aware what it was?

"Seems to be the case. Reid's at the cemetery, brooding." Lucas chuckled.

"With the ring?"

"No." He dug in his pocket, pulled it out, and slipped it back on my finger. I held my hand above my face to examine how the gem sparkled.

"Did Megan get home okay?" I asked lightly.

"Yeah." His stare moved over my face, and I knew something was wrong.

"What happened?"

"Vanessa was unconscious when she got there. Megan's dad called the ambulance, and they were working on her."

"Is she all right?"

"The doctors ran a bunch of tests, but found nothing wrong. They can't figure out why she's dying."

"What about a healer? I mean, it's a magical problem, so it requires a magical remedy, right?" Even I didn't believe the hope in my own voice.

"Several healers have seen her, and they all say the same thing—there is no cure for a dying spirit."

"What if a necromancer shows up? Will that heal her?"

Lucas rolled a strand of my hair around his finger, absently letting it uncoil before he started over. "No one knows that either, Care."

"This is so stupid!" I said, upset about Vanessa, about the lack of information the recog gave, about Lucas's lost soul, about the stupid prophecy, about Stacy, about Mike—about everything. Even the upcoming marriage of Griffin and Ami sneaked its way back into my thoughts. I just wanted to scream and run and scream some more.

A knock on the door accompanied a voice. "Room service."

"I'll get it," Lucas offered.

He ordered my favorites, including a bowl of mint chip ice cream and a Pepsi. I also drank the rest of the bottled water in the mini-fridge. When I finished, I felt better, but not enough to get out of bed. So we found a movie and spent the evening wrapped up in each other's arms.

A couple days later, I felt like myself again. Lucas was right about these episodes draining me more and more. The recovery too was taking longer.

"Adelia's coming here this evening," Lucas said in the morning.

"You think she'll have some answers?"

"I think she has *all* the answers."

I rolled over onto my stomach to see Lucas better. "You think she knows about your soul too?"

Lucas clenched his jaw. "I think my soul is the last piece of this giant puzzle."

"Why do you say that?"

"Because it's what brought us here. It's what's kept *me* here." He flattened his palm over my heart. "It's what bound us together."

"Seems like this mess began with us. It only makes sense that it will end with us." As I said it, my heart sank deep into my stomach. I'd encouraged this conversation, but I was already done with it. I threw the blankets off me. I needed to get out of this cramped hotel room.

"I'm going out for a run," I said, throwing my hair up into a ponytail.

"I'll come with you."

I shook my head. "I'll be okay. It's the middle of the day, and we both know there'll be no demons about. I just need some air."

He opened his mouth to protest, but I placed my hand against his chest, stopping him. "I'm a big girl. I can take care of myself."

"I'm only—"

"An overprotective boyfriend. Yeah, I know." I smiled to lighten my tone.

"I know you can take care of yourself, but that doesn't mean you have to."

"I need out of here for a while, okay? I need to think. I need to process all of this…stuff before I lose my mind. I…*did this. It's my fault,"* I finished in my head before I could stop myself. The rest of my thoughts let go too.

Lucas's jaw clenched.

"I'll be back before Adelia gets here. It'll be before sundown, right?" I said fast, hoping he didn't catch the conclusion of my thoughts.

"She said eight."

I rose up on my tip-toes and kissed his cheek. "Great. I'll be back before eight."

When I left, I felt his gaze piercing into my back.

***

I ran until my lungs were about to explode. I still had one of Lucas's car keys, so instead of going back to our room, I decided to drive. I'd only been to my destination once, but I easily remembered how to get there.

St. Paul's Cemetery was situated on the edge of his hometown, away from the noise and distractions of the city. Peaceful and serene, it offered a place to sort through the thoughts I buried during my run.

I parked the Jeep in the same place I had on my previous visit. Lucas's grave was on the other side of the cemetery, but I enjoyed the walk. It gave me time to think.

If the Opal of Veritas was the real deal and could do what the warlock Matthias intended, then Megan could use the potion stores she had to bring Lucas back to life. Maybe it would work on Vanessa and Reid too. Then Marax could have the gem for all I cared. I'd offer another deal: the gem in exchange for our lifelong safety. His legions of demons and *all* legions of demons would leave us alone.

It fit the prophecy too.

One will come to save them all: Vanessa, Reid, Lucas, Mike…myself, maybe? Other than that, I didn't know who else needed saving.

An otherworldly connection will grow her, and when she is strong, evil will pursue her: Incenamus had grown me, and this power I seemed to have had clearly strengthened. Evil ran beside me, but my plan would nix that. *Poof.* No more evil chasing after us.

A choice will be before her and the decision must be hers: to live or die: I made the choice with Marax, and so far I was still alive. Unless it wasn't my life the prophecy referred to…

Only one will bring life to those without: Again, Lucas would be given life with the Opal of Veritas. As would Reid.

Problems solved. Most of them, anyway.

My mental explanations were shaky, sure, but Lucas's soul would be safely inside him *and* he'd be here on earth with me.

The only thing was…it all seemed so small. A prophecy spoken for Lucas to get his soul back? What about the army of angels? How did any of this mean I needed to see auras of supernaturals? And why would Marax care about a single ghost?

I shuffled through the lawn, distracted by my

own thoughts. I passed gravestone after gravestone, not really seeing them. A cool breeze circled around me, and at first, I figured that was all it was—a cool breeze. Then it happened again and goose bumps prickled over my skin.

I looked up, half-expecting to see Lucas. But there was no swell of his soul inside me indicating he was near. I turned around, peering down the rows of headstones. I wondered how many were resting in peace and how many had been left behind.

The breeze circled me a third time.

"Hello?" I asked.

Nothing.

"Anyone there?"

Icy air brushed across my cheek, and I froze. That wasn't a breeze. *That.* Was a spirit.

I waited, silent, as the chill crept over my face. I watched, hoping to catch a glimpse of the silver aura that had to be there. If I could see Lucas and other spirits, then I should be able to see this one too.

I focused hard in front of me, willed myself to see, but the breeze floated slowly away from me.

Shivering, I continued down the path. When I reached Lucas's stone, I sat down on the grass in front of it. Crazy to think only his body lay under me. His spirit was back in the hotel room, and part of his soul rested beneath my ribcage.

He was here, on this earth with me. Yet—

He wasn't.

How can I save him when I can't put him back together?

Engrossed in my thoughts, I didn't hear a vehicle park alongside the road. Or the doors slam shut. Or the brush of shoes against the grass. It wasn't until someone spoke to me that I realized they were there.

"Beautiful day, isn't it?"

The woman spoke softly, nostalgia evident in her voice. She stood behind me, dressed in a long, pink sundress that flowed easily in the wind. She had her dark hair twisted into a French knot behind her head. Wrinkles stretched deep from the corners of eyes, giving her the appearance of a woman older than she was. In her hand, she held two bouquets of flowers.

The man beside her smiled at me, and I assumed that before the years had passed, his hair had been dark. Sunken eyes moved away from me and rested on the gravestone. I recognized them from their pictures.

"Very beautiful," I said, pushing the words through the lump in my throat. They came out small and shaky, and I immediately wished I hadn't come. I rose to my feet and dusted off my shorts. "I'm sorry, I was just leaving."

"It's okay." She nodded at Lucas's tombstone. "Did you know my son?"

A pitchy "yes" was all I could manage through the lump that had doubled in size.

She extended a hand to me. "I'm not sure we've met. I'm Clary Reynolds, Lucas's mother. And this"—she motioned to the man beside her—"is my husband, his father Eric."

"I'm, uh, Carrie. Carrie Reese," I said, forcing

myself to look into the eyes of my soul mate's mother. For years she grieved her son, praying for just one more minute with him. One more time to tell him she loved him. One more touch. One more smile. One more anything. And here I was, having spent the last year with him. Fate could be so unfair.

"How did you know him?" Her question was one of curiosity. Like I could be another link to her son. Tell her something about him she might not already know.

I swallowed. "School." I hated lying to her. So hated it, but what choice did I have? "I'm sorry for your loss."

"Thank you. Both children the same day," she murmured. "You don't get over that." A tear rolled down her cheek and her husband pulled her to his side. A small gust of wind carried the sound of her muffled sob.

Their home, the pictures, the angels, the untouched bedrooms flashed into my memory. This was a woman who was still grieving, still hurting, and I had everything and nothing to offer her. Words seemed so meaningless.

"I'm sorry," I repeated, suddenly cold.

She forced a smile through the tears. "I miss them. Every day I miss them. But I know that wherever they are, they're happy."

"How do you know that?" I asked, my voice turned hoarse.

She patted her chest, over her heart. "Because I can feel it. The ones we love never truly leave us. We carry a piece of their soul, right here, forever." She touched her heart again.

Mine dropped at her words.

I nodded, desperate now to leave before I started to cry. “I better go. It was nice to meet you.”

“You too, dear. Thank you for coming and caring about our Lucas.”

“Forever,” I whispered, because I couldn’t speak any louder.

***

I made it back to the hotel room before eight, as promised. I closed the door behind me to find Lucas at the desk, working on his laptop. He stopped typing when I entered, his stare pinning me in place. He offered no greeting, no smile.

“I’m here,” I said lamely.

“Adelia will be here in thirty minutes.” Then he returned to his work. He’d never acted like this before, and it made me uneasy, especially because it was my fault.

“Okay, well, I’m going to jump in the shower.” I pointed toward the bathroom like a dork.

I figured I’d upset him earlier when I denied his company. Okay, so it wasn’t *just* his company I denied. I left with the thought that I was so tired of everything, all because I fell in love with a ghost.

Would we be in this mess if I hadn’t?

These thoughts were like unwanted relatives; they showed up regardless of an invitation and didn’t give a damn about the damage they left behind.

I slipped out of my sweaty clothing and stuck my hand under the running water. Normally I preferred lukewarm temperatures, but tonight I cranked it to a hotter setting. I needed to feel the burn on my skin and let the steam saturate my lungs.

With so much uncertainty, all I wanted was to hide from reality. The so-called light at the end of the tunnel was now shaded by doubt. So much so I could barely see the light anymore.

I let the water run over the nape of my neck and down my shoulders. I closed my eyes and the tears that had threatened to spill over finally made good on their promise. Too much weight bore down on me, and the tiny pieces that had floated away didn't make much of a difference. More worries piled on. More, more, and more, until I wouldn't be able to carry it all. Until I was finally—

Broken.

That was me now. I never asked for a prophecy. I never wanted to be the chosen one or save anybody. When I'd been coaxed up to Villisca from Texas over a year ago, all I wanted was to cover up my pain and anger and pretend it didn't exist. After my parents, I wanted to finally have a say over how my life turned out.

Instead, I had a prophecy to control my life, and my only role in it was to make a choice. The right one meant life. The wrong one, death. How would I be able to live if I made the wrong one?

Lucas's fate too seemed to be in my hands. We weren't any closer to finding his soul, nor had we discussed what to do if we found it. And if we didn't, he would fade out of existence. Every second spent not searching was a second lost.

Finally, I turned off the water, toweled dry, and

got dressed. When I opened the door, I saw that Adelia had arrived. She'd perched herself in the desk chair, her legs too short for her feet to touch the floor.

"Your dinner is on the nightstand," Lucas said as I entered, halting his conversation with the oracle.

"Thanks." I rounded the bed and sat on the opposite side of him. He followed me with his gaze, but said nothing else to me. It made me think I interrupted them. In the far corner, I tucked my legs under me and placed the tray on my lap, trying to make myself as small as possible. Because that was how I felt—small, vulnerable, weak.

I was hungry, but all I wanted was to melt into the mattress and disappear. Forfeit all my responsibilities and cease to exist.

When I looked up at Lucas and Adelia, she held the ring up to the light. She hummed as she examined the jewel. Lucas focused on her, his brows lowered in expectation. For a second, I wondered why Reid wasn't here.

"Yes, yes," Adelia said, nodding. "This is indeed the Opal of Veritas."

"What can you tell us about it?" Lucas asked, sparking my interest.

"The Opal of Veritas was a gift from Matthias's wife in the short time she was reunited with him. In return, she made him promise not to use the one-time power on her."

"One time?" I repeated. "As in *one* life?" Our possibilities suddenly crashed down.

Adelia motioned to me. "Life crystals such as this are once-in-a-lifetime, Miss Carrie. And only once-in-a-lifetime can they be used."

"Why wouldn't she let him use it on her? Didn't she love him?"

"Very much," Adelia said. "You see, she was ready to cross through the veil. She'd moved on to the next life; she no longer belonged in this one. But he did, and she wanted him to live even if that meant without her."

"The power of love," I murmured to myself.

"Yes, Miss Carrie. The greatest power in the universe, and it is given freely to all."

"Can you tell if the gem has been used?"

Adelia nodded. "I can." She paused while giving the ring back to Lucas. "It has not."

"So it holds the power of life?" I asked. "It can be used?"

"With the correct combination of ingredients, yes, it can. But heed this warning—" her eyes moved between Lucas and me "—it is called the Opal of Veritas for a reason. The potion and the opal will only work with one who is true, one whose life was unjustly taken. Any other use and the spell becomes worthless and the Opal dead."

What did that mean, and who determined it? Lucas died in a car accident. Did that count as unjustly taken?

Lucas nodded, like he understood. His eyes flicked to me for a moment, holding me silent. He probably heard the questions in my mind, and from the slight hint of sadness in his stare, I assumed the same questions hit him as well.

"The ring belonged to my sister," Lucas said. "Do you know who gave it to her?"

"The stars are aligning. Mercury, Venus, Earth, Mars, Jupiter, Saturn, Uranus, and Neptune. Surely you have seen this?"

"I have," he confirmed.

"Destiny is putting her soldiers in order. A war is coming, one that has been foreseen for centuries. Many years ago, she put her hope in the wrong person to end the war before it began. This time, however, she left little to chance."

"You're speaking in riddles. All I want to know is who gave my sister this ring."

"No, Lucas." Adelia placed her hand over his. "You want to know why, not who. Who is not important. But why? Why means everything."

"I want to know both."

"I can offer the answer to only one. The other will come when the time is right." She paused, a motherly expression on her face. "I gave Rachel the ring, and I erased the ring's memories."

Lucas jerked away from her, his eyebrows narrowing over anger-riddled irises. "You? Why?"

Adelia shook her head. "These things were put into motion before you died, Lucas. Before Miss Carrie was born."

"I refuse to believe that," I said, sitting up taller.

"That is the way of fate." She looked at Lucas. "Of destiny."

"Fate, destiny, whatever, can be changed. It happens all the time," I countered, even though I couldn't come up with anything specific. But it had to be true.

"That is not how it works. You have been told that the future changes, but there are some things that cannot be changed," Adelia said, repeating what Susan Taylor once told me. "Some things are meant to be."

"How would you know that? Have you been spying on me too?"

"Like I said before, I know many things."

"Rachel getting the ring? That was meant to be?" Lucas asked. "Or did you force that to be?"

"The ring was always meant to be your sister's, Lucas. And I was always meant to give it to her."

"Did she have a prophecy too?"

Adelia's gaze roamed over Lucas's angered expression. He was hurting, but we both knew prophecies were only meant for those they were about.

"You are on the right track, Lucas. Keep going, and you will find the answers you so desire." She touched his face, her lips spreading into a sympathetic curve. "The end is near."

Chapter 24

I couldn't sleep. Lucas disappeared after Adelia left, and her words still sprinted through my mind. The Opal of Veritas had the power Lucas needed, and dying in a car accident couldn't be considered natural causes. The potion and the gem had to bring him back. Except—

My soul—Lucas's soul—weighed me down. I didn't feel right, and it wasn't the sorrow burning inside me. That, I knew, belonged to him.

No, this was something else. Something that had been bothering me since I walked in on the two of them conversing.

I gathered up the blankets on one side of me, hugging them to my chest. Unlike Lucas's body, these were warm and uncomfortable and I hated them. I hated the scratchy sheets, the musty scent of the duvet, and the brightness of the streetlamp that snuck through the curtains. I hated the smell of this room and the too fluffy, too small pillows.

And I hated that Lucas hadn't returned yet.

I threw off everything I hated, put on a bra under

my black tank top, and slid into my flip-flops. It was after dark and technically I was supposed to stay in this horrible room—alone—but screw that. I ditched him to be alone earlier, now he'd done the same to me. Game over. We needed each other. I was going to find him.

At the door, I closed my eyes and concentrated on Lucas's soul. I needed Incenamus to come through for me. I cleared my mind of all thoughts and focused on what I felt. Let your heart guide you, right? Only it was Lucas's *soul* guiding me.

I sensed him close, in the building. I opened the door and launched myself into the hallway. It was a risky move, but I hated that Lucas had taken the same risk.

Incenamus steered me to the elevator and down to the lobby. At two o'clock in the morning, only the desk clerk people and a few straggling patrons dotted the space. I walked by the waterfall and seating area.

I continued toward the lounge. They closed an hour ago, but Incenamus drew me forward. And then I heard it: music. Dark and enchanting, it poured out into the foyer, beckoning me to come closer. I stood outside the double glass doors that separated the lounge from the atrium. One door had been left ajar. I checked the few people in the lobby. No one seemed to notice me, so I widened the door and slipped inside.

Shadows darkened the room. The circular tables were cleaned off. The barstools empty.

A small light illuminated the stage, and there he sat. Lucas. At the piano.

Mesmerized, I watched him. Bright irises hid behind closed eyelids. His fingers glided over the keys like they'd done so all of Lucas's life. As he played, his body swayed, letting the music consume him, and never once did he fade from reality.

This, him playing, was another thing I never knew about him. I debated whether or not to stay. This moment seemed too intimate, and I didn't want my presence to ruin it for him.

But my feet wouldn't take me back toward the door.

I recognized the piece he played—Beethoven's *Moonlight Sonata*. The ghostly notes filled the room, and I shivered. The last time I'd been in here, Marax gave me seven days to trade the book for Mike's life.

I waited until he played the final note, the haunting tone of the chord suspended in air. Then, as if sensing my presence, he turned toward me. His gaze found mine and settled there.

"Hey," he said, and the low husk of his voice stabbed me. The burn of emotion flushed my cheeks.

"Hey," I replied, still unable to force myself forward. "I didn't know you played piano."

"I didn't either."

My feet began to move on their own. "Does this mean your memory is returning?"

"Maybe. Maybe not."

"This is dangerous," I said, pointing behind me at the entrance. "It's after dark."

"We are surrounded by angels. Come here," he said, sliding back on the bench. I hadn't realized I'd walked all the way up to the stage.

I stepped up and sat down, Lucas's thighs on both sides of me, his stomach pressed against my back. He circled his arms around me, returning to the keys.

He began to play. I didn't recognize the piece, but it was slow and beautiful and melodic. I listened and watched him move with ease.

"Play with me," he whispered into my ear.

"I don't know how."

"You don't need to."

He lifted one of my hands and placed it over his. With only his right, mine on top, he kept playing. Stiffly, I tried to mimic his motions.

"Close your eyes," he murmured, sweeping hair from my neck and leaving it bare. He kissed me at the nape as I did what he asked. "Relax into me."

I exhaled. I didn't try to play the notes. Didn't copy his movements. Didn't think.

I just fell deep into him.

My hand never left his. The music didn't stop.

Gently, he added his left, filling the unknown piece with depth. He said nothing. I said nothing. I placed my other hand over his and our four became two.

I sat against him, letting the melodies and harmonies consume me too. Our fingers glided over the keys together, creating magic.

I don't know how long we sat there. An eternity. Longer, I hoped. With him, time ceased to exist. We were one.

One spirit. One body. One soul.

Whole. Complete.

Fingertips smoothed over the surface of my skin. Up my arms, then down and around my torso.

"Open your eyes," Lucas breathed against my neck.

Slowly, my eyelids lifted, and I realized the only hands on the keys belonged to me.

"Incenamus," Lucas whispered at my shock. "Keep playing."

He skimmed over my shoulders, tracing the outline of my straps with his mouth. Heat delved into my abdomen, and I ached for him. My heart beat faster, and my body responded to his touch. But somehow, I continued to play the music that resided in Lucas's mind.

Gently, he tipped my head to one side, exposing my neck. Cool lips pressed against me, and I inhaled. Goosebumps appeared on my arms. The tip of his tongue trailed over my shoulder, then back up to my earlobe.

I must have fumbled at the keys, because Lucas dipped down. "Play."

Whatever awareness I had on my movements floated away. My only focus was on Lucas's caress. Somehow I continued to play.

The volume increased, along with the intensity. I remembered Stacy once compared classical music with sex. The beginning introduced the mood. Not overwhelming you, like foreplay. Then, gradually the tension built as the themes developed and wove together. Climbing, climbing to the climax, when the tension finally released in all its magnificence.

Lucas joined me again, his breath blowing icy air onto my neck and sending little pinpricks down my spine.

My own hands fell from the keys to his thighs. I massaged them, squeezing my own together to relieve the growing pressure. He moaned, the sound vibrating throughout his chest. I tilted my head back to peer up at him. His lips partly open, his mouth caught mine in a kiss that shot down to my core, shattering me.

He hit the climax.

I grabbed at his hair, pressing him harder into me. He answered back by deepening the kiss, making me forget where we were.

The music began to slow, the intensity shrinking into the wonderful realm of bliss.

Lucas's kisses also slowed to sweet and satisfied.

The last note resonated in the air, circling us in the afterglow of the beauty we created.

Then, he lifted his hands from the keys and gathered me to him. He didn't have to say anything, he just held me, and I him.

Finally, he sighed. "We have some choices to make, Care."

"I don't want to," I admitted. "They'll affect everything."

"Fate seems to trust you."

"I don't understand why."

Lucas dragged two fingers down the side of my cheek. "I don't think that's for either of us to understand. Like it or not, we got pulled into this war, and there's no walking away from it. We finish it, or it finishes us."

"Crappy odds with what's at stake."

He puffed out a chuckle. "Our odds aren't

getting any better."

"So what do we do now?"

"Same thing we've been doing: searching for my soul, keeping you safe, finding answers. We're closer than we've been."

I swallowed, averting my gaze. "Closer to losing you, you mean?"

He lowered his voice. "I never said that."

"Sometimes no words speak louder than the spoken ones."

***

Back in our room, I couldn't sleep. Lucas's arm draped around my body before it disappeared, leaving only a whisper of coolness over me and letting me know he'd fallen asleep.

I lay on my side, one arm tucked under my pillow and the other fidgeting with a crease in the sheet. Sometimes, mindless activity lulled me to sleep. I rubbed the cotton against my nails, considering what Adelia said about love being the most powerful force in the world. This was the second time she'd talked about its power.

If I loved enough, would I fulfill the prophecy? How would that work?

I chewed on the inside of my cheek as thoughts invaded my brain. Adelia had given Rachel the ring. Did that mean she'd seen the future, that this moment would happen? Megan said Adelia was an oracle, not a precog. Maybe Adelia simply let each prophecy guide her. I bet that was why she gave Rachel the ring. The prophecy may not have been about Rachel, but it concerned her on some level.

I grabbed the ring off the nightstand and turned it over, studying the contours and the design as if I knew anything about jewelry. The silver band sparkled under the moonbeams. I circled my fingertip around the edge, the smoothness glasslike. As I flipped it over, something on the inside caught the light seeping in through the window.

I switched on the lamp and held the ring up.

"Lucas," I said, knowing he'd wake up at the sound of my voice. The frigid air stirred beside me, and he materialized.

"Yeah, what's wrong?" he husked out in his sexy, sleepy voice.

"Check this out. There are numbers engraved on the inside." I squinted to read them. "3116327471…" I squinted harder, trying to read the rest. They'd been worn off and I couldn't make them out.

He reached around me as he sat up a little, and I dumped the ring into his palm. He examined the inside like I had. Having perfect eyesight, maybe he'd be able to read what I couldn't.

"What do you think it means?" I asked.

"Hard to say," he murmured. "The next number is a three, but after that I don't know."

"Why would there be numbers inside a ring? Sayings, names, declarations of love, I get, but numbers?"

"Beats me. Maybe it's code for something."

"Sounds pretty sci-fi to me," I grumbled.

"Stranger things have happened."

"Hmm. Code for what?"

He focused on me, making a pleasurable shiver race down my back at his nearness. I loved how he affected me.

"Well, it's Matthias's ring, right? So my first instinct would be to check his book…"

"But Marax has the book." I said each word slow.

"Yeah. At this point, it's a guessing game."

"I hate games." I groaned at our dead end. "By the way, Adelia said something about the planets aligning. What was that about?"

"The stars, the planets aligning is a mythological science. Some say certain patterns mean things, and others disregard the whole system of thought. But what's happening now has even the skeptics wondering.

"They're all aligning. Every planet in our solar system with the sun. Proponents say this kind of convergence is the ushering in of an Earthly cleansing of evil. Where there's a shift in spiritual energy from war to peace."

"Here." Lucas took my hand and slid the ring back on. "That's better."

I studied it for a second, then nuzzled up against Lucas's chest, sighing out my restlessness. My brain needed a break, and enjoying Lucas's closeness usually did the trick.

"Maybe Megan…might have an idea," I said with a yawn.

Then I drifted off to sleep.

Chapter 25

Knocking at the door tore me from my sleep. Eyes half-open, I fumbled for the clock on the nightstand. 6:30 AM. What the…? Who knocked on someone's door in the middle of the night?

Lucas must have answered it, because I heard the door open and what sounded like the crumbling of a paper bag.

"I brought breakfast."

Reid.

"I appreciate the thought," Lucas said.

I pulled the blankets over my head as they walked into the room and Lucas opened the curtains, allowing the stupid sunlight inside.

Two more hours. Please let me sleep for two. More. Hours.

"Late night?" Reid said, and I could almost hear the approving grin plastered on his face.

"Speak for yourself," I mumbled.

Thud. Reid probably dude-slapped Lucas. "Early morning nookie, huh? Nice, man."

"Shut up, Reid," I grumbled, then I flipped the

blankets off my head. “See? I’m dressed.” Whether it was pent-up frustration or the ungodly hour, I didn’t care. Reid got a body full of daggers.

He did a fake grimace at Lucas. “I didn’t give you enough time, did I? Sorry about that.”

Lucas chuckled until he noticed I was so not laughing. “I hope you brought a peace offering in that sack, Reid. You might need one,” Lucas said.

“I brought something better.” He opened the bag and pulled out two Styrofoam boxes. He gave me one with an extended arm, like I’d bite it off if he got too close. “See for yourself.”

I glared at him for a second before I opened the box. “Pancakes?”

“Oh no. Not just pancakes.” He tossed me some plastic silverware. “The best damn pancakes in the South, baby! You remember these things, buddy?” he asked Lucas.

“Can’t say that I do.”

“Ah, man. Mama Rita’s pancakes are to *die* for.” Reid snickered. “Hell, I’d do it again for these things.”

“You’d die for pancakes?” I deadpanned.

He stuffed a whole half a pancake in his mouth, I swear. “Fr tease n’s, ah. Oh esten.”

“I didn’t understand any of that,” I said.

Reid swallowed. “Shut up and try them.”

I cut off a piece and examined it first. It was Reid, after all.

“Don’t die on me, baby,” Lucas said, smiling.

“Blame Reid if I do.” And I ate it.

Hmmm. Buttery. Fluffy. Wow!

Reid nodded at me with brows perched high.

"Huh-huh. Listen to Reid."

"Peace offering accepted," I confirmed, slicing off a larger chunk this time. "So where were *you* last night?" It wasn't my business, but he woke me up, damnit!

He hesitated before answering. "The potion Megan cooked up for me works wonders, but it doesn't change who I am. It helps control the cycles; it doesn't stop them. I'm still an incubus."

"Oh," I whispered, understanding. He'd been out doing what incubi do—seducing people to steal their souls. Last night, Reid probably killed someone.

"Let's enjoy breakfast," he said, dropping his gaze.

I didn't argue with that. Lucas even had a few bites of my pancakes. He couldn't taste them like I could, but he nodded at me like he enjoyed them.

When we finished, Reid resumed Megan's role in the group. "We need to figure out what we know, what we don't know, and how the pieces connect." He opened his laptop, and soon Megan showed up on Skype. To say she looked exhausted would understate her appearance, dark circles under her eyes, a yellowish tint to her skin.

"You met with Adelia?" she asked, getting down to business.

Lucas and I went over what Adelia had told us last night, leaving out nothing. When we finished, Megan shook her head in slow movements.

"Let me get this straight: we only get one shot at using the Opal?" she asked.

I nodded. "That's what she said."

She massaged her temples. “Okay, we’re operating on the assumption that the Opal of Veritas is somehow connected to Carrie’s prophecy, right?”

“Adelia gave it to Rachel for the purpose of it coming to us at this very moment,” Lucas confirmed. “Fate is in control here. We are meant to have it.”

“I was meant to fulfill this prophecy,” I added.

Reid shrugged. “I’m here for the ride. And, I guess, for the fact that Adelia said I had a part to play in the upcoming events. What the hell that is, I have no clue.”

Megan tapped her finger on her lower lip. “Okay, okay,” she repeated. “We’re all connected and have been since—” she locked onto Lucas “—before Carrie was born?”

“Adelia’s words,” Lucas said.

She sighed. “I don’t see how, if we only get one chance to use this Opal with the potion, how it will ‘save them all,’ according to the prophecy.”

“Who does ‘all’ refer to?” I asked. “All what?”

“Here’s what I think. I think it’s all those who are dead and stuck here,” Megan said. “The end of the prophecy says that only one will bring life to those without.”

Reid’s eyes flicked from me to Megan. “Is that ghosts or all of us dead supernaturals?”

“Prophecies never side with evil. When your change is complete…” she trailed off.

“I’ll belong to Hell,” Reid finished for her. “There’s no salvation for things like me.”

“I’m sorry, Reid,” Megan whispered.

The sadness in Lucas’s stare probably matched

mine. Reid didn't deserve what had happened to him, but he'd suffer anyway in the worst possible ways.

I rubbed Reid's back. He didn't move at my gesture, and there was nothing that any of us could say. His fate was sealed.

"Just ghosts, then, it seems," Lucas murmured.

"That would explain the pairing between you and Carrie. Incenamus is only found between humans and ghosts. So yeah, it seems Fate has chosen Carrie to save ghosts. Tip the scale away from Hell."

"Which is why Marax said that I coming into my power would disturb the balance," I reasoned. "If, somehow, I could reunite all ghosts with their souls—"

"—or bring them back to life…?" Megan suggested.

"Hell would lose its next recruitment class," I finished. "Balance shifted."

"If I were a demon, I'd be concerned about that too. But the Opal of Veritas can save only one, not all."

I recited the prophecy in my mind again: *A choice will be before her, and the decision must be hers: to live or to die.*

A choice.

Between life and death.

Only one will bring life to those without.

Then it came to me.

"It's not the Opal," I murmured into the air, hating my own voice. Hating the stupid prophecy for making me choose. "The Opal of Veritas isn't what will save anyone." I twist to Lucas, my Lucas, my love. "It's my choice, my decision. It's a freaking test, Lucas!" I sucked in a shaky breath.

This was torture. Slow, agonizing torture.

Why did Fate have to be so cruel to put us together only to tear us apart?

"Carrie, you're not making sense. What's a test?" he said.

"It's you," I cried, my sob barely making it past my lips. "You are my choice, and mine alone."

Beautiful greens peered into mine as cool palms cupped my face to reassure me. But not this time. This time there was no reassurance for me. "Shhh, Carrie. It's okay."

Tears wet my cheeks. "No, you don't understand. It's not okay, Lucas, it's not! I can't let you go."

"You don't have to, baby. I'm here, I'm right here, and I'm not leaving."

I shook my head in quick movements, because he didn't understand. None of them understood. My stomach tightened into a heavy ball, making it impossible to breathe. This couldn't be happening.

This wasn't fair!

I closed my eyes, because I couldn't bear to see him. Couldn't bear the betrayal in his eyes when I told him the truth.

"My choice? It's you or everyone else. To save the rest, Lucas, I have to give you up. I have to let you die."

Chapter 26

Dead silence met my forgone conclusion. There was no other possibility, no other way. The only question left was how my letting Lucas go would send the other lost spirits through the veil and to their eternity.

And why me?

I wanted to run and hide from those beside me, especially Lucas. How could I meet his eye after this, knowing his fate was in my hands?

"What are you saying, Carrie?" Megan asked.

I felt my lips tremble as I worked up what I needed to explain. "I'm saying: the Opal of Veritas is my decision. In the prophecy, it's the choice I have to make. I can use the power to bring Lucas back to life or I can let him reunite with this soul and cross over."

"The prophecy says only one choice will bring life to those without, but it doesn't say which one," Megan said, but even as she did, her expression told me she'd come to the same conclusion I had.

"Lucas's life puts him back on earth with me. No

longer in the spiritual realm. I don't know how, but it's like he's supposed to be the first one to go home."

As soon as I said it, a cloud of smoke rose from floor to ceiling in a twister of green. Then as quickly as it appeared, it seeped back into the floor as if it had never been. In its place stood Adelia.

"Carrie," she said, beaming at me. "Now that you understand your mission, allow me to fill in the rest."

Reid backed away as if she were contagious. "That was wicked, ma'am. Can you just appear, you know, anywhere?"

Adelia ignored him and regarded Megan. "How is your mother, Miss Megan?"

Megan slumped in her chair. "She's stopped eating and drinking. She sleeps twenty hours a day, and can no longer get out of bed."

"Chin up, Miss Megan," Adelia commanded. "Vanessa Pouvoir has done beautifully."

"With all due respect, dying isn't beautiful," Megan said, a hint of ice in her tone.

"No, my dear, it is not. But her bravery, her stamina, her outpouring of love is. And of those things, she has much. Those things are her legacy, and they are beautiful." Adelia faced me next. "The decisions must be yours, Miss Carrie, and yours alone."

I shook my head slowly. "No, the prophecy only cites one choice."

"For the prophecy, yes. For this to be over, there will be another."

"What if I say no to all of it?" I defied. "What if

I'm done playing your stupid game?"

"That is your choice," she said, frowning. "If that is what you want, a new prophecy will be born, and another savior will be sought. In the meantime, Marax will continue his quest of devouring lost spirits and Miss Megan will take her mother's place."

My attention snapped to the computer screen. "Her place?"

"Yes, dear. Villisca will need a necromancer, and Megan is next in line should you refuse your calling."

Megan's eyes widened as she stared at me. I stared back, unbelieving.

"It's Carrie?" Megan murmured.

"I'm…a necromancer?" My voice failed me halfway through, and I had to force the rest out. Was this real?

"You have been chosen, yes, but with powers beyond those currently called. Fate, Carrie, has given you special abilities for this time to see those whom you are to help, and those who can hurt. Incenamus has sealed you and Lucas together, and Lucas splitting his soul further strengthened that bond. As you've already figured out, he is the first in your charge to ferry through the veil. Unlike other necromancers, your rare knowledge and experience will lead all spirits seeking rest to their afterlives."

"This was my destiny from before I was born? That Fate would put Lucas and me together just to rip us apart?" Hurt didn't come close to describe the fire burning deep inside me. Had I ever had any real choices, or had everything I'd ever done led me to this moment?

"Everyone has a purpose, Miss Carrie. This is yours."

"What about me, then? Did I ever have a choice in this so-called purpose? Did Fate ever consider asking me what I wanted?"

Adelia smiled, and I despised the simple action. "Every day. All the choices you've made have led you here."

"But you said Fate decided my path."

"Both are true, my dear. Fate decided *and* you chose. That is why we are having this conversation."

"You're saying that had I made my choices differently, my path would be different?"

"We live in the 'what is.' 'What could have been' never happened and never will happen. You live the life you were given, and you only get one. Don't get hung up in the past that was or the past that *might* have been. They were never meant to exist."

I glanced at Lucas. Glowing greens intensified, a mix of pain and concern weaving through his gaze. My focus remained on him, but it was Adelia I spoke to. "Then what was his fate?"

"You needed each other," Adelia said. "You could not have come to be who you are without him and, likewise, he would not be here without you. The strength of your love is what has grown you, will continue to grow you, and is what will lead the both of you home."

Sensing the turmoil within me, Lucas crossed the

room and gathered me in his arms. He pressed my head against his chest, and I let the first tear fall. How could I make this kind of decision? How could I say goodbye?

"Shhhhh," he murmured into my hair, hearing my thoughts. I wished I could hear his right now, but the other end of our connection remained silent.

"The angels will protect you until your calling, my dear," Adelia said.

"And Marax?" Lucas asked.

"His time of control is waning. He grows weaker as Miss Carrie grows stronger. For now, the angels have him and his legions contained."

"How about after her calling? What happens to him then?"

"That all depends on Miss Carrie." Silence hung in the air as Adelia scanned the faces in the room. "My part in this has now ended. The rest now lies with you."

"What about me?" Reid piped up. "You said I had a role to fill."

"You have done well, Reid, and this is not over for you yet. Miss Carrie will need you before it is, and you will need her."

With a nod toward me, Adelia vanished the same way she'd come.

***

"Well," Reid said, breaking the tension that had dropped into the room. "That was enlightening."

"I think Carrie and Lucas need some time," Megan murmured from the computer screen.

I heard them both, but I didn't care what they said. I clung to Lucas, inhaling the scent of him and committing it to memory. Nothing else in the world mattered to me now. Hell could come for all I cared. As long as I got to keep Lucas.

In the distance, what seemed like a million miles away, I heard the clap of the laptop closing. Seconds later, the click of the door behind Reid faded into the space around us.

Lucas's mouth found mine, and I returned the kiss like it was our first, our last, our only. When he finally drew back, I fought to fill my lungs. Again, I didn't care. He could take every last ounce of oxygen from me if that meant I didn't have to lose him.

"What am I going to do?" I whispered. A half-sob burst from my chest, and I held my breath to contain the rest.

He held my face between his palms. "You're going to do what you've always done, Care."

"I don't know what that is."

He pressed his cool forehead against my warm one. Icy breath brushed over my face, and I inhaled the wintery air.

"You'll be alone with your thoughts. You'll examine your heart, your soul, and you'll realize what has to be done, and then you'll do it."

I peered up at him. "What do *you* think I should do?"

The corner of his lips lifted and he brushed nonexistent hair away from my face, my skin cooling at his touch. "You know the prophecy; this is your decision to make."

"But you have an opinion, right? Can't I base my decision partly on that?"

Lucas pressed a kiss against my mouth, then stood up to shift the curtains to the side. "It's a beautiful night. Have you ever watched the stars from the top of a mountain?"

"I haven't…"

"A memory came back a while ago. One I didn't think was important. When I was alive and I needed to think or clear my head, I'd drive as high as I could and stare up at the stars. Up there, with the universe hanging above you and the Earth below you, the world seems bigger, and our decisions seem so insignificant in comparison." He twisted to face me. "Sometimes what seems impossible to us in one moment of time is nothing but a grain of sand on the beach, a drop of water in the ocean, a single star in the vastness of space. The choices we think are too big to handle become smaller in that perspective."

I quirked a brow at him. "You're telling me to stand on a mountaintop?"

Lucas grinned. "I'm telling you it used to work for me."

"In the dark, though…"

"Adelia said the angels will protect you."

Protect me. Not Lucas.

"It's the planets aligning," Lucas said, breaking into my thoughts. "Ringing in a period of peace on earth, settling the war between good and evil."

"They're aligning in hopes that I…" I couldn't finish out loud. *"…choose to let you go and accept my calling."*

Lucas nodded. Then he threaded his fingers through my hair, bringing me closer. "You don't have to come to a decision tonight, okay? I'll be here when you get back."

"You won't come with me?" I asked, my voice failing me again.

"Oh, Carrie," he said, closing his eyes. "I want to, but this, I think, you need to do alone. This is your path, your calling. Your destiny."

"It's yours too."

"That, my love, is up to you." He pressed a soft kiss to my lips. "I'll love you forever."

I grabbed the infinity necklace around my neck and squeezed. "Forever."

***

Golden forms of splendor unknown to this earth followed me as I drove up, up into the Appalachians. I tried to ignore their presence, but like a little sister, they seemed to be constantly at my heels, beautiful or not. I parked the Jeep and stepped out onto the rocky terrain.

The spot I picked looked out over the city. This high up, I could barely make out the vehicles and bustling nightlife of downtown. Up here, I was truly alone.

My thoughts jumbled together in a mess of emotion and logic. If I relied solely on emotion, my choice was easy: I'd pick Lucas. Based on logic, though, I couldn't be selfish. Other spirits needed me. Other *people* needed me. How could both win?

They can't.

Lucas spoke of the stars. Of the mountains. Of the immensity of the universe around me. It was all there, yet I found solace in none of those things. They all reminded me of him and what I'd lose if I let him go.

An evening breeze raced past me without stopping to caress my skin. It didn't linger to create goose bumps or whip up feelings of nostalgia within me. Overhead, an owl glided through the air as if the world below him moved on as usual. Nature had no need to cry over would-be broken hearts and lost time. They understood their path. They didn't question it.

I didn't know how long I stood there, gazing out at the world beneath me. At my back, a car drove higher and higher upward, but I no longer registered the sound. I stepped over the metal barrier and sat on the other side, my knees hugged to my chest.

My mind was as clear as it was gonna get. Time to allow one thought at a time to roll back through.

I did what Lucas said and gazed into the magnificence above me. The stars and moon lit up the sky, reminding me of all the nights we laid together and did this. Lucas would tell me about the constellations as if he belonged up there with them.

Down here, though? Down here he fought his own spirit and soul as they tried to reunite. From the beginning, the choice before him had been me or his soul. What had changed was that the choice was bigger than us.

Deep down, I'd known the answer all along. Since last summer, it had tugged at me, and now it stared me down like a demon at its prey.

I wasn't ready.

I wasn't ready for Lucas to go. Wasn't ready to be Villisca's necromancer. Wasn't even ready to deal with Griffin and his upcoming wedding.

I thought about Megan. How her mother's life, *her* life, depended on me. Megan had done so much, so much she didn't have to do for us. She'd risked everything too. Like Jessica.

No, Jessica *gave* everything, down to her last breath. *"A soul was never meant to be separated from its spirit,"* she'd told me. *"I want to help you, help Lucas, find his soul."*

Instead, she found herself in a coffin.

Then there was Reid. If Adelia was right—and I had no reason to doubt she wasn't—then Carver turning Reid into an incubus wasn't coincidental. He'd been part of Fate's conniving plans too. As had his brother, Parker. No longer did I believe, out of all the supernatural creatures in the world that Carver's involvement with both Reid and Lucas was by chance. No, this was all Fate's doing.

And Rachel. She died too.

How many lives did Fate need to destroy for me?

What if...

Adelia's words rushed back at me: *"We live in the 'what is.' 'What could have been' never happened and never will happen."*

I shivered and hugged my arms around my chest. I closed my eyes and envisioned that my own arms belonged to Lucas. That he was here, comforting me. Except instead of a cool embrace, the arms he wrapped me in were warm. He took away the chill seeping into my bones.

He leaned around me and turned my face to him. The smile he wore displayed his lone dimple and drew heat to my face, flushing it. His eyes sparkled in the moonlight, casting beams of glittering light over his irises. He nuzzled his cheek against me. The warmth it created overwhelmed me, and a sigh slipped out. He kissed me and hummed at the sensation.

The kiss lingered long after he let go.

"I love you," I whispered.

"I'll love you, Care. Forever."

I reached out to touch his face, but my hand faded into his skin like it wasn't there. I tried again. My fingers sank into the illusion. Frantically, I pushed into him over and over, desperate to get his warmth back.

But it was no use.

He was only a silhouette. A transparency—a ghost.

When I opened my eyes, I was alone. Just me, the mountain, and the starry sky above me.

I hadn't come out here to make my decision, but then again, maybe deep down, I had. Because the choice in front of me really wasn't a choice—

It was destiny.

Chapter 27

I found Lucas standing at the window in our room, doing what I'd been doing—gazing up at the stars. He told me once they weren't the same stars in the city as they were out in the country. Away from the lights and noise, they shone brighter.

I didn't say anything when I entered. I simply stood in the room and watched him. He knew I was there, of course. His shoulders rose and fell, and after a few silent moments he turned around. His eyes landed softly on me, and I felt my chest lurch. Suddenly, I couldn't breathe.

He knew my choice.

A knife stabbed my heart then, and I cried out in pain. The grief in Lucas's eyes disappeared, instantly replaced with fear. He ran to me.

"Carrie!" He cocooned me against him.

The knife twisted, gutting me further. My knees wobbled.

I'm going down.

We both understood. As Adelia had said, the end drew near.

"I'm fine," I said, catching my breath and attempting to straighten.

Another slice. Sharper and deeper.

I screamed in agony. It had never hurt this much before. It was as if Lucas's soul wanted to rip itself from my body. I doubled over and dropped to the floor.

Lucas dropped with me. "Stop saying that, damnit!" He held me tighter and kissed the top of my head. "You're not fine."

I shook my head, but Lucas clasped his palms over my cheeks, stopping me. Green morphed into icy grey.

"You're not fine," he repeated, his voice achingly soft. "You're dying. I can feel it."

"No. You saved me. Your soul brought me back."

He gave a slight nod. "Yeah, and it will be for nothing if I don't unite the halves. You weren't meant to bear this burden, Carrie. We have to end this."

Love wasn't supposed to be selfish. If I wanted to keep him, I'd have to let him go.

"I decided, Lucas," I said, weak. My eyelids falling.

He picked me up and carried me to the bed. Gently, he laid me down. Brushed hair away from my face and kissed me.

"I know, Care. It was the right choice."

I nodded once before darkness enveloped me.

***

When I awoke, it wasn't Lucas waiting for me; it was Reid. He sat at the desk, his attention buried in his laptop.

"Where's Lucas?" I asked, my throat dry. I tried to gather saliva into mouth, but there was only cotton.

Reid swung around on the chair. "You look like hell."

"I didn't ask for your opinion," I breathed.

"He's out," Reid said, grabbing a water bottle from the mini-fridge. He untwisted the lid and handed it to me. "He should be back soon."

I glared at him for not answering my question, but I was too thirsty to make an immediate come back. So I downed the water and threw the empty bottle at him. He caught it.

"More?" he asked.

"Yeah, like, three more. And food."

Reid gave me another bottle and set two more on my nightstand. He picked up the hotel phone. "One of everything on the menu?"

"A burger. Fries. Salad with Italian dressing. Extra, extra large Pepsi," I said.

Reid dialed and rattled off my order.

"Oh, and a slice of apple pie a la mode," I added.

"And a slice of apple pie a la mode," he said into the receiver. "Yes, please. Room 532. Thank you."

He hung up and chin-upped me. "Happy?"

"Happy as I'm gonna be without food or a shower."

Reid pointed. "Bathroom's over there."

I tossed the blankets off me. "I'm glad you told me. I'd forgotten in the…how many days?"

"Twelve."

"Right. In the twelve days I've been passed out."

"You're welcome." He spun back around and went back to whatever he was working on before I'd interrupted him. Great babysitter.

I wobbled to the bathroom and locked the door. Since I gained sight and Reid had returned to my life, he'd been only human around me. But best to not take chances.

Did his powers work on necromancers?

Though, technically I wasn't one. I hadn't accepted the calling yet.

I washed my hair and body twice and brushed my teeth for, like, an eternity before I got out. A few minutes ago, I heard a knock on the door and Reid thanking the room service people, so I wasted no time getting dressed.

Hair still wet, I whipped open the bathroom door and spotted the plate Reid put on my bed faster than a vampire could smell someone bleeding out. I had the burger in my clutches before I even sat down.

"Ohmygodthisisdelicious," I said, the words muffled by hamburgery bliss.

"You have ketchup dripping down your chin," Reid noted. "I can see why Lucas is so attracted to you."

"Speak for yourself," I said after swallowing. Really, he could say whatever he wanted. The burger was so freaking amazing, I didn't care about his lame teasing. "You're just jealous."

I wiped the ketchup off my face with a napkin and took another bite.

"So jealous," he deadpanned.

I flashed him a puffy-cheeked smile.

After I swallowed the last bite, sucked dry my Pepsi, and savored dessert, I collapsed backward on the mattress.

A swoosh of cold zipped around me before it settled at my side. Lucas materialized in its wake, and I laughed. Man, I was in a good mood. Strange, considering what happened right before I passed out.

I rolled on top of him and kissed him hard.

"Great to see you too," he murmured, his fingers tangled in my hair.

"Glad you're back," Reid grumbled, gathering up his stuff. "I'll be next door if you need me."

"Thanks, man," Lucas said, genuine appreciation in his voice, but I caught the melancholy that lingered too.

"Yeah. No problem." Reid's tone matched his friend's. A few tense seconds passed before I heard the click of the door behind him.

"What was that about?" I asked.

Lucas pulled me back to him, ignoring my comment. He kissed me again. "You feeling all right?"

"Better than ever."

"Good."

"Where did you go?" I asked, propping myself up over him.

"Soul searching."

"For how long?"

"A few hours a day. I've looked everywhere. Old high school, college, home, Reid's house, the hospital, parks. Everywhere."

"No luck, huh?" I read by his tone.

Frowning, he shook his head. "Nothing."

"If we can't find it, then what?"

"You fail the test and don't get called."

My heart dropped into my stomach. "And Vanessa dies, and Marax's legions are released."

"Until the next prophecy."

We couldn't let that happen. Not only would that scenario mean Jessica's and Susan Taylor's sacrifice, Rachel and Parker's deaths, and Reid's turn to evil would be for nothing, it would also mean Lucas would fade away and cease to exist. He wouldn't cross over.

I slipped off him and sat cross-legged on top of the duvet. I grabbed one of the bottles of water and chugged it down before I twisted the cap back on and played nervously with the plastic.

Lucas sat up too, taking me in. "I think I know where it is, though."

"Where?"

"The cemetery."

Mixed feelings accompanied his words—pain, regret, relief.

"What makes you say that?" I whispered.

"Because we've searched everywhere else. It's the one place I haven't been."

I dropped my gaze to the water bottle I dented with my thumbs. "I went," I admitted. "I've been there twice."

I expected him to be upset because I hadn't told him, but he lifted my chin and I met his stare. "I should have gone with you," he murmured.

"I had to see for myself," I said, my voice

cracking at the memory. "The second time…I, um, I met your parents."

Lucas's face went blank. His hand fell away from my chin. "What did they say?"

"That life's been hard for them, losing both of you. But they find comfort in knowing—" I breathed in a sob and focused on the carpet.

"Knowing what, Care?"

"Knowing you're happy. That—" I paused to inhale and blow out the emotion clogging my throat. "—that you and Rachel have each other."

Lucas nodded, his head low. Their comfort was a lie. "I've checked in on them often since we've been here. I can't explain it, but I think my staying on earth affects them too. It's as if they can't move on fully."

We sat in silence, not speaking, not touching. I the only one of us breathing.

Finally, I looked at him, and something deep inside me opened. A light switched on, the veil between us floating away.

"Susan Taylor said your soul would attach to an object linked to whatever is left unforgiven," I thought through the open connection. *"You think that's at the cemetery."*

Lucas's eyes lifted to mine.

"I know it is. It's where Rachel is." His voice sounded the same in my head as it did in my ears.

"You haven't forgiven Rachel?" I asked, confused. Technically, Reid had killed her.

"Rachel is the object of my unforgiveness," he clarified. *"The reason she died."*

"Reid…"

"Yeah, Reid. But I knew something about him seemed off. He hadn't acted like himself for months. Rachel, she, uh, she sensed it too. We talked and she decided to break up with him. He scared her. I told her I'd be at home that night, but I wasn't."

"Carrie," he said out loud, "the person I couldn't forgive—is myself."

Chapter 28

The plan was for me to get ready for our last date together while Lucas and Reid drank some beers in the lounge. I was to meet Lucas in the atrium. They decided this was the best way to say goodbye while I'd been asleep. In fact, Lucas made quite a few plans during the last several days.

He talked to Megan about his house, his belongings, and the Jeep. He paid for our entire stay at the hotel, plus an extra day for me. He closed down his online business and emailed his former customers.

Lucas insisted that the reuniting of his soul needed to happen sooner rather than later. Vanessa's situation hadn't improved, and the pain within me still lingered two weeks after the last seizure. My chest had a constant ache, to the point of needing to lie down a few times during the day.

"Seems you thought of everything," I told him, frustrated by how simple he made it sound. "Getting your ducks in a row," Grandma used to say.

He hugged me close to him. "Easy stuff first.

None of that matters."

Tonight, though? Tonight mattered.

"As long as the other half of my soul is on this earth, you won't be free," he said. "I'm not taking any chances. Not on your life."

"But…tonight?" My voice shook, and I had to sigh to steady myself again.

"Prolonging it will only make it harder," he insisted.

I pulled the curling iron down until the lock of hair did a perfect spiral. Turning my head to one side, I examined my work. I rarely did this sort of thing, and when I did, I had Stacy around to perfect it for me. So far I hadn't set my hair on fire, so I considered that a success. Satisfied, I coated the curls with a thin layer of hair spray. Then, carefully, I applied my makeup. Lucas had specified "not too much," which didn't make sense because I never put on too much. Maybe he figured I'd go all out for tonight. I kept to his request, though, only highlighting my natural features. I did all this wearing only my bra and panties. It was the only matching set I owned—a birthday gift from Stacy a year ago.

When I finished, I exited the bathroom and sat down on the bed beside the box Lucas left me. The note on top read,

"Do me the honor of wearing this tonight."

I assumed he did this because the dress I bought for a special night with him was tainted as soon as

Marax requested it. Besides that, I burned it and buried the ashes.

Inside the box laid the exact opposite of that dress. Instead of black, Lucas chose white. Strapless and simple, it reminded me of a more elegant sundress. Light, flowing material that felt like feathers against my skin. The skirt curved up short in the front, but fell to the middle of my calves in the back. Thin rhinestone cording around my middle accented the bodice.

At the bottom of the box were matching shoes. White. Simple. Basically flip-flops with a slight heel. Lucas knew me well.

I'd spent my shower pep-talking myself. All I wanted was to have a memorable evening with the man I loved without my brain reminding me it would be our last. I did a little twirl in front of the mirror to see the skirt swirl around me.

A quick check of the clock told me I only had time for one more twirl before I had to meet Lucas in the lobby. I made it a quick one and left our room.

Downstairs, Lucas waited by the waterfall. Debonair and sophisticated, he wore his green button-up shirt with the collar unbuttoned, sleeves rolled up, and a black suit jacket flung over one shoulder. I laughed, because he probably planned the pose.

His gaze slid up my body until he reached my stare. Then he let his full smile assault me, his lone dimple sinking deep. My skin prickled at his appreciation.

"You look…*wow*!" he murmured, taking my

hand and kissing the back of it.

"A very gentlemanly gesture," I noted.

"Only the best for you."

I wrapped my arms around his neck and pulled him to my mouth. "All I want is you. It's all I've ever wanted," I said before I kissed them.

"Come on, I don't want to waste a single second with you."

He led me to the Jeep, and I couldn't help noticing the army of angels guarding the hotel. I also couldn't help noticing how their heads turned as we passed them. I swore they beamed at us.

We had a five hour drive to Wilmington. As Lucas drove, he held my hand and skimmed his thumb over the skin there. Soft little caresses that made my heart fill with even more love. I didn't care what happened tonight as long as he kept touching me.

Dressed as we were, I anticipated some fancy restaurant by the beach with candlelit centerpieces and sparkling champagne. But nope. I laughed when Lucas pulled into a burger and pizza joint.

He grinned, amused with himself. "Google said they have the best tenderloins in town."

"Recreating our first date, are we?"

"The best I can. With better clothes."

"Nicer. Maybe not better." I winked at him, because *dear. God.* He looked good in jeans and a button-up. Anything, really.

Or nothing.

I bit my lip at the thought. He heard it, and the sexy glint in his irises proved it.

"Special," he clarified. "And you? In *this* dress?

I didn't want to miss that."

I blushed.

Inside, I let Lucas order for both of us. Two tenderloins with fries and two Pepsis. I loved this man!

People crowded the dining room. Music blared upbeat songs from the jukebox and pre-teens stood shoulder-to-shoulder inside the arcade with video games on sixty-inch screens on the walls. A little different than Dan's Bar & Grill in Villisca. Plus we were the only patrons not wearing shorts and t-shirts.

But I didn't care. I barely heard the noise around us, barely noticed the kids running from their parents to the arcade in the side room. All I saw was right in front of me: dark, disheveled hair, creamy, pale skin, a smile brighter than the sun, and glowing green eyes. Always the glowing greens.

We talked, ate, and avoided all things supernatural. Instead, we laughed about the time I burned popcorn in Lucas's microwave and how he burned breakfast for me. How I sucked at playing min-golf and how he remembered Reid and him with plastic golf clubs as kids in their backyard.

"Neither of us had our front teeth, and we couldn't stop licking our gums. That night, my dad made corn on the cob just to watch us try to eat it." He shook his head at the memory.

"Jessica lost both of hers first, and Stacy and I teased her about it. We always came up with stuff for her to repeat, then we'd laugh at the lisp. She got mad once and punched Stacy in the mouth. That night, both of Stacy's fell out." I giggled. Mine didn't fall out for three months after that.

"I bet you three were neighborhood terrors."

"We were. Probably like you and Reid."

"Eh. As we got older, we just blew things up in the backyard. Did stupid shit like jump off Reid's porch roof onto an old mattress and skateboard off ramps we built. You know, we probably both should have died sooner than we did."

I grew silent at the mention of death. I cut my eyes out the window to see two angels keeping watch on the sidewalk, and I immediately looked away. Unwanted reminders seemed to appear everywhere.

Lucas noticed the change in me and reached across the table, slipping my hands into his. With his thumbs, he caressed the backs of mine. His touch sent shivers down my spine, shivers I'd come to love and associate with comfort.

"Come on. Time for the next part of our evening." His low voice soothed me. It wiped away the sorrow before it settled into my stomach.

He scooted out of our corner booth, and I followed, taking one last sip of my soda before I left. Lucas ran, yes, ran to the car, pulling me along with him. Against the wind, I heard him chuckle.

"What are you doing?" I yelled, but then I noticed I was laughing too.

My flip-flop heels clacked against the cement as I pushed myself to keep up. When we reached our destination, Lucas spun and swept me into his arms, lifting me so my head tilted down to his.

"Tonight is for happy. We're celebrating," he said, keeping me above him. My hair fell around both of us.

"Celebrating what?"

"Life. Love. And everything that comes with it."

I focused on him, thinking about how he was right. Our last night shouldn't end in tears or goodbyes. For the next twelve hours, Lucas belonged to me and me to him.

"I'll celebrate that," I said.

Slowly, he lowered me until we met in a kiss. When my feet found ground again, he opened the door for me.

"Wait. After dinner, we took a walk," I reminded him.

"Yes," he answered, neither confirming nor denying our next adventure. He shut the door and as he drove, he continued to be mysterious.

He pulled into a hotel on the beach. "Do you remember when we walked around the square?"

I searched my mind. "Yes. A band of some kind played on the bandstand."

"Jazz, actually. But I thought you'd like this better." He led me through the hotel and out the back where they set up a stage on the deck, overlooking the ocean, the canopy lit up with strands of white lights. People in suits and cocktail dresses sipped on flutes of champagne and picked hors d'oeuvres off silver platters carried by hotel staff.

On the stage was a grand piano. A man stepped up and went to the microphone.

"Ladies and gentleman, if you'd kindly take your seats. Kai Hung Lao will be out momentarily."

Lucas grabbed two flutes of champagne off a

tray and handed one to me before we sat down. I leaned into him and lowered my voice. "You mean *you'd* like this better."

"I could have taken you to a leaf-blowing seminar tonight and you would have loved it," he replied.

Yeah, he was right. My perfect night included only him. Nothing else necessary.

The concert reminded me of Lucas in the lobby of our hotel. How his fingers glided over the keys like magic. And then, how he pulled me into that magic. That night, for a single moment, we'd been united in a slice of Heaven.

Lucas sat mesmerized, closing his eyes and letting the music stir within him. He told me once that touch and taste and smell couldn't be felt with his conjured body. Not like mine could. But that he felt those things deep inside his spirit. They burned and shone and overwhelmed him from the inside out.

That was how he looked now. Entranced, filled up from the inside out. The content expression he wore was enough for me.

When the music ended, Lucas rose to his feet. I did the same, though no one else did. We probably seemed silly, but we didn't care. Tonight wasn't about the dinner or the concert or anyone else. We were in our own world, a moment in time that would last us forever.

"That was beautiful," I said.

Lucas threaded his fingers with mine. "Now comes our walk."

With a nod toward one of the hotel servers,

Lucas opened the gate and motioned me through. Below us stretched out a sea of sand. I held on to Lucas's forearm for balance as I slipped off my shoes. In my Texan opinion, sand was meant for one thing only: to get stuck between your toes.

"Okay, your turn," I said, holding my fancy flip-flops.

"Me? Take off my shoes?"

"Pfft, no." I made a face, like he was being absurd. "Who walks through sand in their socks? That's ridiculous. Socks *and* shoes off. Go."

With a smirk on his perfect face, he did what I told him. He stuffed his socks into his shoes and dangled them in front of my face.

"Happy?" he asked.

"Very. *Now* we can walk."

He held my hand again, because neither of us wanted to be too far apart. I nudged him a little closer to the water's edge.

"Okay, hang on," Lucas said. He knelt down and rolled up his pants like they did in the movies. "Ready."

Soon, both of us walked ankle deep along the shore. Warm water lapped at my calves, and wet sand folded in around my toes.

Moonlight shone around us, and I lifted my face to it. Lucas and I, out bathing in the nighttime glow. For a while, I didn't think this would ever be possible. I ignored the few angels tailing us. In fact, I'd completely forgotten about them during the concert. Hopefully I could trick my brain to forget them again for the rest of the night.

"We stargazed that night, remember?" I asked

him, continuing to bask in the salt-water air.

"You almost sprayed me with pepper spray. Remember that?" he asked, laughing.

I giggled too. "If I didn't apologize then, I'm sorry."

"You did."

"Okay, then I'm not sorry."

Lucas hung back and circled his arms around my waist, picking me up. I kicked my feet, happily squirming inside his embrace. He spun me around before setting me back down. But we continued to spin. I wrapped my arms around his neck, and we danced there, in the water, under the moon.

I rested my head against his chest. The absence of a heartbeat didn't bother me anymore. Mine beat for the both of us.

Unbidden, thoughts I'd been holding back flowed into my mind. How had it come to this? Most people got a lifetime to love each other. To learn everything there was to learn about each other.

I didn't even know Lucas's favorite color. I never asked him if he preferred dogs or cats. Who was his second grade teacher? Did he like him or her? Had he played with dinosaurs or cars or zoo animals as a child? I'd seen him drink coffee, but how had he prepared it? Sugar? Cream? Nothing?

Tears I'd fought all day began to sneak their way to my eyes, but I refused to let them fall. My chest lurched though, before I could stop it.

"Carrie." Lucas's pitch shook as he spoke my name. His lips pressed against my head, kissing me over and over again. He held me tighter, like he too was afraid to let go. I lifted up on my toes and kissed his neck. His skin tasted like the purest snow, and I never wanted to forget it.

"I don't want to do this," I breathed out. My voice sounded so small in my ears, so not mine.

"It's time, Care. For both of us."

"What happened to forever?" Absently, I went to the necklace I never took off. I fisted it and squeezed hard enough for the metal to dig into my palm.

"Forever never ends. It goes on and on and on." He tipped my chin up until my gaze met his. He brushed his thumbs under my lashes, wiping away moisture. "We still have forever. This, right now, doesn't change that."

"Of course it does. You're leaving me." Another tear fell as I said it.

"It means my time here is over, yes, but yours isn't. Look at me, Care. I'm proof that there's life after death. That forever goes on. I'll be waiting for you when you finish down here. Life was meant for the living, not for the dead, so live."

I held my breath to stifle the next sob. He was here, right in front of me, so why did I already feel so empty?

"Without you?"

Slowly, Lucas nodded. "Yeah, without me."

"What am I going to do?"

The love of my life stared at me, his eyes searching mine as if the answer to my question pained him to say. But then a small smile broke free. "You, my Carrie, are going to go to college and major in something amazing that you love. You're going to take care of your grandparents, ride

Goldie every chance you get, make up with Stacy, and have her over for a girls' week and do whatever it is girls do. You're going to go to your dad's wedding in Texas. Forgive him for hurting you, and move on with your life."

I opened my mouth to protest that last one, but he silenced me by placing his index finger to my lips.

"You can't hold on to pain. It will eat you up and destroy you. I know…well, because I know." He faded into transparency, proving his point. When he solidified, he combed through my hair. "Forgive him."

I nodded, because how could I argue with that?

He continued, "You're going to accept the calling when it comes, help lost spirits reunite with their souls, and you're going to be great at it. That's why they picked you, you know—because you're great."

"I'm scared," I admitted.

"That means you're wise. Fear gets a bad rap sometimes, but it's necessary. Fear fuels us to become better and reminds us who we are—human. It's okay to be scared. I am too."

"You make it sound so simple."

His Adam's apple bobbed as he swallowed. His voice came out soft and steady. "Fall in love. Get married. Have babies and throw them birthday parties and hug them every day."

"You want me to love someone else?"

"I do. And I want you to grow old together, like your grandparents." He dug his fingers deeper into my hair. "Live, Carrie."

"What about you?" I asked, because how could he want me to replace him? How could I? I had his soul, and Incenamus connected us.

Lucas bobbed his head slightly as I asked all the questions inside my head. Then, one by one, he answered them. "You never replace love. You hold on to what you had in your heart, and new love will form when it's ready. You'll always have my soul, but it will be your soul now. I don't know what Incenamus will be like once I'm gone, but my guess is neither of us will feel it anymore."

"What makes you think that?" I said, already feeling empty.

"Because its work is finished. I'll no longer be in this world with you."

I broke away. I didn't want to hear this. More so, I didn't want to believe it. Lucas had changed me, and I'd never be the same after him.

Lucas saw me—the real me. Not whom he wanted me to be or the person I pretended to be. He saw through my fears, my tears, my insecurities. I couldn't hide or run from him. No matter what he saw—how childish or silly—he loved me regardless of the flaws.

Would I ever find that kind of love again?

He gave me the time I needed to hurt and to question, and when I peered back up at him, he smiled. His beautiful, one-dimpled smile that had the power to melt me regardless of my mood.

"Can I ask you something?"

"Always," he answered.

I let out a breath. "How do you take your coffee?"

The serious lines on his face disappeared and laugh lines replaced them. "With a tablespoon of sugar."

Oh.

Now I wanted to know the answer to every question inside me. Find out everything about him I could.

"If you could visit anywhere in the world, where would it be?" Tears continued to blossom.

"As far north as I could get, where I could gaze up at the stars and see the northern lights."

"Football or basketball?"

"Basketball."

"Favorite team?" I asked, even though I knew the answer from the posters in his bedroom.

"Blue Devils, baby."

"Second grade teacher?"

"Miss Crowler. I had a crush on her too." He winked, and I giggled.

"Favorite color?"

"Yellow."

"Yellow?" I asked. I would have never guessed that.

"Why not yellow? You look good in yellow."

"Do I?" Stacy once said I looked good in yellow.

"Stunning. Almost as stunning as you do in white."

"Favorite season?"

"Summer—when I met you."

My shoulders fell as I ran out of questions. Stupid too, because before tonight, I had a million of them. Crazy how you think you have all the time in the world to know someone, until that time sneaks up on you and—*snap!*—it's gone.

"I don't want to say goodbye," I murmured. If I did, wouldn't I forget everything we shared? What if I forgot the color of his eyes? The coolness of his arms around me? The sweet scent of his icy breath?

Lucas lowered himself to the sand, tugging me down with him. He tucked me in between his legs and circled an arm around my waist.

"See that row of stars, there? The three smaller bright ones in a line?" He pointed toward the sky, over the ocean.

"Yes."

"It's the easiest way to find Orion—by his belt. All right, now expand out." He traced something bigger around the small row. "Do you see him? He's hunting."

"I think so," I murmured, waiting for the story he'd tell now. I loved his stories. Well, I loved his voice when he told the stories. And how his face lit up. And how he held me.

"Orion was mortal—not a god. He loved to hunt and chased hard-to-get game. This attracted the goddess Artemis. One day, they were both hunting in the same place and their attention landed on the same game. Even though Artemis was the goddess, it was Orion who shot and killed the stag before she could. Along with his good looks—" Lucas paused as if waiting for a reaction from me. He got it too, when I twisted to him. He winked at me. "Good looks, you know. Important."

"You're vain, you know." I laughed.

Irises sparkling, he lowered his head until his lips found mine. "Hmm. All right, where was I?"

"Good looks."

"Dark hair. Green eyes. Guy was hot." He smirked, clearly happy with himself.

I rolled my eyes.

He continued. "Okay, along with being attractive, his skill with a bow impressed her further, and she befriended him. They went hunting together, camping, teased each other. Became best friends.

"Artemis, though, had taken a vow of celibacy and promised to never marry. Her twin brother, Apollo, knew this, and her growing relationship with Orion angered him. He thought she broke her vow. So when he saw Orion swimming in a lake, he went and got his sister."

"That sounds counterproductive," I noted.

"If only. Orion was far out into the lake, with only his head bobbing on top of the water. Apollo pointed out some creature out there and dared Artemis to shoot it. Greek gods were vain, and she didn't question the challenge. She aimed, fired, and hit."

"Orion? She killed her best friend?"

"She didn't know what she was doing. When she learned what she'd done, she threw Orion's body into the sky and he broke into stars. There, she could always see him, and he could always see her."

I caught onto his point faster than I ever had, and it killed me. I bowed my head and held my breath, hoping the pain cradling my heart would vanish. It didn't.

Lucas tilted my head to him. Kissed me. Peered into my eyes.

"I'll love you forever. Whenever you need me, Carrie, look to the stars. I'll be there waiting for you."

Chapter 29

A part of me died when Lucas disappeared to retrieve a blanket from our hotel room back in Asheville. True, he was gone for less than a minute, but it was the longest fifty-six seconds of my life. They felt like fifty-six years.

What would fifty-six years feel like without him?

The ache in my chest pulsed, and black fuzz rounded the edges of my vision. I massaged the skin over the area, hoping for a little relief. I got none. Instead, the weight of Lucas's soul bore down harder.

I won't pass out, I won't.

Determination pushed my hand away. I had a few hours left, and I wouldn't spend it with Lucas worried about me. I straightened, pulled myself together, and filled my lungs with fresh ocean air.

Once he returned, it became easier to ignore the pressure filling me. I watched as he laid out the blanket over the sand, how the muscles in his forearms made him seem so alive. He placed two pillows at the top for us, but who needed a pillow when Lucas's chest was right there? I cuddled up beside him, one leg over his. I didn't care that next to him I shivered from the coolness he exuded. The coolness belonged to him, and I wanted him all over me.

"I don't want to fall asleep," I said, exhaustion tugging at me. I'd been awake too long already, which probably half-explained the throbbing pain.

"Me neither."

So we lay there, staring up at the stars. Lucas pointed out other constellations and told me the stories that accompanied them. In slow, tender strokes, he trailed the length of my bare arms, leaving ripples beneath my skin that I committed to memory. I breathed him in, listened to his voice, and melted deeper into his embrace. If it were possible, I would have melded myself to him so I never had to be without him.

This night, under the stars and with the sound of the tiny waves rolling over the water's surface, was as close to perfection as this world would allow. It fit us. Who we were as a couple and who we were as individuals. Strange how two totally different people from two totally different places who lived in two totally different worlds could become so in sync with each other. We didn't need Incenamus for that. We didn't need Incenamus for anything.

Lucas and me, our love, our bond. *That* was the real power.

Love. The most powerful thing in the universe. Stronger than good; stronger than evil; stronger than Hell itself.

Love was what cocooned us, held us, grew us. And it would be love that would set us free.

Heavy eyelids plagued me, and I had to work to keep them from falling. I kissed Lucas's neck and nestled in closer. And listening the low tone of Lucas's voice, I drifted off.

***

He loved watching her sleep. So peaceful, so beautiful. It was a guise, he knew, because inside she was breaking. And there was not a damn thing he could do about it.

She made the choice, and she made the right one. The one he hoped she'd make. The one he *would have made. Not only for the spirits she'd eventually save, but for her. She deserved a life with someone who could give her the love and life he couldn't. The dead couldn't do much for the living.*

Sometimes, he wished he could turn back time and do what Megan asked from the beginning—leave. He would have kept her from all the danger that had opened up around her. Saved her from this heartbreak threatening to shatter her.

One year. One measly, short year. That was what he got with her.

But in that year, he'd loved more than he had in a lifetime. Carrie, who she was, her love, the way her chocolate irises delved into his soul, had saved him in so many ways.

Most of his memories from life had returned. He wasn't a perfect guy during life. Hell, he'd made his fair share of mistakes during death as well. But

Carrie was his redemption. She stood by his side, kissed away his pain, and made him live for something other than his guilt. And tomorrow morning, she'd reunite his soul and spirit and send him home. Yes, she was his salvation too.

What gutted him was that he wasn't hers. Not like they had both wanted. It would take time, of course, but she'd move on. Find someone to love who would love her back with the warmth he couldn't give.

To him, that someone was obvious. He'd loved her as long as Lucas had. Risked his life for her, for those she loved, just to see her happy.

Lucas felt a little lighter knowing he would be waiting for her. He'd get her through this. Plus, she had Megan and Reid. Hopefully Stacy too. She'd be all right.

He breathed out a contented sigh, combing his fingers through her hair. So gorgeous, so amazing. He never deserved her, yet here she was. His for another hour. He pressed a kiss to her forehead. She shifted slightly but didn't wake.

Holding her against him, he closed his eyes and slipped into her thoughts. Most of the time it wasn't hard to get through. Tonight was even easier. This time wasn't about listening in, though. He'd show her images of his fondest memories, those that had been and those he only dreamed of. It wouldn't stop her emptiness, but maybe he could soothe her some from the inside.

He showed her his most treasured memories from death; they all involved her. How she giggled. How she tucked her hair behind her ear. How she blushed when he flirted with her. How she kissed him, and how he felt when she straddled him and gave him that sexy little smirk of hers. He doubted she really understood what she did to him.

Soft snores escaped her when he finished. Then she bit down on her lower lip in the way that drove him crazy. He knew what memory she was watching. He'd give anything to relive that moment with a warm, working body. He would never have faded from her arms.

He peered out over the ocean. Way out, the fin of a dolphin broke the surface before going back under. A few more dolphin fins appeared, and he watched until they swam away. Then he turned to the stars. They sparkled and reflected off the water in a sea of glitter.

Out here, life seemed peaceful and perfect. No one died. No one hurt. And the world was beautiful. Out here, under the stars, life made sense.

He turned back to Carrie, hating that he had to wake her. But the sun would soon rise, and they had somewhere else to be.

***

I heard my name on Lucas's tongue. Oh, the way he said it! My eyes fluttered open, and his gaze shined back at me in the darkness.

Then it hit me: I'd fallen asleep! How much time had I wasted not being with him?

Lucas noticed the fear on my face, because he cradled me and kissed me and soothed me.

"Not long," he promised.

"It seemed like a long time," I said, touching his cheek. Cool, smooth skin felt like satin under my fingertips. "My dreams…you were there."

"I'll be there forever, and in your memories too."

Before I drifted off, there'd been a hint of sorrow in his stare, but it was gone now. Now, the only thing I could see was hope. Acceptance. A new beginning.

I didn't know how to feel about that.

"He doesn't belong here, Carrie," Jess had said. *"A soul was never meant to be separated from its spirit."*

Soon, he'd be whole again. Where he belonged. That thought should make me happy, right? So why didn't it?

Lucas rose to his feet and offered his hand. I took it, and he pulled me up with him. In silence, we brushed the sand off our feet. Gathered our shoes, blanket, and pillows. Then Lucas wrapped his arms around me.

"Ready?" he murmured.

I squeezed my eyes shut and nodded against his chest. My nod was a lie. I wasn't ready. I'd never be ready.

The feeling of being sucked through a small tube encapsulated me, and I couldn't breathe for a few seconds. When we both solidified, I sucked in the sweet, humid oxygen because my lungs made me. But I didn't open my eyes.

I didn't have to in order to know exactly where we were—at the cemetery.

I clung to Lucas, and he pulled me to him like he never wanted to let me go.

We stayed like that, holding each other, until the early morning light hit my face. A sob formed in my chest, but I held it back. I promised myself I wouldn't cry.

Lucas let go of me first. He looked over his shoulder to the identical headstones standing side by side—his on the left, Rachel's on the right. I peeked around him, and my heart hammered against my ribs. Faster and faster, it raced as if it wanted to break out of my chest.

Am I having a heart attack?

I dropped to my knees, clutching at my chest. Fear creased Lucas's brow, and he lowered himself to the ground. I could see my name on his lips, but I couldn't hear the words. I couldn't hear anything.

I could only feel.

It wasn't pain I felt. Pressure, yes, but no pain. It was more like…like—

Fusion?

I lifted my head. Golden light of the most radiant glow formed a shape in front of me. Slowly, the intensity faded until the form became distinguishable. A soft facial expression accompanied the whitest, purest light. More breathtaking than even the sunrise.

An angel.

The angel wasn't looking at me. He motioned toward the ground under Rachel's headstone, and the grass began to shift. The ground trembled. Suddenly, silver light sprang up like a geyser, reaching higher, higher into the sky.

A beam of silver shot out from my chest, taking my breath with it. I expected pain, but instead serenity filled me with a peace, a beautiful, soul-resting peace I'd never experienced before. The strands of silver light twisted around each other, braiding into one heavenly strand.

Lucas's soul.

"Lucas," the angel said.

Frowning, he nodded. He understood, and so did I. It was time.

Lucas cupped my face. Peered into my eyes like he'd never see me again. I finally let the sob loose, and the tears flowed fast.

"Don't go," I murmured through a gasp.

"Remember Orion and Artemis?" he asked.

A weak "yes" slipped from me.

"Good. Take care of Reid, okay? He wasn't himself, and I don't blame him." Then he leaned in and whispered instructions into my ear.

"What if I'm too late?" I asked when he finished.

"You won't be, Care. You won't be."

And then he crushed his mouth against mine. Of all the times he'd kissed me, this one didn't remind me of any of them. It wasn't a simple brush of his cool lips. There was no lustful hunger behind it. It wouldn't go anywhere. Passionate, yet thoughtful. Urgent, yet sweet. Blissful, yet grounded. It was a kiss made from love, pain, regret, desire—and goodbye.

He pulled away slowly, me already missing him. His touch traveled down my arm to my hand. Floated over my fingers to the ends of my fingertips until he let go completely.

He backed up, away from me and into the silver light of his soul. He never broke his gaze away from me though. Out of the corner of my vision, I saw other forms of silver mist lined up along the edges of the cemetery watching.

Lucas pressed a palm over where his heart should be. "Forever," he said.

"Forever," I heard myself say.

I rose to my feet, ready to run to him and pull him away from the light. I wanted to scream at him. Tell him I'd changed my mind and all I wanted was him. I'd take Marax's deal, no matter the price.

But I couldn't move forward. I couldn't speak.

I couldn't stop him.

One more step and the beam immersed him. His feet lifted off the ground, and the silver light disappeared into his chest.

The angel turned to me, offered a small smile, then faded into the air.

Lucas rose higher and higher into a ray of sunlight that poured over the horizon. His eyes remained on me until I could no longer make them out.

And just like that, he was gone.

Chapter 30

I stood there, staring up into the clouds. Tears streamed down my face. He was gone. Really gone.

Tonight, he wouldn't be there to hold me while I slept. Never again would I peer mesmerized into those eyes of his or hear his voice inside my head. I'd never hear him say my name again. Never feel the butterflies in my stomach go wild at the sound of his voice. He'd never do that thing where he combed his fingers through his hair when he was anxious.

I didn't hear the car pull up or the person who came up behind me. I didn't move when that person placed a hand on my shoulder. Whoever it was gave me a light squeeze and let go.

They stepped around me, and only then did I realize the person was Reid. He held two bouquets of wildflowers. He crouched in front of Rachel's stone first. Pressed two fingers to his lips and then against her name on the granite. He said something too, his voice too low to hear. Then he leaned his forehead to the rock before he laid the flowers at the base.

"I love you," his lips seemed to say.

He remained there for a few moments before he went to Lucas's grave. There, he bowed his head like he was praying. When he finally lifted it, a tear slid down his cheek. He wiped his face and held his fist to his mouth, his jaw trembling.

My feet moved on their own, and I knelt beside him. He reached for my hand. I let him have it. We said nothing to each other, just gazed at the cold representation of Lucas's life.

Finally, Reid gave me the flowers. I shook my head. I couldn't do it. I couldn't lay them there, as if Lucas cared about flowers on his headstone. The gesture wasn't for Lucas, anyway. It was for Reid, and clearly Reid needed it.

"You," I whispered.

Reid arranged the bouquet as he had Rachel's. Then he sat back on his haunches.

"I'll be in the car whenever you're ready," he said.

I nodded, no longer able to speak.

He stood up and left me there, at Lucas's gravestone. Lucas and me. Forever.

I pressed my palm to the smooth surface. The coolness reminded me of Lucas's skin, and right there, with that small detail, I broke down. Emptiness consumed me, and I curled up on the ground. I used the bottom of Lucas's headstone as a pillow as if it were his chest. Hard and cold and not even close to how he felt.

My favorite place in the world, now taken away. I'd never touch him again.

Humidity slunk along my skin as the heat of the sun drove down over me. Hours must have passed by now, but that didn't matter. The only place I had to go to was an empty hotel room.

Reid must have pitied me, because eventually the Jeep door slammed shut and his arms slid under me. He carried me to the car and laid me in the backseat, and I remembered the last time he'd done this. Carver had stolen my soul, and I was at the edge of death. That was when Lucas gave me his.

I clutched my heart. The silver light that had poured from me disappeared when Lucas floated away, and with it, the ache that had been Lucas's catalyst for leaving so soon. I closed my eyes and tried to break through the veil. I needed to hear his soothing voice in my head, telling me it would be okay. That *I* would be okay.

Lucas, can you hear me?

Nothing.

Please. I need you.

Nothing.

Of course not. Words didn't bring people back from the dead.

When we arrived at the hotel, I walked myself inside. Reid stayed close, and I wondered if he thought I was a flight risk. But where would I go?

I pressed the button in the elevator and leaned against the back wall. Other people entered, and got off, and entered. Some nodded at me, but most didn't. It was like they knew my heart died today.

The doors opened on the fifth floor, and I nudged past a lady with a stroller to exit. I barely noticed that Reid left right behind me. At my room door, I slid the keycard in until the light turned green, and I opened the door. I stepped out of my shoes on the way to the bed. I threw down the blankets and lay down.

Empty. That was how the bed felt. Warm and empty.

I grabbed the pillow Lucas used the night before and hugged it to my chest. I breathed it in, but only a slight hint of his scent remained. By morning, it would be gone.

I don't know what time it was before I realized Reid was in the room with me. He sat at the desk, head in his hands. Sleeping, maybe?

It didn't matter. Not now, anyway. Tomorrow, though, tomorrow I had something to do. Something to start doing.

For Lucas. Because I promised.

But tonight?

Tonight, I needed to grieve for the man I lost. The man I loved. The man who now lived among the stars.

Chapter 31

I didn't have much to pack, as I'd been living out of my suitcases the last two months. In fact, I felt like I was leaving with less than I came with.

Because I was.

I zipped up my luggage and plopped down at the edge of the bed. The one I shared with Lucas until two nights ago.

Why did doing the right thing hurt so bad?

I toyed with the ring on my finger. Without the rest of the numbers, the Opal was unusable. Plus, we didn't know what the numbers meant.

That was my mission now. My promise to Lucas—to figure it out. But I had no idea where to begin.

I checked my phone out of habit. I had fifteen minutes until I was to meet Reid in the lobby. Because *maybe* Mike or Stacy had called and I missed it somehow. I hadn't exactly stayed close to my cell lately. Honestly, I wasn't sure what I'd say to either of them right now anyway.

I scrolled through my log, and something lodged

itself in my throat. Six missed calls from Stacy.

I was about to check the voicemails when someone banged on my door.

"Carrie Anne Reese," the Texan drawl hollered. "You better open up. I didn't fly all this way for nothing."

Stacy?

I leapt off the bed and to the door. I ripped it open. With one hand resting on her hip and the other clutching her pink rhinestone phone, Stacy stood on the other side. Her baby blues bored holes into me.

"Uh…how did you find me?" I stammered, the shock making my voice hoarse.

"It's the twenty-first century, darling—the GPS on your phone is active. You gonna invite me in or not?"

"Yes, of course." I motioned her inside and closed the door.

She turned to face me. From her purse, she pulled out what resembled a diary.

"I've been trying to call you for days," she said.

"Sorry. I…have been busy," I finished, suddenly aware that I'd have to mention Lucas at some point.

"Well, *Miss Busy*, I think I found what you wanted." She tossed me the book, and I caught it before it smacked me in the face.

"What's this?"

"Jessica's diary. But Mrs. Phillips didn't know where to look." Stacy grinned wide, proud of herself.

"And you did, of course."

"Yes. After our visit to see you over Christmas,

she asked me to stay over one night. She said she needed help. She wanted a hiding place for her diary, one that no one but her and I would know about. I figured she wanted to keep her sister out of some of her stuff. So I helped her loosen a few boards in her floor—under the rug, you know—and we made the perfect secret vault."

I opened the book and skimmed the first few pages, because I wanted to make sure it contained what I thought. It did. They were Jessica's dreams—her nightmares. The ones of me last year and others too. At the top she'd written the date of the dream; at the bottom she scrawled the dream's completion—when it actually happened.

I peered up at Stacy. "Did you read this?"

She rolled her eyes. "You think I'd find that for you, fly halfway across the country to give it to you, and *not* read it? Have you lost your damn mind in this humidity?"

"And?" I asked, nervous of her answer. This book, this diary, was proof that what I told Stacy was true. In it, Jessica had written about her own foreseen death.

Stacy shuffled her feet on the carpet. "It's why I'm here in person," she said. "I owe you an apology."

That lasted for one second.

Her icy gaze pinned on me. "But you owe me one too!" Tears brimmed over her lashes. "You should have told me. You both should have told me! I trusted you two with everything."

"We *were* protecting you, Stacy. We didn't want you to get hurt."

"I'd have died for you too, you know," she said, her voice cracking. "I loved both of you that much."

"Oh, Stacy." I closed the distance between us and wrapped her into a hug. "I loved both of you too much to lose either of you."

"I miss her," Stacy sobbed against me.

"I miss her too. And you. I've missed you so much."

Stacy held me tighter. "I saved all your stupid messages, just so I could hear your voice when I felt lonely. Thank you for calling me so much."

I choked on a laugh. "Welcome."

We let go of each other, wiping our mascara-tinged tears from our faces.

"Okay, let's get what you need out of this diary," Stacy finally said.

She scanned the left-side pages and I scanned the right. The numbers 314 showed up a few times, but Jess never elaborated on them. They were only numbers she mentioned in passing.

"Whoa!" Stacy exclaimed. "Check that out. Jessica dreamt I'd fail accounting months before I actually did."

"You failed accounting?"

Stacy shot me a pouty face. "It was hard! But Mr. Browner let me off with a D minus on account of Jessica's death." Stacy pointed to the page. "See? Like Jess said he would."

"That was nice of Mr. Browner."

Stacy shrugged. "Didn't matter anyway. I didn't need the class."

We continued reading until something caught my attention at the bottom of a page. "What does your side say?" I asked Stacy.

"Um…'Written inside the band of a silver ring. 3116327471,'" she read.

"Wait," I said, stopping her. I slipped off the Opal of Veritas. "Read me those numbers again."

"3116327471."

I turned the ring so Stacy could see. "They match."

"Crazy. She never saw this ring, did she?"

"No. I only saw it for the first time a few weeks ago."

Stacy flipped it over to see the gem. "Dayum, girl! Did Lucas give this to you? Are you two officially engaged? Ohmygod…but why would he engrave numbers in it?"

"Not exactly." Emotion rose in my chest, creating a new swell of emptiness. I breathed it out in a long, silent exhale. "The ring belonged to his sister, Rachel."

I did a quick explanation to bring her up to speed about the ring, the Opal of Veritas, Adelia, and even Reid. I couldn't get Lucas's name past my lips.

"This whole…whatever it is, is freakier than I thought," she said, making her signature "ew, gross" face. No one did it better than her.

"It gets freakier, trust me," I said.

She quirked a brow, waiting for more.

"Later," I promised. "Now, though, we need to see if Jess has any more on this ring."

"Wait, Jess had other numbers earlier. What if they go together?" Stacy asked, skipping back a few pages. "Here. 314."

I reached around Stacy to grab a pen from the

nightstand. At the bottom of the page, I wrote the numbers from inside the ring and added 314 at the end.

Stacy cocked her head to the side. "So…what is it?"

"I have no idea," I admitted. "The numbers go with the ring, obviously, but how?"

"Coordinates for a matching one?" Stacy suggested.

"It's a one-of-a-kind," I muttered to myself. "The final ingredient for a potion to bring the dead back…"

A thought began to form in my mind. Something Adelia had said. Something Megan had said. Put it all together, and—

That was it. *That* was the missing piece.

"…to life," I finished. I sucked in air. "I gotta call Megan."

I rushed over to the desk and swiped my phone off it. "Megan," I said, before she had a chance to say anything. "How many ingredients are in the *Restitue Animam Ad Inferos Deducentur* potion?"

"Uh…" she hummed, thinking. "Seven. The Opal would make eight, but it's the last thing to be added. I think it activates the potion. Why do you ask?"

I held out my palm to Stacy and she gave me Jessica's diary. I skimmed over the full set of numbers I scrawled at the bottom of the page. The highest number was a seven.

I almost laughed out loud. Seemed so obvious now.

"I think I know how to make the potion work."

***

"I'll change my flight," Stacy said, Googling the number to the airport. "I can spare the time." She dialed the number and put the phone up to her ear. "By the way, where's Lucas?"

I inhaled, steeling myself to answer when she held up a finger and started to talk to the operator on the other end.

"Yes, ma'am. Out of Omaha a week from today, please." She pulled out some plastic from her purse and rattled off the numbers. "Thank you."

She hung up and nodded at me, ready for the answer to her question. I couldn't meet her stare. Instead, I swallowed the lump that had materialized there. It returned immediately, and a matching one settled in the pit of my stomach.

The sparkle in Stacy's irises dimmed until it burned out completely.

As usual with Stacy, I didn't have to say anything. She pulled me into a hug, and the tears I thought had run dry returned. "Oh God, Carrie. I'm so sorry."

I cried on her shoulder like I'd never cried before. This was the kind of crying I saved for my best friend.

I crumbled. Shattered into a million pieces on the floor. It hurt. Oh God, it hurt so bad. Every beat of my heart broke off another piece. Soon, all I'd have was a hole where my heart used to be.

I buried my face into Stacy's shirt to muffle the sobs, and Stacy smoothed my hair. She didn't try to tell me everything would be okay or try to quiet me.

She didn't tell me a story of when someone broke her heart. My best friend did what best friends do—she cried with me.

For a second, I thought I sensed Jessica's presence. Her sadness enveloped us into shared embrace. But when I glanced up, she was gone.

"*Take care of him, Jess,*" I mouthed into the air.

When I finally got myself under control, I realized that we'd both lowered ourselves to the floor. I wiped the tears and snot from my face and wiped them on the carpet. Stacy did the same.

She shrugged. "It's okay. The carpet is hideous anyway."

We looked at each other for a second, then let out a chuckle.

"Thanks for being here," I said, a fresh tear for her presence rolling down my cheek.

"It's what BFFs are for, remember?"

I nodded, sniffling. "I remember."

Stacy wrapped an arm around my shoulders. "It's you and me, girlfriend. We gotta stick together."

Pounding on the door interrupted us.

"Carrie!" Reid yelled from the other side.

Crap.

"Who's that?" Stacy asked.

"Our ride back to Iowa," I said, standing up. "I was supposed to meet him downstairs, uh, twenty minutes ago."

"Whoops."

I pulled open the door. "Hey!" I greeted, aiming at a smile so he'd forgive me quick. He probably expected the red cheeks and swollen eyes I knew I had. “I lost track of time. Sorry.”

He’d left in the first place because a twenty-four hour road trip with a human female, an incubus needed to do what an incubus needed to do first.

Reid narrowed his eyes. “What’s going on?” he asked. Instead of waiting for my answer, though, he pushed past me into the room.

“I don’t do well with redheads,” Stacy said. “Too hotheaded for me.”

Reid turned to me but thumbed at Stacy. “Who’s this?”

“Our new vehicle buddy?” I shot him an unsure grin.

He stared at me, unblinking.

“She’s my best friend from Texas. Mine and Jessica’s friend,” I clarified. “Stacy, this is Reid. Reid, Stacy.”

“Oh…Reeeeeeiiiid,” she drawled out, backing up so that the bed separated them. “Nice to meet you…I think.”

His eyes flicked from her to me. “She knows me? How does she know me?”

“She flew in this morning,” I explained. “She brought Jessica’s diary.” I picked it up off the bed and gave it to Reid.

“So?”

“She wrote down her visions. Stuff we might be able to use, you know, about the Opal.”

Reid’s gaze dropped, and he shoved the diary back at me. “Doesn’t matter. Lucas is gone.” He moved toward the exit, picking up my suitcase as he went. “Let’s get out of this town.”

After the door clicked shut behind him, Stacy

grabbed her bag. “What’s up his ass?”

I sighed at the door. “Lucas was his best friend, and he blames himself for Lucas’s death. And now that he’s actually gone, I think Reid’s hurting.”

“Did Lucas blame him?”

I shook my head, saddened. “No. He never blamed Reid.”

“Does Reid know that?”

“Yeah, sometimes, though, it’s not about knowing. It’s about believing.”

***

Reid slammed the trunk over our belongings. I only had one bag and one suitcase; Reid brought one suitcase; and Stacy, crazily enough, only brought a carry-on.

She shrugged. “How often do you get to go shopping at the beach?”

“Knowing you? A few times a year,” I said.

“Yeah, well.” She opened the back door. “Did Lucas give you his car?”

“Yeah, but I don’t think I can keep it. I can’t afford the insurance on this thing. Heck, I can barely afford the insurance on my own car.”

What I didn’t tell her was that I planned on giving it to Reid. The Jeep and a few other things.

I slid into the passenger seat and buckled up. “I want to check on Lucas’s parents before we leave town.”

“Yeah, well, I don’t.” Reid started the Jeep and backed out.

“I’m not asking you to get out of the car. Only to

drive by slow."

"You want to check on their house, then, huh?"

"Just…please?"

He didn't answer, but he turned right instead of left.

"Thank you," I murmured.

Reid did better than I asked; he pulled over on the side of the road. For a moment, I worried that they'd see us, but then I remembered the tinted windows would keep us hidden.

Mr. and Mrs. Reynolds were in the front yard pulling weeds from the flowerbeds. She wore an oversized floppy hat with a blue and white polka dot bow tied around the base, but when she turned her head to speak to her husband, I could see her face. Her eyes sparkled as a beam of light hit them. Pink lips curved up into a smile, and she laughed. She pointed to something in the other flowerbed. Mr. Reynolds acted as if he didn't understand, so she got up, brushed her gloved hands on her pants, and went to kneel beside him. When she did, he pulled out from his side a bouquet of flowers he probably picked. She gazed lovingly at him and kissed him.

"That's how they acted before," Reid said.

He didn't have to tell me before what.

"They seem happy now," I said.

We watched them for a few more seconds. Mrs. Reynolds went inside with her flowers, and Mr. Reynolds' stare followed her before he too tossed off his gloves and hurried after her.

Reid puffed out a chuckle. "Yeah, they do."

Chapter 32

Other than pit stops for gas, food, and restrooms, we drove straight through. At night, I noted how the splendorous blaze of angels lit up all sides of the car. Better than the demons we had on the drive down.

Reid didn't say much during the trip. Other than filling in Stacy on my being the new necromancer, I remained fairly silent as well. My time was spent lamenting over how empty my hand felt without Lucas's holding it. How the air conditioner did nothing but remind me that he was gone.

"Drop us off at Megan's," I told Reid once we entered Villisca's city limits. "You can take the Jeep back to"—I swallowed—"the house." Lucas's house.

I texted Megan that Stacy and I would be there in five. We actually made it in three. Yeah, Villisca was *that* small.

Megan met us outside and helped unload our luggage. "You want to come in?" she offered Reid.

"Nah, not tonight. I—" He stopped himself from

finishing whatever else he was going to say. "Good night."

He backed out of the driveway without another word. The difference between us right now was that he'd started grieving, and I hadn't. Not completely. I had a purpose. I needed to do what Lucas had asked. After that, I'd allow myself to break down.

"How's your mom?" I asked Megan as the Jeep's taillights faded into the darkness.

"The same. Not better, not worse. I guess that's an improvement."

"Do you think she'll be cured once I accept the calling?"

Megan looked at Stacy, unsure of how to answer my question in front of her.

"It's fine. She knows," I said. Megan nodded once, her expression telling me how she wasn't fond of the idea, but she didn't argue.

She yanked open the basement door. "I have no idea, Carrie."

She led us into the downstairs den. At the bookcase, she opened a hollow book and typed something into a keypad. The bookcases split down the middle and pulled apart, giving us entrance to a secret room I'd never seen before. Once I stepped inside, though, familiarity crept in. Lucas had been here; I'd seen it in a dream.

A laboratory took up most of the space. At the far end of the room was a lounge chair, television, and a bookcase filled with leather and cloth-bound books. I recognized a couple of them—the angel one specifically stood out with its golden lettering.

"So what's your theory?" she asked, leaning on

her palms on her work table.

I moved to stand next to her while Stacy examined the books. "Okay, there are seven ingredients you said, right?" I said.

"Plus the Opal, yeah."

"Opal makes eight." I took off the ring and gave it to Megan. Then I opened Jessica's diary to the page I'd taken notes on. "Check out the numbers. The Opal, the ring, these numbers here, the potion—you said they were all connected. The numbers go up to seven if we see them as individual numbers and not one big number. The original potion had your scribbles on it, about how you changed the formulas each time you and Lucas tried it."

"Yeah. Most of the time the adjustments extended how long he stayed alive."

"Because you were getting closer in the *amount* of each ingredient needed." I pointed to the ring. "But what if it was the wrong order? What if *this* is the order? Like the secret code or something. So see here? You put in however much the formula said, but you don't start with the first ingredient. You start with the third one. Then the first. Then the first again."

I peered up at her to see what she thought. She had a hand over her mouth and her eyes shifted back and forth between the ring and my notes. Finally she dropped her hand, and a grin began to form across her lips.

"You might be on to something. Hmmm, something I read about Matthias linked the Opal to the Seven Sisters—one ingredient per sister and then one more to activate the potion."

"The Opal of Veritas."

She laughed, shaking her head. "Good God, Carrie, I think you're right. How did I miss that?"

"Thank Stacy. I wouldn't have figured it out without her."

She chin-upped her thanks in Stacy's direction. "All right, ladies. Let's get this potion put together!"

Megan and my gazes locked and we both smiled. What if this actually worked? Deep inside me, I swore I could feel Lucas's soul dance.

"First things first," Megan said. "There were special spells put on the book to keep those who saw it from remembering what the ingredients were and how much of each was needed."

"Wait, so we don't know what to put into this cocktail?" Stacy asked, frowning.

"Technically, no," Megan answered. "But…" She went to her mini-fridge and pulled out a test tube rack filled with vials. "Lucky for us, I thought ahead."

"What are those?

"I made a few extra mixtures. You know, just in case." Megan winked at me. "And this one—" She removed a tube labeled *original*. "—has one serving of each of the seven ingredients."

"How does that help us if we don't know what they are?"

Megan held the vial up to the light. "In this case, science can tell us what magic has erased."

"Science?" Stacy asked, a hint of fear in her tone. She turned to me. "She means chemistry, doesn't she?"

"Afraid so," I said.

"If it hadn't been for Jessica, I would have failed chemistry," she groaned. "She's torturing me from the grave."

"Ah, it's not so bad," I encouraged. "Megan's awesome at this. We'll get it figured out."

"It'll take all night, but yeah." Megan's eyes glittered with excitement. "We're doing this."

Stacy clapped her hands. "All right then. Let's bring a dead person back to life. What do you want me to do?"

***

Three of the seven ingredients we found easily, considering. The amounts, though, were a little trickier. They had to be precise, so all three of us titrated the same solutions to compare. When we got five of the same answer, we considered it to be true.

"Fourteen point six milliliters of witch or warlock blood? That's disgusting!" Stacy cringed.

"A human being is made up of three parts: spirit, body, and soul," Megan explained. "All three must be present for life to exist. My guess is there is a representation of each part in the formula, and witches and warlocks would represent the soul portion."

"Why's that?"

"Witches and warlocks have two souls each," Megan said, shrugging. "At this point, it's only a guess. Apparently I used my own blood for this."

Megan showed me the DNA match on her computer. “Four ingredients down, three to go,” I said.

We went back to work, the three of us shuffling around each other. Megan turned on some music, but other than muffled singing and a few questions, we stayed focused on our task.

My mind enjoyed the break from the constant memories of Lucas flowing through it. Now, his face only appeared every few minutes instead of every single second.

By the time most people would consider morning, we only had one ingredient left to solve for. We were so close.

Megan nervously tapped her nails against the monochromater. I tapped mine against my teeth, and Stacy examined hers for minor imperfections.

The machine hummed, and the infrared printout slid out from the printer. Megan snatched it up. I didn’t bother reading it. All the pointy red lines made no sense to me. She compared it to the previous one.

“Gotcha.” She chuckled, bobbing her head. “Tricky one.”

She wrote down the last ingredient and pushed the paper across the table to me.

“You ready to mix this?” she asked.

I scanned the list. “You have everything?”

She did a slight shoulder shrug. “Of course. I’ve made it before, remember?” She had a point.

“This is the correct order of the original? Are you sure?”

Megan placed a clean beaker on the table. “One

hundred percent."

"I'm ready, then," I said, suddenly breathless. Stacy nodded with me.

Megan rummaged through the fridge and cabinets, grabbing what we needed. Once all seven items were on the table in front of us, I shivered at the power it represented. To bring a person back to life—my mind couldn't comprehend it.

One by one, I read off the ingredients and how much we needed in order of the numbers inside the ring. I added Jessica's 314 to the end.

Megan dumped in the last one. "The Opal?"

"What do we do, drop it in?" I asked, unsure.

"Yep. It's what activates the potion."

"So, how long do we have to administer it before it, you know, won't work anymore?"

"This isn't medicine; it's magic. There is no expiration date." Megan glanced at the door. "But before we act, I'd like to make sure we got it right."

"How will we know?" Stacy asked.

"I'm hoping it will be obvious," Megan said.

I held the ring between my forefinger and thumb. The magic inside the gem would flow out and do its thing.

"For you, Lucas," I whispered in hopes that this would fulfill my promise to him.

Then I dropped it into the solution. Instantly, the potion began to glow and pulse as if it had its own heartbeat. Golden smoke swirled inside the glass. Stacy's face went slack, her eyes widening.

"Holy shit," Megan whispered in amazement.

"I don't think most people consider shit to be holy," I murmured, distractedly.

"What?"

"Never mind."

We stared in silence until the golden smoke disappeared and the potion stopped beating. The glow remained, though, beautiful and bright like new life.

"That. Was. The coolest thing. I've ever seen," Stacy let out slowly.

My heart thudded in my chest. This was it. The moment of truth.

I pulled my phone out of my pocket and looked at Megan. "Do you want to make the call or should I?"

***

We had to wait, so Stacy and I made a run to the Coffee Shop in town. It didn't escape me that this was where Lucas and I first met. Well, the place where I first saw him. Gleaming green eyes had peered at me from the doorway, and I'd freaked out a little.

Now—now I'd give anything to see those beautiful irises of his again. To look into them just one more time. Touch his face. Kiss his lips. Feel his coolness against my skin.

"Are we going to go inside?" Stacy asked.

I tore my attention from the Coffee Shop. I didn't remember how long ago I parked and cut the engine.

I shook off the nostalgia and heartache. My job wasn't finished yet. "Yeah, let's go."

This early in the morning, The Coffee Shop

garnered a long line. Everyone in town who worked on the square stopped in before eight. When we finally reached the counter, Stacy had changed her mind five times.

"Spiced apple latte, double shot, extra cinnamon, and an egg and ham sandwich," she ordered. She cocked her head toward me as she dug into her purse. "And whatever she wants."

"I can get it," I said.

"I know you're capable, darling, but as you admitted earlier, you can barely handle your own car insurance. Let me get your breakfast."

"I have Megan's order too."

"All of it. A friend of yours and Jess's is a friend of mine."

I smiled. "I love you."

She swept her hand out to the side, palm up, Stacy-style. "Obviously. Now order."

"Cappuccino—large. Chai-crème latte, also large, a blueberry scone, and an egg and bacon spinach wrap."

The barista gave Stacy her order first. She sipped her latte, and I'm pretty sure she coffee-gasmed right there in the store. Her eyes rolled back in her head and a satisfied sigh breathed out.

"We are coming here every day," she said. "Hell, I might even move in with you so I can come to this place every day. *Dayum*!"

I giggled. Girl loved her coffee.

She snapped into a point. "Seriously, better than Starbucks."

"That might be considered blasphemy in some parts of the world, you know."

"It's not blasphemy if it's true."

Outside, I shuffled toward the car, hoping for a whirl of a cool breeze to encircle me. But only warm, summer air pressed in on my skin. I paused at my car, looking back at the sidewalk. My insides fell at the absence of what I longed for. I opened my door and got inside. I buckled up and took one last glimpse at the front door. Nothing.

Emotion welled inside my chest, and I inhaled deeply. What was I doing? He was gone and he wasn't coming back.

I backed out onto the street and drove until the empty Coffee Shop entryway disappeared from sight.

***

We congregated in Megan's living room, eating and drinking our breakfast. And waiting. Megan seemed nervous, her eyes flicking up to the clock several times a minute. I'd be lying if I said I was fine. Stacy, though? Stacy kept Megan and me from going crazy.

"Senior year sucked without you, Carrie. Just saying," she said. "I mean, lunches in the courtyard weren't the same. You listened to people, you know? Like, really listened to them, and I think they knew that, and since you left, they didn't talk about their lives as much. It was boring."

"It wasn't the same here without you, either, Stace."

The knock on the door made me jump. Stacy's perfectly-shaped eyebrows flashed upward at my anxiety. It was time.

“Relax,” she mouthed to me as Megan got up to answer.

I wiped my palm over my face and rose too. Stacy followed me to the foyer to greet our guest.

Dressed in the same clothes he wore yesterday, Reid more closely resembled a zombie than an incubus. From the scent of his breath, it was clear he’d spent the night drinking. He probably hadn’t slept. I couldn’t blame him. If it were me in Lucas’s house, without Lucas, I wouldn’t have slept either. I would have lain in his bed, my head on his pillow, covered in his blankets, and wept.

“So, what are you going to do now?” I asked after Megan invited him inside. Being half-demon, I knew he didn’t want to go home. He hadn’t even visited his parents while he was in North Carolina. Before Lucas sought him out, he’d been wandering the country, warring with the monster within and hating himself for past mistakes. The last thing Lucas wanted was for him to return to that.

It was the last thing I wanted too.

“I don’t know,” he answered. “Maybe go back to Canada. Wait for the change to complete itself.”

His golden irises fluttered, but they never met Megan’s or my gaze.

“Please don’t,” I said.

“Where else can I go, Carrie, where I won’t hurt you or…anyone else I care about? I can’t be trusted.”

“Adelia said you had a part to play before this was over,” I reminded him.

“I drove you home. It’s over.”

"You really think that was your role in this thing? That Fate determined you would drive me back to Villisca?"

Reid sighed in a shrug and slapped his legs on the exhale. "What can I say? She's a bitch."

"You didn't die just so you could drive me across the country. I refuse to believe that," I said, my tone hardening at his acceptance of the situation. "Lucas didn't believe that either."

He bowed his head. "Yeah, well, Lucas is gone, and I'm the one who killed him. Fate may be a bitch, but she's a fair bitch."

"You didn't kill Lucas, Reid. This, right here? This is an intervention," I explained. "*You.* Didn't. Kill. Lucas."

He snorted. "An intervention, huh? You three?"

"It's what Lucas wanted," I said, straightening my back for confidence.

Now he laughed out loud. "Lucas told you he wanted you to host an intervention for me? Carrie, you might be a lot of things, but a liar isn't one of them. I know for a fact he didn't tell you that. We met too, remember?"

"Okay, well, maybe he didn't use the word 'intervention.' But he approves of this. You are his best friend—"

He cut me off. "Was. I *was* his best friend."

"Are," I insisted. "He once told me that friendships like that never die. He wouldn't have wanted his best friend to grieve for him forever, and he sure as hell never wanted him to drown in blame and regret for something he couldn't control. Lucas chose to escape the hospital. He chose to drive. He chose his speed. Not you, Reid. Not. *You.*"

"I may not have pulled the trigger, but I was the reason he held the gun."

I looked at Stacy. "Is this what it's like talking to me?"

"Sometimes," she admitted. "You're stubborn."

I turned back to Reid. "If anyone gave him the gun, it was the demon inside you. Still, Lucas had a choice. We all have a choice. Lucas made his. I've made mine. And now, it's your turn to make yours: you can go back to the way things were, living with your guilt, or you can forgive yourself, and live the life your best friend wanted you to live."

I was determined.

Reid's jaw clenched, his voice dropping on the next word. "It's not that easy, Carrie. I wish it were."

"I didn't say it would be easy. I said it was a choice."

"I don't have a life to live anymore. A demon took it from me, and a demon is what I've become."

"An unjust death," I reminded him.

"Just. Unjust, doesn't matter. I'm a dead man."

I stared at him. "What if you don't have to be?"

"Don't have to be what?"

I opened my mouth to answer, but Megan spoke first. "Come downstairs. We have something to show you," she said.

Megan led the way.

"Impressive," Reid said when we entered Megan's secret laboratory.

"Sit," she instructed.

Stacy and I rounded the table so the three of us

faced Reid from the opposite side. He scanned the room, but otherwise said nothing. After few moments of silence, he lifted his thumbs. "So…what's up?"

"Remember the ring Adelia gave to Rachel?" I asked.

Reid nodded.

"We figured it out," I finished.

He tilted his head to the side, reminding me of his demon side. "Figured it out? Like, how it works?"

"Adelia said you had a part to play. That Fate took no chances this time around. Adelia gave that ring to Rachel, because it was fate for her to do so," I explained. "It came to me so I could make my choice, yes, but I believe the reason it went to Rachel first was so you could make yours."

Reid shook his head. "Rachel didn't know the truth about me."

"Doesn't matter. You found the ring in her room, right? That simple act set off a series of events that has ended here. With you."

"And my choice?"

I nodded. "This is your second chance, Reid. But life isn't worth living if you can't forgive yourself."

"This is Lucas's doing, you said?" he asked, half-chuckling.

"Yeah. I think Fate meant for this potion to belong to you. I think that's how this ends—bringing life to those without. To you."

"Son of a bitch," Reid murmured to himself. He pursed his lips and moisture glistened in his eyes. He lowered his head and not-so-subtly wiped his face with the back of his hand. "During life, Lucas always had my back. I guess he still does."

I touched his arm. "You had each other's."

"It's what friends do," Stacy said.

"Will you help me?" Reid asked, his stare resting on Megan.

"That means you'll have to stick around, you know?" She grinned back at him, like the thought made her happy.

"I guess it does."

I grabbed the potion from the mini-fridge. The glow seemed to have brightened, as if it realized its time had finally come.

"That?" Reid asked. "Do I have to drink the ring too?"

"Uh, no. We just didn't know if we should take it out or not." I grimaced at Megan, who shook her head. "Yeah, please don't drink it," I told him.

Megan motioned him over to the armchair in the corner. "You might want to lie down. This might sting a bit."

Reid obeyed, kicking his feet up on the ottoman like Lucas had.

I walked over, a mixture of grief and nostalgia pressing in on my lungs. Not because this would actually work, but because Lucas couldn't be here to see it happen. This was his request, his final wish.

Reid and I regarded each other, as if we shared something the others didn't. "What did Lucas say to you?" I asked. He knew what I meant.

He paused, studying my expression. I needed to know, and he must have seen that, because when he spoke, he spoke only to me. "That he was sorry for turning his back on me at the hospital. It was what he regretted most, because it didn't just hurt him. He said Rachel's death wasn't my fault, and that I needed to stop blaming myself. He asked me to make sure you were okay. And he said…" Reid swallowed. "He said life is a gift. Second chances at it only come once in forever."

I gave him the beaker, emotion cracking my voice. "So do it. Use it well."

Reid studied it for a moment. Then he lifted it up to the ceiling, his eyes lifting too. "To you, man."

Then he tilted his head back and drank.

Chapter 33

I spent the first week back readjusting to life. Stacy stayed with me, and I loved her for it. She kept my mind off things. I hated the day I had to take her to the airport, but she needed to get back to work.

After she left, I picked up my old shifts at Renae's Antiques. My grandparents gave me the space I needed, probably thanks to Grandpa.

I thought that because the soul inside my chest belonged to Lucas, I'd somehow feel him. I didn't. Incenamus seemed to have died with him, leaving this gaping hole inside me.

Reid slept for a day, and it was the longest day of our lives. Like Lucas had, Reid writhed in pain as the potion worked its magic. Reviving a dead soul didn't happen easily, but we let out an audible sigh of relief when Megan got a steady heartbeat.

He camped out in Megan's laboratory so we could keep an eye on him. Slowly, pale skin turned golden, and scars I'd never seen before appeared on his arms. Other imperfections too, and I couldn't help liking this version of Reid better than the previous one. Humanity, though vastly imperfect, had a kind of beauty not found elsewhere. And now Reid had it back.

After that it was like he'd never been dead. Unlike Lucas, he retained all of his memories. Because he'd been cycling, Megan thought. Had the demon taken over completely, he would have forgotten who he used to be too.

He kept his word to Lucas about me, and I enjoyed the company. Coveted it, even. We made it a point to see each other every day—meet at the park, go out for lunch, or hang out on my grandparents' porch swing. We talked about Lucas. Swapped stories, laughed. Afterward, my heart always felt lighter.

I gave Reid the keys to the Jeep Compass and signed over the title to him. Reid needed a place to live since he'd now be staying around, so the house worked perfectly, but I didn't want to be there when he and Megan cleaned out Lucas's things. The day they finished redecorating, Reid brought me two items: a framed picture Lucas had taken of me, and the book of constellations I'd given him for Christmas. The pages were worn, and most had notes Lucas scribbled in the margins. I placed both on my dresser, and sometimes looking at them momentarily filled the hole in my chest.

One day, I decided to do laundry. I piled all my dirty clothes into a basket and took them downstairs. I stuffed what I could into the washing machine, leaving one pair of jeans at the bottom of the basket.

I picked them up to smell them. Maybe they weren't too bad. As I brought them to my nose, something crinkled in one of the pockets. I stuck my hand in the back one and pulled out a folded envelope with my name across the middle.

Mike's letter.

Megan gave it to me weeks ago. Without closing the washing machine, I walked to the living room and sat down before opening the envelope.

Dear Carrie,

I know what you're going to say: I should have called instead of written a letter. But I didn't think I could talk to you, hear your voice, and still be able to get out what I need to say. I guess that makes me a coward.

Megan tells me I'm in danger, that demons are watching me, and I'll be used as a hostage if they get me. I should be scared, I guess, consider some of the precautions she talked about, but all I can think of is you.

It's stupid, considering the situation, but I keep thinking about you without makeup in your pajamas, your hair thrown up on top of your head in one of those, I don't know, messy buns or something? Your legs curled up under you on your grandparents' sofa and a bowl of popcorn in your lap and a can of Pepsi within reach. And how you laugh at all the dumbest parts of the movie, even when they're not funny. It's the cutest damn thing.

I think about how you helped me with my homework over the phone, and how I said stupid stuff just so I could imagine you rolling your eyes. Eating lunch in the cafeteria, how you mixed your vegetables with your mashed potatoes because you said they tasted better together than apart. And how you always brought a stash of pink unicorn erasers to class because you knew I'd ask for one. Probably why you always bought pink unicorns anyway.

I think about riding Goldie and Stardust or Roxanne out in the pasture, talking about nothing important. Remember the time we discussed what the babies of rabbits and cows would look like? Your guess was the best. I only answered to hear you laugh.

I don't know what you're doing right now, while you prepare to meet this son-of-a-bitch demon. I asked Megan to keep the details to herself, because I want no information in case they try to get it out of me. I don't want to break and put you in more danger than you're in.

Carrie, whatever happens from here, I just want you to know that I'm sorry about graduation night and all the nights leading up to it. I acted like an asshole. I meant what I said, though, about not wanting to be your friend. I'll always want more than that, but if your friendship is all you have to offer, then I'll take it.

I don't like my life without you.

Mike

I read the letter twice, considering each word. When I asked Megan about him, she said he was fine. He'd asked about me, and she told him about Lucas. She left out the rest though, and apologized to me for telling him what she did. I didn't care. It was probably better coming from her. I probably couldn't have gotten through the explanation without breaking down.

Mike wasn't in Villisca now. Grandpa had told me. After high school baseball season ended, he went on to college for some summer baseball clinic, for those interested in walking onto the team. Grandpa expected him back next week sometime.

Next week couldn't come soon enough.

By the end of my second week back, I thought about the promise I made to Lucas. About forgiving my father. I wasn't there, but I'd taken the first step—the one my mother talked about.

Lucas said the same thing. They were right, and it was time.

I made a mental note to call Dad in the morning. Tonight, I wanted to spend time with Lucas the only way I could.

I adjusted my pillow so it supported my neck. Lying in a field behind the house, I gazed up at the stars and imagined Lucas looking back down on me. I studied some of the constellations in the book, the ones he showed to me, and tried to find them myself. I felt confident about Orion's Belt, but the others? Yeah, not so much. I wished now I'd paid more attention to his lessons.

I thought I'd have more time.

I was shining my phone's flashlight at the book to figure out where I'd gone wrong with Pleiades when a blinding light blasted out from somewhere around me. I shielded my eyes with my arm, burying my face in the crook of my elbow.

Instead of fear, peace flowed through me.

"You may open your eyes now," a voice said, soothing and beautiful like the calm of the ocean.

I did what the voice asked and slowly lowered

my arm. Enough that I could clearly make out her features. Her golden aura shone around her like a dimly lit halo, but it was still the most glorious of light.

"You have done well," she said, smiling.

What do you say to that? To an angel?

"Thank…you," I breathed out.

"Do you know why I am here?"

I nodded, words failing me.

"You have proven yourself, Carrie. Your selfless act of love has brought Lucas safely home. And tonight, your own spirit has begun to heal. You are ready. Do you accept your calling to reunite lost souls so they too may come home?"

This was it. My calling, my final choice, what Lucas died for.

What Reid, Jessica, Susan Taylor, Parker, and Rachel died for. And now, it was what I would live for.

"I accept the responsibility," I said.

The angel's glow brightened slightly, and I could sense her delight in my answer. She extended her arms out from her sides. Her glow continued to swell until I could no longer make out her form beneath it. "They will find you. Farewell, Carrie, until we meet again."

With a final smile, she vanished into the darkness.

***

No ghosts came to visit me the first night of my officially being the necromancer, but in the morning, I received a phone call from Megan.

"Carrie!" she yelled into my ear, and I had to hold out my phone until my eardrum stopped ringing. "Carrie, when I woke up, my mother was in the kitchen, cooking breakfast. What the…? Do you have anything to do with this?"

"Your mom—she's okay?"

"My mom's freaking *better* than okay. She's going *crazy* over here. I hope you're hungry, because she's making enough food to feed the island of Malta."

"I got a visit from an angel and accepted the calling," I said. "I guess that makes me the town necromancer, and your mom's off the hook."

I expected excitement at my announcement, but instead Megan went quiet.

"Hello?" I asked.

"I'm here. If you're the new necro that means the angels' protection of you has ended. We need to get demon barrier spells put up immediately."

"I thought they were already up?"

"No, we need different ones. Necro ones."

"Great…I think."

"Get ready and get over here. We can discuss it over breakfast."

In the background, I heard Vanessa holler, "Ask Carrie how she likes her eggs."

"How do you like your eggs?" Megan asked.

"Scrambled."

Megan repeated my order to her mom, then got back on. "Better hurry or it'll get cold."

***

After breakfast at Megan's, I clomped into the living room and fell onto the sofa. Vanessa was indeed feeling better, and I wouldn't be eating for another week. Apparently, she thought her family hadn't been fed in all the time she'd been laid up. I'd never eaten so much food in all my life.

All I wanted was to go back to sleep, but I had a phone call to make and I wanted to do it while Grandma and Grandpa were out. I blew out a breath and fumbled to pick my phone off the floor.

I scrolled through my contacts until I found Griffin's cell. I stared at the screen for a minute before I convinced myself to follow through.

For Lucas, I thought as I listened to the computer-like ring.

"Carrie, are you okay?" His voice sounded rushed and breathless. I'd heard the same emotion in my own voice too many times—fear.

"No, no," I started, then I backtracked, realizing I just told him I wasn't okay. "I mean, yes. Yes, I'm fine. That's not why I called."

He breathed out a sigh. "You've had me so worried, princess. I called your mother, and she reassured me you were fine, but…next time, you need to send a text if you're set on not answering my calls. I need to know you're okay."

I used to roll my eyes at my parents' concern over my safety. I'd tell Mom how each time she worried about me, it took years off her life with the stress it caused. Her answer to me remained the same: "I worry because I love you. It's my job as a parent."

Dad was never that dramatic, but by the way he

nodded when she gave me her mini-speeches, I should have realized he agreed with her assessment.

"I'm sorry," I said, meaning it. Maybe that was the second step to forgiveness. "I'm calling to ask you…to ask both of you…if you still wanted me to stand up with you at the wedding?"

Chapter 34

Dad connected me with Ami, who cried over the phone at my acceptance. It would have been annoying if she weren't actually kinda sweet.

"Have you tried on your dress yet?" she asked.

"Where would I do that? Should I get an appointment somewhere?" I asked, because I had no clue how these things worked.

"Oh." She sounded surprised. "Did the package I sent over Christmas not arrive?"

The package over Christmas?

Then it dawned on me. Of course! I'd taken one look at the return address and tossed it into the back of my closet.

"Um, yes," I said, letting out a nervous laugh. "It's upstairs. In my room."

I expected a hint of disappointment when she answered. But none came. "Great! Let me know if the shoes don't fit, and I'll overnight a different size. And if you need alterations, Griffin mentioned that…maybe your grandmother could handle it?"

With only a few weeks until W-day, I'd be

cutting it close if I had to take the dress somewhere, I assumed, but Ami was right. My grandmother rocked at sewing, a trait I hadn't inherited.

"I'll figure that stuff out today. Thank you."

"You're welcome. And…Carrie?" she asked, suddenly timid.

"Yeah?" I held my breath, hoping she wouldn't go into some kind of Mom speech.

"I wanted to let you know that…well, you're an adult, and you don't need another mother. You already have a wonderful one. But…I'd just really like to be your friend."

The woman was only eight years older than me, so having her act like my mom would be the definition of awkward. But friends? Friends I could live with.

"We can definitely work on that," I said.

"Good. Well, if you need anything, feel free to call."

"I will. Thanks."

After we hung up, I grabbed the box out of my closet. Ripped off the packaging tape and slid the inner box out of the shipping one. Ami had gone all out, covering it in shiny, red wrapping paper. I opened it the way I always did, gently and carefully.

I lifted the lid and unfolded the white tissue paper. A yellow satin dress lay inside with a card on top. Like Dad once taught me, I opened the card first.

Dear Carrie,

I realize you haven't accepted the offer

of being a bridesmaid, but this is in hopes that you will. If you don't, know that it's okay. We understand. Please keep the dress anyway. It might come in handy for something.

With love,

Dad & Ami

I wondered how long it took her to decide how to close the note. It was clear that Ami had written it, and I'd been so rude to her.

The people you love in your life aren't around forever. A snap of a finger, a small twist of fate, and they're gone.

Family. Friends. They're the ones who were there for you when life sucked.

Adelia, once again, got it right. The power of love overcame anything.

I smiled as I lifted the dress from the box. I held it up against my body and admired the way the material flowed like a waterfall down to the floor. Stacy told me one year how yellow worked for me. Seemed the fashion queen struck gold on her assessment.

It was Lucas's favorite color. This dress couldn't be more perfect.

I stripped down and put the dress on. A few acrobatic tricks later, I had the thing zipped up and the halter top fastened. I dug the shoes out next and stepped into them. Perfect fit. Then I turned to face the mirror.

The bodice hugged me in all the right places, and the skirt rippled down over my legs in a cascading sea of fabric. The straps at the top needed tightening, but that was all. Even the length worked!

Turning slowly, I imagined him peering down at me right now, his lips curving up on one side and exposing his dimple. He would have had some flirtatious comment, yet his adoration would be clear in the way he looked at me.

Whatever fate had in store, I knew one thing for certain: Lucas would be the man I compared every other to.

I opened my door to call down the stairs to Grandma when my phone rang. I smiled at the country-pop tune I'd set for Mike. It reminded me of the high school dances where he'd shown off his line dancing skills.

I missed how things used to be between us.

"Hey," I answered. My smile grew at the anticipation of hearing his voice.

Last year when Lucas disappeared from my life, I'd leaned on Mike. He brought me mint chip ice cream, watched movies with me, laughed with me. He kept me from falling apart, and now I needed that more than ever. Only this time, my mind kept reminding me that Mike wanted more than just friendship. He had back then too, but this was different.

"I'll be at your house in twenty minutes, and I expect you to have good riding clothes on. And a jacket. Because we'll be out late." From the sound of the breeze in the background, I suspected he was outside. Maybe even on his way over.

"What if I already have plans?"

"Cancel them."

"What if they're important plans?" I teased.

"There's nothing more important than rekindling a friendship with a horseback ride in the sunset." I could hear the grin in his voice.

"Yes, because riding into the sunset is what friendships are made of."

"You're the smartest woman alive."

"Flattery might earn you an affirmative answer."

"I didn't ask." His voice deepened as he said it. "Get Goldie saddled up. See you soon."

He hung up before I could ask for a few extra minutes. Oh well. If he got here and I wasn't ready, he'd have to wait. I still shook off the shoes and trotted downstairs to find Grandma quickly.

After she pinned the material and I texted Ami, I dressed in jeans and a t-shirt and ran out to the barn. Goldie whinnied at me.

"I'll take that as you're happy to see me," I said, collecting her equipment.

It had been a while since I'd ridden her, but she didn't mind that it took me longer to get her ready. I was only half-finished when the hoof pounds of another horse sounded at the barn gate.

"I'll be out in a sec!" I shouted.

Seconds later, Mike's palms glided over mine as he adjusted Goldie's bridle straps. The warmth of his touch made me pause. Heat, flesh, bones, a heartbeat. Those were normal things on a person, and they shouldn't feel strange. They should feel good.

"Your place is among the living."

I bowed my head to hide the flush in my cheeks. Then I stepped back so Mike could finish getting Goldie ready for me.

"Girls are always late," he said to my horse, which made me snicker because Goldie was female. But horses were different, I guessed. Maybe they didn't have the same stereotypes as us human females?

"If you hadn't hung up so fast, I'd have asked you to give me extra time to get ready."

Mike walked toward me, and I stuffed my hands in my pockets to avoid an accidental brush of skin. Caramel irises burned into me with a heated stare. I swallowed the nerves bubbling into my throat, but they returned times a thousand.

"Time isn't of endless supply, Carrie. We never get enough of it."

I swallowed again and dropped my gaze to the hay scattered on the ground. He knew Lucas was gone, but that didn't mean my heart was free. We both knew he wasn't talking about today. I wasn't ready to go there yet—to what he said in his letter.

"I accepted Ami's offer to be in the wedding," I said, not meeting his eyes. "Grandma's fixing my dress."

Mike tipped my chin up to him. "I didn't say I was done waiting. I'm saying I don't want to wait forever."

In Texas, after Jessica's funeral, Lucas had bared his soul to me. He showed me the memories he cherished of the two of us and his private thoughts during those moments. He showed me his dreams too, the things that would never be between us, because an eternity of miles separated the living and the dead.

The final image hadn't included him. It had been of me. And Mike.

Together.

Was this what he wanted if he couldn't be here?

In front of me now was the man I met on my second day in Villisca, the one who risked his life for me not once, but twice. He never stopped fighting for me.

I stared at him, taking in the subdued hope in his eyes. "You won't have to wait forever."

***

We talked about stupid stuff. His little sister, Mandy, who in his absence had called dibs on his larger bedroom. We talked about him leaving for college and my plans to take classes at the community college in Red Oak this fall. He was concerned about being a walk-on to the baseball team, and how he'd have to work harder to get noticed than the guys with scholarships.

We discussed my grandparents and what Grandpa would do without his help. Mike asked about the wedding in Texas, even wondered how my mom was. I mentioned Stacy, and how we mended our friendship. When we broached the topic of Megan's upcoming witch trials, we agreed that she deserved to bypass them.

The two things we didn't talk about were Lucas and my trip to North Carolina. We'd have to, eventually, if he wanted a significant place in my life. We had a ton to talk about if that happened.

For now, though, I was glad to be two friends, to ride horses like we used to. Funny what could happen in a year and how fast lives changed.

"We'd better head back," I said.

The sun set an hour ago, and it was strange not fearing the dark. I knew what lurked in the shadows, knew the evil nighttime posed, as did Mike. Yet, it didn't seem as strong anymore. I'd fought it head on and won. Didn't hurt that now I could see the evil's aura.

Mike checked his watch. "Wow, it's late. Time flying and all that." He smirked, his gaze dipping to my mouth before returning to my eyes.

I moved the reins so Goldie did a lovely U-turn on command. "Race ya?"

"Awe, baby. You want to lose?" he teased.

"Who said anything about losing?"

"It's cute that you think you can beat me. I remember when trotting scared you."

"Yeah, well, I'm not scared anymore. And least of all, of you! Winner picks tonight's movie." I snapped the reins and kicked Goldie's side. "Go!" I yelled behind me, and she dashed forward. I laughed as the wind whipped around me in the beauty of freedom.

Stardust, Mike's black American Quarter Horse, closed the distance in seconds. He lowered himself over her mane as he passed me.

"*Rocky*, baby!" he hollered. "A classic!"

Moonlight brightened the field we raced over, and I mimicked Mike's posture, hoping to reduce resistance. I had no clue if it helped. Mike beat me regardless.

At the farm, he reached up to help me off Goldie, and I accepted, because if I didn't, I would have kicked him in the face. Last time that happened, we ended up on the ground, Mike on top of me.

"I'm not going to mention the fact that I won and the fact that you cheated," he said, catching me by the waist.

I felt his breath on my neck, and my body didn't know what to do with its warmth.

I turned to face him and playfully jabbed his shoulder to stay inside the "friend zone." "That's kind of you."

"Anytime."

"I got this," I said, motioning toward Goldie. "Go ahead and take Stardust home. You'll be about an hour, right?"

"You sure?" His inflection made me think he'd rather help me with Goldie first.

I nodded. "I'm sure."

He patted Goldie's side. "Yeah, an hour will work." Then he spoke to my horse, "Nice job tonight, Goldie."

He moved in closer to me. The glint in his eyes told me he wanted to kiss me. Instead, he brushed his thumb over my cheek as he walked off.

"See you soon."

"Bye," I replied, focusing on my horse. That way I wouldn't know if he sent me a glance over his shoulder before he left.

I blew out a sigh and finished unsaddling Goldie.

I stroked her mane. "Why is it that as soon as you think life finally makes sense, something shakes it back up again?"

Goldie's black eyes pinned on me. She swished her tail.

"I guess I always thought my life would look…different than it does."

Goldie neighed and stomped her back foot.

"Yeah," I answered as if she could understand me. "I'm not saying it's a bad life. Just a different one."

I gave her one last pat before I hopped the fence and jogged across the yard to the house. Grandma left a few hours ago to attend an auction and wouldn't be home until late tomorrow night. She put food for Grandpa and me in the fridge, going so far as to label each container by what was inside and how long it took to warm it up for. Grandpa probably hadn't waited for me to eat his, not when Grandma had made her absence insanely easy on us food-wise.

I expected to hear the news on the television when I entered, but the eerie silence gave me pause. I checked the clock. He always watched the weather before he turned in, and that started in two minutes.

"Grandpa?" I said and listened for an answer. Maybe he was in the shower?

I didn't hear the water running, and in this old farmhouse, you could hear everything.

"Grandpa?" I tried again, wandering into the kitchen.

He wasn't at the table, but his worn dirt-ridden boots lay on the floor by the cabinets. Fear took hold, jabbing me in the chest. Boots didn't stand up like that when they weren't on someone's feet.

Heels on the floor and the toes pointed outward, a few inches off the linoleum.

"Grandpa?" I choked out.

I rounded the table. My grandfather's body was sprawled out behind the table, his arms lifeless, one over his chest and the other laid out beside him.

I don't know how long it took me to call 911. It all happened in a haze of involuntary motions. I dropped to my knees at his side as the operator asked me a bunch of questions regarding his condition, most of which I couldn't answer. I wanted to call Mike, because I couldn't do this alone, but she made me stay on the line with her.

"How about now?" she asked. "Can you still feel him breathing?"

I held my trembling hand under his nose and closed my eyes. Soft, barely-there breaths puffed onto my skin.

"Yes," I said, my gaze roaming over his paling form.

How long has he been like this?

Another question I wanted answered I didn't have the courage to think. When it began to slip through my mind, I pushed it away immediately.

The wail of sirens filled me with a ray of hope. I told the operator the ambulance was here. She must have heard them too, because she finally let me hang up.

"Where is he?" an EMT asked when I got to the door.

"Kitchen…"

I followed them. Stood out of the way. Maybe I should have gone outside for air, because their silence scared me. They put tubes into his nostrils and an IV in his vein.

"Does he have any allergies?" someone asked me.

I shook my head. "I don't know of any. Cats?"

"To any kind of medications?" he specified.

"I don't know."

"Any history of heart disease, diabetes, high blood pressure?"

Again, I shook my head, unable to peel my eyes from my grandfather's face. "He…has a pacemaker. The rest, I don't know. My grandma would know, but she's not here," I babbled.

"It's okay," he assured me, speaking calmly. "We're going to take him to the Red Oak hospital. Can you get a hold of your grandma?"

I nodded, fresh tears sliding down my cheeks as they strapped him onto the gurney. Had I been back from our ride earlier, would this still be happening? Was it my fault?

The front door slammed open, and Mike's terrified voice called out my name. The EMTs wheeled Grandpa out and I wanted to follow them. From the corner of my vision, I saw Mike swing around the corner and into the kitchen. He stopped in the entryway, his eyes moving from Grandpa to me.

"Carrie," he breathed, swallowing the distance between us.

I said nothing as I fell into his arms and let go.

Chapter 35

Mike drove me to the hospital. On the way, I called Grandma, who said she'd meet us there. The news seemed to have pumped her full of adrenaline. I, however, had no focus to even think. Mike didn't push me, nor did he ask a bunch of questions. He just drove.

When we finally got there, Mike folded my hand into his and walked me in the emergency entrance—where I'd waited for him after his football accident. He led me to the receptionist and did all the talking. Dazed, I didn't hear much of what he said, but soon he had me sitting in a chair with a coffee between my hands.

"They're running tests," Mike murmured. "They'll come and get you when they're finished."

I nodded, focusing on the linoleum, but not really seeing it. I couldn't handle anyone else dying. I was on the edge. If the doctors came in with the worst, I'd fall. A soul could only take so much before it broke.

Weren't angels supposed to be watching over

him? What good were they if they let people die?

I didn't realize I was crying until Mike gathered me into his arms and pressed a kiss to my temple.

"There was nothing you could have done, Carrie," he said.

"I could have been there," I whispered.

"You can't be everywhere. And even if you were, you couldn't have stopped it."

The thought I'd worked to avoid tumbled out.

That's not true. I could have taken Marax's deal.

Were demons behind this? Was this one of the consequences of my actions?

We sat there, me sipping coffee and Mike gently rubbing my back for what seemed like years. Minutes felt like that when all you wanted was for them to move faster. I stiffened when a nurse in green scrubs emerged from the double doors.

"Carrie Reese?" she asked into the room. She sounded neither hopeful nor depressed.

Slowly, I stood up. "Yeah."

Mike circled an arm around my waist as I walked toward her. My legs were weak, and if it weren't for his support, I might not have made it that far.

"Follow me," she said.

We did so, and I dumped my mostly full, now cold coffee into the closest garbage.

"He's stable," she continued. "The damage to his heart is considerable, though. The doctor will be able to tell you more."

"When will he be in?" I asked, thinking of Grandma and how she should be here to hear this.

"It'll be a while."

We turned down hallway after hallway, the walk

seemingly endless. Finally, she came to a closed door and tapped her knuckles on it. Then she opened it.

Once inside, the nurse proceeded to ask me check-in questions. Mike took care of as many as he could, like my grandfather's full name and address. He'd had the wherewithal to grab Grandpa's wallet off the desk before we drove over. He pulled out an insurance card and gave it to the nurse.

I sat at Grandpa's side and held his hand as Mike answered her questions. The skin there seemed thinner than the last time I'd touched him. Dark shadows clouded the area around his eyes, and a large purple splotch discolored his temple. I wondered if he'd hit his head on the counter on his way to the floor.

Strangely enough, the steady beep of his computerized pulse calmed me. He was alive.

"I'm here, Grandpa," I murmured. "And I'm sorry."

I hadn't ruled out the possibility of demons. If that were the case, Grandpa lying here was my fault.

The nurse left, and Mike pulled up a chair beside me. "How're you doing?"

"Fine, I guess," I answered.

"Can I get you something?"

"Water?"

"I'll be right back." He kissed my head before he got up, as if I was now his responsibility.

My attention stayed on my grandpa. I listened to the machines help him so his body didn't have to work so hard.

Beep. Beep. Beep.

Then, a cool breeze circled at my back. It lingered behind me, and I twisted in my seat. A woman a few years older than me sat on the other bed, watching me. Her eyes were an unnatural shade of blue, like the blue of a swimming pool. Almost turquoise. Her silver aura floated around her in a shiny haze.

This was my purpose. Ferry lost souls across the veil. The angel said they'd find me in time, and from the look of it, my time was up.

"Hi," I said.

Her gaze narrowed in confusion. "You can *see* me?"

"Yes. I also know why you are here; you're dead."

Her shoulders slumped. "That's the conclusion I came to as well. But then, why am I still here? Is this what happens when you die?"

I shook my head. "No. This is what happens when you don't crossover to the afterlife. When your soul has separated from your spirit."

"Why would it do that?"

"Because in life, you held on to guilt and pain, and that leaves a void."

The explanation came out almost too easily. As if I'd said it a million times.

"What do I do, then?" She nodded toward the door. "That person on the surgical table, she's me, but I don't know her. I don't remember anything before this."

"You must reunite your spirit—what you are now—with your soul."

"How do I do that? I don't belong here."

"No, you don't," I said. "Close your eyes."

She did.

"Now, search your spirit. Find the hole inside yourself."

She remained silent, her eyelids fluttering.

"You'll know you've found it because you'll be able to feel it. It'll hurt," I told her softly.

Suddenly, her shoulders hunched over like someone punched her in the gut. Her aura trembled.

"You found it. Concentrate on it," I instructed. "Let it consume you until it fills every part of you. Out to your fingertips, down to your toes. Leave nothing untouched."

She squeezed her eyelids together until creases spread into her hairline. Her hands balled into fists, and her face contorted.

"You're doing it," I encouraged. "A picture should form in your mind. It might be a place or a person or an object. Tell me when you see it."

She scrunched her face. "It's a ring. An engagement ring."

"Study it. Memorize it," I said. "Then open your eyes."

While I waited for her, I searched the end table drawer for a piece of paper and a pen. As I did, I noticed Mike watching me from the doorway, his expression thoughtful. I must look strange talking to someone who wasn't there.

"I've got it," the ghost said.

"Okay," I answered, turning away from Mike. "Describe it to me."

As she spoke, I drew. I made several small

changes until she nodded her approval.

"That's it. That's what I saw."

"Your soul is attached to it. Do you think it might be yours?" I asked.

"It might be."

"You said you died on a surgical table. Was it here, in this hospital?"

"Yes."

"Today?"

"Yeah, it sounds crazy, but an angel told me to come here and find you."

I smiled. "Doesn't sound crazy at all. Keep a hold of the feeling that showed you the ring. It'll grow stronger the closer you get to it. Try the room you came from first. They usually keep your personal belongings somewhere."

"What do I do when I find the ring?"

"It'll be obvious to you," I said, remembering the silver light erupting from Rachel's grave. "Your spirit will know what to do."

"Thank you," the ghost said. "Thank you so much."

She stood up, and I watched as her silver haze breezed through the wall. Slowly, I returned to Mike. His presence hadn't altered what I told the spirit, but I didn't forget that he was there either. He hadn't moved from the doorway. Caramel irises met mine from across the room and held my stare.

I had no guidebook for this sort of thing. Who was supposed to speak first? My brain slammed words into my thoughts, but my mouth rejected them all. Or maybe it was my heart. Sometimes every part of you blurred together, becoming indistinguishable from each other. Kind of like they all worked as one. Like now.

"All they had was Dasani or Aquafina. I didn't know if you had a preference," Mike said, holding up the plastic bottle of water.

"Thanks," I said, finally allowing a single word to pass through my lips.

Mike closed the distance between us, his gaze moving to the empty bed behind me. He held out the water, and I took it from him.

"You want to tell me what happened in North Carolina?" he asked, not sitting back down. Instead, he leaned up against the wall and crossed his arms.

I fidgeted with the cap of my water. "Can we discuss this later? Like, when we're not in the hospital?"

With Grandpa and all...

"I just caught you speaking with—what I can only imagine—was a ghost. And not Lucas. We have time now." He wasn't angry. Concerned, maybe, but not angry.

I took a deep breath and released my anxiety with the exhale. "I see ghosts," I explained. "They don't have to want me to either." I swallowed the cotton in my mouth, but more took its place. "And it's not only ghosts. I can see demons, cambions—vamps, werewolves, incubi, and the rest of them. I can tell if someone is a witch or a warlock by looking at them."

"Their auras, right? That's what you can see?" Mike asked, remembering what had been explained to him in the past.

"Yes."

"So what does that make you?"

"An anomaly," I half-chuckled, using a word Reid had used about himself.

"A witch?"

"No, no, I'm human. Nothing extra, nothing missing. Seeing the supernatural world is the only power I possess. I'm..." I bit the inside of my cheek, quickly calculating the possible ramifications of telling Mike the truth. But not telling him at this point wasn't an option. Besides, he already knew more than most people. "I'm a necromancer."

Mike bobbed his head a little, absorbing what I said. "Like Susan Taylor."

"Yeah. Though she didn't have this sight I have. I was a part of a prophecy. One who'd be able to help ghosts reunite with their souls, because I lived it with Lucas."

"So you're special?"

"Not the word I'd use. Cursed, maybe?"

Mike snickered, the corners of his lips tugging up into a grin. "Nah," he said, sauntering over to me. He stood in front of my chair and peered down into my eyes, like what I'd told him suddenly sparked a newfound respect. "Special. I saw it the first time I met you, and I see it now. You shine, Carrie. When the world around everyone else goes dark, you still shine. Because you care. You care so *damn* much, and that's what makes you special."

He lowered himself into a chair and reached for my hands. "You've never let me down when it mattered."

"I could say the same about you," I murmured, because it was true. In stubbornness, I'd met my match. But he always came through to the point of sacrificing his life for me, for Lucas, for all of us. If anyone cared too much, it was him.

"Heaven trusts you. You're going to do one helluva job."

"It doesn't weird you out? That I can…you know…see things?"

Mike laughed. "After everything that's happened, you seeing ghosts and helping them might be the only thing that does make sense. The other shit weirded me out."

"Yeah, well. I had a five-star dinner date with the president of Hell. He went so far as to dictate my wardrobe for the evening. Talk about weird."

"That. Is very weird," Mike agreed. "Was that the night I was kidnapped and tied up in the Moore House basement?"

"Yep."

"The demon had good taste then. Because you looked hot." He smirked.

I wiggled away from his grip and slugged him playfully in the shoulder. "I saved your life that night, and all you have to say is that I looked hot? Chauvinist pig."

Mike waggled his eyebrows as he gave me a onceover. "Hotter than hell."

"I rode a horse in these clothes."

"I know. Sexy."

I giggled, then breathed out a sigh as the sound of Grandpa's machines brought me back to earth. I glanced at him and the tubes surrounding him.

"This is my life, Mike," I said, serious again. "I don't know if a demon did this or not. But what I do know is they hate me, and if they can kill me, they will." I peered at Mike again. "You don't want to be a part of that."

"I'm already a part of that." He scooted his chair closer to me, until our knees touched. "Listen, Carrie. I don't have a lot to offer you. I'm a simple farm boy, who's majoring in agriculture and will one day take over my father's ranch. My dream is to settle down and have two point five kids with a woman who loves me. I don't need more than that."

"Being with me is dangerous."

"Life is dangerous. In fact, there's a one hundred percent death rate attached to it. Doesn't mean you stop living because you fear what might be around the next corner."

He wanted to be with me. After everything, Mike didn't run away screaming, like he should have.

Like most guys would have.

No. Mike did the opposite.

He stayed.

Chapter 36

Grandma beelined to her husband's bedside. She caressed his pale cheeks as she scanned him, assessing the damage. I'd never seen her like this before, on the verge of crying. She dipped down to him and whispered something meant only for the two of them. She pressed her forehead against his.

"Come back to me, Rob," she whispered. "I need you."

My grandmother, the strong one, was broken with fear. Suddenly, I felt like an intruder. Mike must have felt the same thing, because he took my elbow to get my attention and nodded toward the door. Quietly, as to not disturb them, I slid my chair away from the bed and followed Mike out of the room.

"It's strange seeing Rob like that," Mike said, sitting down with a cup of coffee secured between his palms in the cafeteria. "I didn't think anything could slow that man down."

"Grandma used to say he was as stubborn as a mule. I guess that trait passed down to Dad and me."

"You, stubborn?" Mike made a face, which quickly morphed into a smirk. "Nah. Never."

"Shut up," I said without commitment.

I sipped on the hot coffee Mike got for me. Knowing Grandpa was stable didn't deter from the seriousness of what occurred today. Or what it might mean if Marax decided to visit.

"Should you call your dad?" Mike interrupted my thoughts.

"Oh, uh. I guess I don't know the proper etiquette for this stuff. Should I? It's really late."

"He'd want to know, I'm sure."

"I suppose." I pulled my phone from the back pocket of my jeans, thinking of an action plan. No need for anyone to come tonight. I made the necessary calls to family, answering their questions the best I could.

After I hung up with Dad's voicemail, we decided to go back up to the room. Maybe the doctor had been in. But when we got there, all the lights were off, and Grandma slept in the reclining chair at Grandpa's side.

"Want me to take you home?" Mike asked after we'd slipped back out.

"I feel like I should stay close. You know, in case Grandma wants me for something," I said, noting the lack of a nearby waiting room.

Mike must have noticed too, because he led me to the elevators. "I've got a solution."

I followed him outside to the parking lot. At his truck, he opened the drivers' side door, and I crawled over the seat.

"Hotel?" I asked, wondering about his so-called solution.

"Hotel del Mike," he said. He flung his seat forward and pulled out a couple of blankets, a pillow, and an old, dirty hoodie from behind it. "We have only the best amenities here. Six-star worthy."

"Um…" Was he serious? "We're sleeping in your truck?"

He dumped the pile of "bedding" into the middle seat, climbed in, and slammed the door. "Done it a hundred times. Best sleep you'll ever have."

I watched as he sorted through his stash, wondering why he slept in his truck so much. More than that, if he usually slept in here alone.

"You can have the pillow," he said, tossing it into my lap. "The sweatshirt is kinda dirty"—he sniffed it, then shrugged—"but it'll work." He rolled it up around his forearm and tucked it between the headrest and the window. Next, he examined the two blankets. "This one has oil on it." He stuffed it back behind the seat. "The other is okay, though," he concluded and held it out to me.

"You'll be okay without?" I asked, feeling bad over getting the only blanket. It wasn't big enough for two.

He situated himself, resting his head against the sweatshirt-pillow. "Not all blankets are made out of cloth."

He grabbed the pillow he gave me a second ago and put it on his own lap. "Lay down," he said.

I hesitated, considering his offer. His heavy eyelids already drooped from exhaustion and I didn't see a hint of flirt on his face. This was kind, gentle, friendly Mike. The one I'd adored since the first time I met him in the barn. The one who had my back during my senior year in a new school.

This was genuine.

"You sure?" I asked, because I'd get to stretch out over the seat, and he'd probably wake up with a sore back.

"Absolutely. Come here."

I obeyed. Head on the pillow, I was surprisingly comfortable. I extended my legs and adjusted the blanket over me. Mike helped a little, leaning over me to make sure the end went over my bare feet, since I kicked off my shoes the moment I got in.

"You all right?" he asked after I got settled.

"I'm good. You?"

"Better than good," he whispered.

I smiled. He'd waited for over a year to get me to sleep with him, and here I was. In his truck, of all places. Feeling warm and safe and tired, I fell asleep to Mike gingerly combing his hand through my hair.

***

Sunlight poured in through the windshield, waking me. I shifted a little and rolled onto my back, my face pointing up. Mike's golden stare peered down at me.

"How'd you sleep?" he asked.

I grinned. "Best sleep I've ever had."

"Told you." The flirtatious glint had returned, but I didn't mind it so much this morning. Maybe I was getting used to it.

Mike trailed thick fingers over my face, his expression hardening. His lips parted as his attention dipped to my mouth. A part of me wanted to stay there and be mesmerized by him. But I couldn't. Not now.

I twisted away and sat up into my own seat. I stretched the ache out of my back and rolled my head a few times.

"How's the breakfast here?" I asked to cut the tension. He'd had surgery in this hospital back in the fall.

His eyes remained on me. "I prefer Denny's or IHOP, but it ain't bad."

"Good. I'm starving." I forced a small chuckle, then reached for the door handle.

"Carrie," Mike said, grabbing my arm and stopping me.

"Yeah?"

His gaze burned into me. The same look from Lucas would have melted me in an instant. Mike's probably could too if I let it go on much longer.

He brushed loose locks of hair from my face, then snickered. "Your makeup is all smudged. Reminds me of a raccoon."

I flipped down the visor to check for myself. Yep. Raccoon for sure. I let out a groan, popping the visor back in place.

"Bathroom first, breakfast second?" he suggested.

"Good plan."

Inside, I splashed water over my face and used a paper towel to wipe the makeup off. The girl staring back at me in the mirror resembled a much older version of the one who left Texas almost sixteen months ago. That girl had been innocent and naïve. Angry and hurt. Now, the one in the mirror knew what it felt like to ponder and choose life or death. She'd witnessed the beauty of love and the pain of losing that love. She'd seen horrors no human should ever see. She'd fought, and fought, and fought.

And here she was. Still standing.

I nodded at myself, the girl in the mirror. She may not have done everything perfectly—she made mistakes—but she survived. She'd done well. She was stronger and wiser for it.

She'd be okay.

I left the bathroom with my head a little higher and smiled a real smile at Mike when I met him in the hallway.

"Feel better?" he asked.

"Much," I replied. "And I'll be even better with some food in my belly."

We both had French toast, coffee, and fresh fruit. Mike suggested we buy an extra plate for Grandma, in case she hadn't eaten. She was good at taking care of others in a crisis, but she often forgot to take care of herself. Grandpa typically had that part covered. Now, it was our turn.

"Oh, Carrie!" she said, taking the plate of food from me. "Thank you. I'd completely forgotten. Steven called. Vivian called. Your dad called. It's been hectic this morning. I appreciate you letting them all know, honey."

"You're welcome. How is he?" I asked. Honestly, Grandpa looked a little better than last night.

"Weak, but okay."

"Has he been awake yet?" Mike wondered, studying the numbers on the machines.

"Early this morning." She laughed. "Like clockwork. At five o'clock sharp."

I sat in the same chair I had when we'd arrived yesterday. "Has the doctor been in?"

"Yeah, the cardiologist came in an hour ago. The EKG showed some extensive damage to his heart. He'll have to slow down."

"He won't like that," Mike mused.

"No, he won't," Grandma agreed. "But if I want to keep him around, it's the way it has to be."

"So it was a heart attack?" I asked.

"He has two blockages. They want to schedule him for surgery on Friday to put stints in." Grandma frowned, her strong façade thinning. She sniffled.

Mike patted her shoulder. "Don't worry about the farm, Renae. I'll take care of it until other arrangements can be made."

"No, sir, you won't," Grandma said. "You go off to college, young man, where you belong."

Mike laughed. "Let me at least take care of things for this week."

"I'll help," I offered. I had no clue what my volunteering entailed.

Both Mike and Grandma glared at me like an alien had invaded my brain or something.

"What?" I said, half-offended. "I can help."

"I'll find something for her to do," Mike mumbled to Grandma, giving her another reassuring pat on the shoulder.

"You keep an eye on her, then," Grandma warned.

"Promise."

Grandpa coughed, garnering our attention. He coughed again, and Grandma bolted from her seat to stuff an extra pillow under his head.

"Deep breaths," she instructed, smoothing his face with her fingertips. "There you go."

His eyes fluttered open. He blinked, breathing deeply until he found Grandma. He exhaled his relief. After a moment, he used his bed remote to lift himself into a sitting position.

Mike shook his hand. "Good to see you up."

"Hey, Grandpa," I said, getting up and leaning in to kiss his forehead.

"Oh, Care Bear." His soft brown irises glistened with tears. "You saved my life."

I adamantly shook my head. "I should have been there sooner. Maybe, if I had, then…" I held my breath to stifle the rising emotion in my chest.

"Renae. Mike. Could you give Carrie and me a moment alone, please?" he husked weakly.

Grandma kissed his cheek. "Steven should be here soon. I'll go meet him in the lobby."

Mike nodded at me and followed Grandma out.

Once we were alone, my grandfather motioned for me to sit. I did.

He shook a finger at me. "You hide things well, missy."

"What do you mean?" I said, confused at his accusation. Did he somehow know I spent the night with Mike in his truck?

"I wondered for a while, but it wasn't until last

night when I overheard you that I knew for sure."

"Oh, we're not together, Mike and me," I said, brushing off his suspicions. "He wants to, but I'm not ready to go there yet."

Grandpa shook his head. "Not you and Mike talking. You and the ghost talking."

What?

I breathed out a nervous laugh. "Grandpa. Ghosts? Not real. You were dreaming."

He squinted at me, knowing that I was lying.

I stood my ground. "It was just me and Mike in here."

He narrowed them further. I met his stare. One of us would break soon, and it sure as hell wouldn't be me. No way would I put more people in danger by revealing the supernatural world. No. Way.

The machines beeped. The oxygen tank buzzed. The clock ticked off the seconds.

Thirty.

Thirty-one.

Thirty-two.

No...

Thirty-three.

Thirty-four.

He's not backing down.

Thirty-five.

Thirty-six.

This is not possible.

Thirty-seven.

Thirty-eight.

He hasn't blinked in thirty-nine seconds.

Forty.

He knows! Holy crap, he knows!

I finally sighed. "I don't understand."

"I received the calling when I was your age too, Care Bear. It's in my family line—we're Protectors."

Words escaped me. Grandpa got the calling to be a necromancer? Questions exploded in my brain and I couldn't keep up with them. I asked the first one I got a hold of.

"So, did Dad or Steven or Vivian get the calling?"

"No, it doesn't mean we all get the calling. It only means I was available when they needed me. Like you are now."

"How did no one know?" I asked, relaxing a bit. "Lucas, Megan, Vanessa. They should have known. Susan Taylor?"

He frowned. "Because, Carrie, I made the deal you didn't make."

"What deal?"

"Marax's deal. I gave up my powers, my opportunity to help lost spirits, so Renae would live. You see, I couldn't do what you did; I couldn't let her go. Not even for the greater good."

"Wait. Grandma? Grandma was…" I couldn't get the rest out.

"Back in high school, Renae got real sick with cancer. The doctors did all they could, but it wasn't enough. The medicine she needed hadn't been developed yet.

"I'd only received the angel's call a few days before Renae's condition worsened and she slipped into a coma. That's when Marax summoned me. He offered me a deal: he'd save Renae if I released all claim to my power. I didn't think twice—I shook his hand. I made a deal with the devil, and Renae woke up. Doctors called it a miracle. Not a lick of cancer remained in her body, nor has it ever returned."

"He must give all necros this deal," I muttered, appalled.

Grandpa shook his head. "No, only the ones like you and me who possess the special sight, those with a prophecy to be the chosen."

"You had a prophecy?"

"I did. And I fulfilled it, as I'm sure you will fulfill yours."

"And after you…did what you did?"

"I lost it all. My powers, my calling. Susan Bunner, a classmate, accepted the calling in my place."

"Susan Bunner? Mrs. Taylor?"

"She did a better job, I'm sure, than I would have done."

My mind spun, wrapping itself piece by piece around this new information. My grandfather, Robert Reece, had been called as Villisca's necromancer. But he chose to save my grandma instead. He *accepted* the deal.

Marax's deal!

'Don't make the deal, Carrie!' Mike had yelled at me through the demon's phone. Mike had known. He'd known the deal Marax would offer.

But it wasn't Marax's lackey who told him. No—

"You told Mike, didn't you?" I asked, stunned. "It was you who told him about the offer Marax wanted me to take."

"Mike was at the house when Akouk came for him. There was only one reason a demon would ever come for someone like Mike—Marax needed him to get you to comply. He needed a hostage. They knew he would be here, so Megan's enchantments didn't work. I chased Akouk and Mike down the driveway and begged Mike to convince you to not take the deal. At the time, Mike didn't know more than that."

"Does he now?"

"Yes."

It would have stung less had Grandpa slapped me across the face. The way he said it cut me straight to the heart. Like he knew the conflicting emotions I held regarding my best friend. Now I wondered if he had known since the moment I arrived in this town.

No wonder Mike reacted the way he did about my talking to a ghost last night, why he'd been cool with it.

All this knowledge and he wasn't too spooked to stay away from me.

"So all this time you knew about Lucas?" I asked.

Grandpa nodded. "I knew the moment I shook hands with him."

"You didn't say anything."

Grandpa's eyebrows rose. "You know why."

"Did you know how this would end? That he'd leave?"

"Know? No. I hoped, though. He doesn't belong here. *You* do."

I shivered from cold my own body suddenly produced.

"Do you think he's happy now?" I murmured.

"Happier than he's ever been."

I let out a breath, my worries dissipating with it. Grandpa was right. Deep down, I knew it too. Lucas was where he belonged, where whatever guilt he'd retained disappeared. His soul and spirit were finally free.

Like it was meant to be.

I nodded, feeling a smile slowly take over my face. "Yeah. I think so too."

Chapter 37

Chaos ensued following my dad and Ami's announcement.

Because of Grandpa's medical condition and his being stuck in a wheelchair for a few months, Dad and Ami decided to move the wedding to Villisca. It was a crazy idea, but they didn't ask me. I figured most of their decision was because I didn't feel comfortable leaving my grandparents so soon after Grandpa's open heart surgery.

People arrived to take pictures of the barn and clean it out. Painters tidied up the trim, but Ami wanted to keep the red peeling paint because she liked the rustic charm. She scrambled to find decorations that fit the new country theme, and Grandma and I volunteered to make them. I sweet-talked Mike, Megan, and Reid to pitch in too. Stacy said she'd help when she arrived on Thursday.

"You think they need help outside in the barn?" Mike asked, peering out the window. I knew why he asked. He wanted to avoid gluing the mint-green chevron bow onto the burlap wreath I just finished.

"Pretty sure they have it under control out there," I said.

Reid wrapped a ribbon around the arranged candles and secured it with a dab of hot glue. "Dude, if I have to get in touch with my feminine side, so do you. Besides, chicks dig this shit."

He winked at Megan, who gave a one-shouldered shrug.

"He just got his life back," she'd told me at the antique store the other day. "He's remembering what it's like to not have a demon living inside him. That's more than plenty to deal with without adding a relationship on top of it."

I didn't believe her then, and looking at them now, I definitely didn't believe her.

"Yeah…" Mike hummed. "I could, you know, do something with Goldie while they work. I hate seeing her tied to the gate like that."

"The wedding is in five days," I said, half groaning at all the decorations we had left to assemble. "Help me this afternoon, and we'll go riding tonight after Grandma gets back from the store. Deal?"

He twisted, letting the curtains fall closed behind him. His golden gaze skimmed over me, and a smirk appeared. "Deal."

I pointed to the bow. "Glue."

***

Leaves crunched under my heels as I walked through the woods. It had been a year since I was last here, but I remembered where to go.

Nature seemed to know my purpose for being out here too. Squirrels sat on branches over my head, watching as I passed under them. Birds hushed their songs, and the soft rays from the setting sun shone through the leaves.

This place, the place Lucas revealed his secret to me, was where I'd find my rest—where I'd say goodbye.

Full circle.

Funny how life was a never-ending loop of life and death, beginnings and endings.

I held up my yellow skirt, attempting to keep it as dirt-free as possible. Ami might not be pleased if I showed up to the wedding wearing a dress covered in forest powder.

The woods opened up before me, and the two weeping willows swayed their threads in the breeze. I paused between them where their branches interlocked and danced together to the music of nature. Two becoming one.

Lucas's spirit and soul. That's what the two of them represented to me, and here, in their middle, he danced.

So, I danced with him. Clutching the crystal angel frame with the picture I'd taken of him right here, I moved to the sound of the birds and the toads and the wind. Heaven's music.

Beams of light washed in, and I imagined Lucas laughing. I lifted my head to him, closed my eyes, and opened up our soul.

My heart thudded when a cool breeze circled me, catching falling leaves with it. They brushed against my skin. Goosebumps spread along my arms, and the scent of lilacs and vanilla filled my senses. I opened my eyes, my heart content. Lucas was where he was meant to be. And so was I.

I pulled out the pocket knife I'd slid under my bra strap and walked over to one of the trees. I scratched until one word sank into the trunk—***Spirit***. On the other trunk, I etched ***Soul.***

I stood back, the branches gliding over my shoulders. I removed Lucas's picture, the beautiful, perfect picture of him. With eyes I could have stared into forever. But sometimes forever didn't include the now.

Sometimes you had to let forever go.

I flipped the picture over and read the words I'd copied from the Moore House. They meant something different to me now than they had then.

Through Love and Devotion, we are spared a life of loneliness and despair. To have someone to love so greatly and have someone love back so deeply is the only way to live a life of Happiness and Joy. Even in Death, you can still Love in a way that brings Life.

I spoke out loud, letting the words resonate one last time. I'd loved and had been loved. Through Lucas's death, I learned the meaning of love and the power of it. He brought me to life in ways I could never have imagined.

Now, it was my turn to bring life to those without.

"I'll look to the stars," I promised the photo. I held it for a second longer before putting it back in the frame. Then I grabbed the shovel I dropped on the ground and started to dig.

When the hole was deep enough, I gently placed the frame inside with Lucas's beautiful face pointing upward, toward his new home. I covered it and with my finger I wrote his name in the dirt.

"Goodbye," I said, saying the word I once vowed to never say again.

Emotion rose into my throat, and I closed my eyes until it passed. Then, I stood up, grabbed the shovel, and headed back to my car.

Three strides in, someone stepped out from behind a tree. I shot the shovel over my shoulder and swung at the intruder.

He barely had time to jump out of the way. "Whoa, baby! Watch the head."

Mike.

"What are you doing here?" I half-yelled, unable to slow my heartbeat back to normal that quickly.

"Dodging your swing. Might wanna choke up a little there. You get more control that way," he said, giving me batting pointers. He held out his hand in caution as he approached me.

"That's it. It's okay, Carrie."

My heart eased its pounding in my ears. "You still haven't answered my question."

"Sure I did," he teased now that my weapon was safely in his possession.

I looked at him. Hard.

"I followed you," he murmured. "Then, when I realized what you were doing, I wanted to give you space."

"I appreciate the space. Not so much the following part."

"Someone's gotta keep tabs on you. A woman in

a formal dress going into the woods with a shovel tends to involve a dead body."

"Too many horror flicks, Mike."

"I've learned a lot from those things. I may not have survived without them." He slipped my hand into his. With his other, he tucked a loose curl behind my ear. "He was a good guy."

I bit into my cheek. "Yes, he was."

"You all right?" he asked, his tone serious and gentle.

I glanced over my shoulder. The weeping willows swung in the breeze over Lucas's memorial, the tips brushing over the dirt. If I focused hard enough, I could almost make out his form. He smiled at me, and his lone dimple sank into his cheek one last time. Then, with the next gust of wind, he blew away.

Here, I laid him to rest.

Here, I let him go.

"Yeah," I said. "I think I'm going to be just fine."

I squeezed Mike's hand as I returned to him. Warmth spread over my skin at his concern for me. Human, living, amazing warmth.

Together, we left the past behind and moved toward the future.

Epilogue

The party crew did a smash-up job on Goldie's horse barn. I'd never seen the place so clean. They put in fake bamboo flooring over the ground. Square hay bales draped with one piece of light green fabric surrounded the circular tables and doubled as decorations and seating. Grandpa had hay to spare, so it worked nicely. Half the tables had candles with LED wicks as centerpieces, while the other half had the floral arrangements Stacy, Grandma, and I made. At the end of the aisle, the double barn doors became a beautiful backdrop of white Christmas lights, green silk, and white tulle adorning the frame.

Heck, even little Miss City Bride loved it.

"You all set, princess?" Dad asked, giving me a one-armed hug.

"How hard can it be to walk down a barn without tripping?"

"Considering rehearsal last night, maybe not as easy as it looks." He grinned, his eyes lighting up in amusement. I may have face-planted the night before, but in my defense the overly polished floor and the brand new pumps with no traction clearly harbored some kind of vendetta. My walk through the woods hopefully took care of scuffing up the bottoms of my shoes. No way was the floor getting the best of me today!

"How about you?" I asked. "Are you sure about this? I mean, it's not too late to call off the whole thing." I crossed my fingers that he caught the lightness in my tone, because I was only half kidding.

Dad cleared his throat, turning serious. "Second chances are a necessary part of life, Carrie. We make mistakes, we learn from them, and we spend the rest of our lives trying to not repeat them." He peered out over the barn and guests chatting quietly amongst themselves. "This is my second chance."

"I know, Dad. You'll be fine."

"So will you. I'm proud of you, princess." He kissed my forehead. "I'd better go get in my spot. Ami will be here in a few minutes, and she doesn't want me to see her until it's time."

"Off with you, then." I gave him a small push into the barn. As I did, my gaze caught Mike's. He smiled, his eyes brighter than I'd seen in a long time.

Tires rolling over gravel made us both turn. The limo carrying my soon-to-be-stepmom and the rest of her party pulled into the driveway. The matron of honor—Ami's oldest sister—got out first. I'd be second in line as maid of honor. Beside me would be her younger sister, and last, her best friend. The flower girl was my newly inherited cousin, Casey.

Ami exited the limo last. She wore a simple white halter-top gown that flowed elegantly from her hips into a short train, very similar in style to what I wore.

"Carrie!" She beamed, her voice rising in pitch. She wrapped me into a hug and kissed my cheek. "I'm so, so happy you're here with us today."

I live here.

She pulled away from me and wiped away a tear from under her lashes. "Your father was right. This color is perfect on you."

"Thank you," I replied. "And look at you! Radiant."

Ami giggled. She opened her mouth like she was going to respond, but instead, her smile widened and she hugged me again. Tighter, this time. I heard her exhale over my shoulder before she let go.

"It's show time." She winked at me and led me over to the others.

I lowered myself in front of Grandpa, the best man, and gave him a hug. "No wheelies, okay?"

He coughed out a laugh, and I frowned. "Are you all right?"

"I'm fine, fine. You and Renae act like you're close to burying me."

I kissed his cheek. "Not a chance. I can't do this alone. I need you."

"You make me so proud, my Care Bear."

"You make me proud too, Grandpa."

"Eh," he said, but grinned as he shooed me away.

Stubborn, I didn't listen. I adjusted his yellow rose boutonniere, then took my place behind him. I hooked my arm with my Uncle Steven. The music began, and couple by couple, we walked down the aisle. I flashed Mike a grin as I passed, and he shot me a thumbs-up, which made me snicker. Beside him, Stacy waved, and I chin-upped her. This might be my dad's wedding to bond him and Ami together for life, but I needed this day too, just like Lucas had told me I would.

This was what he wanted—for me to live, to be happy.

And I was. I really was.

At the front, I nodded at Dad before I took my place beside Ami's sister. The flower girl spun in circles and threw yellow petals into the air on her turn, a few landing in her hair. The audience giggled and she curtsied when she reached the front. Weddings weren't weddings without some silliness.

The music changed, and Ami appeared at the end of the aisle. Everyone stood. I watched my dad as his new bride made her way to him. His eyes glittered, and I was pretty sure I saw some extra moisture in them. It had been a long time since I witnessed this kind of happiness on my father's face.

The ceremony started, and something drew my gaze to Mike. Maybe it was the fact that he was staring at me? Suddenly, I realized he hadn't taken his eyes off me the whole time. And his eyes?

The gleam in them matched my dad's. They were new, fresh, like he saw me now for the first time. He'd never been quiet about his feelings for me. Hell, he'd never really been subtle either, even with Lucas around. But now the hope he held had grown into more.

Because now he had a chance.

Something stirred in my stomach at the thought.

"You may kiss your bride," the preacher said, bringing me back to the reason I was standing here. Our postlude song began softly and I joined in with the bridesmaids, dancing and clapping to the beat. The party had officially begun.

"Presenting, for the first time, Griffin and Ami Reese!"

Dad thrust Ami's and his linked hands up between them and the DJ jacked the music up. "I Feel Better When I'm Dancing" blared through the barn, and laughter erupted from the crowd. Dad and Ami did the side hip bump thing before they danced back down the aisle. Dad had some moves!

"Whooooooot!" I cheered.

Us girls kept the claps up, and soon everyone joined in. When Dad and Ami reached the end, they spun around and pointed at us—our signal to boogie!

Bouncing and swaying, one by one, we met with our partners and partied our way to the back of the barn. We weaved around the tables, gaining whoops and hollers as we went. At my friends' table, I grabbed Stacy's hand and pulled her up. We shot off some of our best BFF moves, and I winked at Mike as I danced past him.

I met back up with Uncle Steven in the aisle, shook my ass, and joined the bride and groom at the back. God, this was fun! I was still laughing when Dad wrapped his arms around me.

He kissed my head. "I love you, Carrie."

I peered up at him, at my father. Did he deserve my love and my forgiveness? Did anyone deserve that stuff from anyone?

I didn't know.

What I did know was that love was the most powerful thing in the world. It could heal all wounds, calm all fears, allow forgiveness, and erase evil.

I hugged him back. "I love you too, Dad." Ami stood off to the side. I motioned her over. "Take care of each other," I said as if I were the parent instead of the child.

"Oh, princess," Dad sighed, pulling both of us against him. "You are the best thing I ever did."

I shrugged, fighting to keep a straight face. "I know." I ducked out from under Dad's arm. "All right, you two. You have a party to stir up, so get moving. Your guests are waiting."

After a ton of photos and introductions to Ami's side of the family, I kicked off my heels and padded over to the bar.

I skimmed through the wine selections.

"Merlot?" the barista offered.

I cringed. "Uh, no thanks. That's demon wine."

"What?"

Dad snapped his attention at me too, his brow quirked.

"Oh, nothing." I waved them off. "I'll have a white zinfandel, please."

The barista poured my drink and handed it to Dad. Dad passed it off to me, because, well, the law.

"Be responsible," he warned. Parental duty and

all.

"Should I tell you the same thing?"

He smirked. "Wouldn't hurt."

"Be responsible, Dad," I said, holding up my glass and clinking it against his. "Cheers."

Dad returned to his bride, and I crossed the dance floor toward my friends. Mike met me before I got there. With a coy half-grin, he confiscated my wine glass and downed it.

"Hey!" I cried.

He set it down on the nearest table. "I've been waiting all day for a dance with the most beautiful girl in the room."

"I think she's taken."

Mike threaded his fingers with mine. "Not anymore. But she will be soon."

He led me to the dance floor and wrapped his arms around my waist. We swayed to the music amongst the other guests, but I barely noticed them. How could I with Mike's caramel irises trained on me the way they were?

My friend. Who had been there for me through everything.

I glanced at the table in the corner. Megan's auburn updo highlighted her natural beauty. Her worry lines were gone from the corners of her eyes, she seemed free-spirited and happy, like she too had pushed the stress and anxiety of the last year from her mind. Sure, there'd be more later—life was like that—but tonight was tonight. And tonight was about letting go of the past…and about second chances.

Newfound life suited Reid well, I noticed. Still a

smartass, still charming, witty, and loyal. Lucas's best friend until the end.

Megan laughed at something he said, and he chuckled at his own joke. They tipped their champagne glasses, clinking the tops before drinking.

It took a quick scan of the room to find Stacy, but when I did, I wasn't surprised. She twirled a lock of blonde hair around a finger as she flirted with one of Ami's relatives.

New beginnings indeed.

"Hey," Mike said, turning my focus back to him with two fingers against my cheek. He smiled, his eyes sparkling under the strings of white lights overhead.

Happy, I thought, remembering our first evening together on my grandparents' front porch swing. That's how he looked now—happy.

"You stopped dancing," he murmured, staring at me like I'd been gone for a thousand years. "What are you thinking about?"

"That first night we met."

"Yeah?" His lopsided grin made me giggle.

"Yeah."

"I think about that night a lot," he admitted, his voice lowering. "I think that maybe if I'd kissed you then, I never would have lost you to someone else."

"Fate isn't defined by one moment in our lives," I said. "But by all the little ones. The ones that happened and the ones we only wish had happened. They all weave together to create the lives we live." One of the many things I learned.

Mike tipped my chin up, bringing my lips closer

to his. “If it’s fate, then I don’t want to let another moment pass without making up for lost time.”

Then he kissed me. Soft, tender—

No, not happy, I realized. *In love.*

When he finished, he pulled back so the tips of our noses touched, and he grinned. I smiled back, seeing him like I had the first time.

Because maybe, just maybe, Mike could be my second chance.

THE END

Acknowledgements

Surreal. That's the word I'd use as I write this. It's the word I feel ever since typing "The End" in the first draft of this book.

I started writing *The Spirit* seven years ago. I'd always loved to write, and thought, "why not?" I had an idea, so I ran with it. Never in my life did I think it would actually get published, let alone the whole series! I'm amazed.

Thank you. Even though I don't think those two words will ever be good enough to express the gratitude in my heart.

First and foremost, I thank God, for without Him, none of this would be possible.

Secondly, my husband. I will forever be grateful for your encouragement, especially when I'm feeling frumpy about my books and my writing. Your support of me in all areas of my life is astounding, and I'm so honored to be able to spend the rest of my life with you.

To my children, all four of you. You guys are crazy! And I love each of you very, very much. Your vastly different personalities and all the cute things you say are inspiring. Thank you for bearing with me as I worked hard to finish this book. The four of you are the best!

Next, to my parents, siblings, and in-laws for being there for me throughout my life. For all the good and bad memories. Each one has helped shape me into the person I am today.

Thank you to my friends and beta readers who read through this book with a keen eye. I'm glad I can count on you for your honest feedback. I'd like to offer a special thanks to Matthew Wiese for always being willing to talk books with me. Not just likes and dislikes, but *everything* books! Thanks especially for the POV conversation that helped shape this particular book into what it is today.

To Angela McPherson. #Workdates wouldn't be the same without you. Whether I write one thousand words or one word, you are there to cheer me on. Thanks for that!

I've been blessed with amazing CP's, and I'll never be able to thank them enough. Did I mention that they're amazing?

Sunniva Dee: You are my writing rock. This whole writing and editing and publishing journey is crazy, and I don't know how I would manage without you. You know how much I love you!

Laura Thalassa: Your power of positive thinking is definitely your superpower, girl! I love how you seem to know just what to say when I need to hear it. Thank you for your unfailing support of me, of this series, and the writing community.

To my street team for pimping me like, well…uh, anyway. You know what I mean. Thanks for being there for me. Thanks for loving my books. Thanks for promoting my books. Thanks for the fantastic teasers. Thanks for a whole list of stuff that is too long to mention here. I appreciate you more than you know.

To the bloggers and reviewers who have supported me and this series. I'm too scared to list you all because I'll probably leave someone out, but you know who you are. Bloggers are the bread and butter for authors, and I want to thank you for welcoming me with open arms. Keep up the great work!

Okay, I'm almost done, I swear!

To my editor, Toni Rakestraw. You have been a joy to work with. Thanks for picking apart this book and giving me all your fantastic comments. There were a couple things in there that I'd have been seriously embarrassed to have had published if you hadn't have caught them. ☺ Thank you, thank you, thank you.

A huge thanks to Redbird Designs for the freaking sweet cover. It is beyond perfect. Your talent is unbelievable.

Thank you to Limitless Publishing! Jennifer O'Neill, Jessica Gunhammer, Dixie Matthews, Elise Balt. I appreciate all of you. Thank you so much for taking a chance on me.

And last but certainly not least, to the readers. Without you, there'd be no books! So, as long as you keep reading, I will keep writing. A huge, sincere round of applause to each and every one of you. You're the best!

Love Always,
d.

About the Author

d. Nichole King was born with a book in her hand. During her school years, she'd hide books inside textbooks, read during recess, changing classes, and while walking home from school. She wrote her first book at the age of 11, and the re-worked version of that book is her debut novel, LOVE ALWAYS, KATE.

Her YA urban fantasy series, THE SPIRIT TRILOGY, along with her NA contemporary series, LOVE ALWAYS, were acquired by Limitless Publishing and includes a total of six books. BREAKING THROUGH, an NA science-fiction romance, is her first self-published novel.

d. Nichole King currently resides in a small town in Iowa with her supportive husband, four amazing kids, a dog, a cat, a fish, and a turtle.

Facebook:
https://www.facebook.com/authordnicholeking

Twitter:
https://twitter.com/dNicholeKing

Goodreads:
www.goodreads.com/author/show/7762889.D_Nichole_King

Website:
www.dnicholeking.com

Newsletter:
https://app.mailerlite.com/webforms/landing/h8i4k1

www.ingramcontent.com/pod-product-compliance
Lightning Source LLC
LaVergne TN
LVHW041102080826
845145LV00007B/1658

* 9 7 8 1 6 8 0 5 8 8 3 1 6 *